Scarhaven Keep

J. S. Fletcher

SCARHAVEN KEEP

BY J.S. FLETCHER

1922

CONTENTS

CHAPTER

CHAPTER I
WANTED AT REHEARSAL

Jerramy, thirty years' stage-door keeper at the Theatre Royal, Norcaster, had come to regard each successive Monday morning as a time for the renewal of old acquaintance. For at any rate forty-six weeks of the fifty-two, theatrical companies came and went at Norcaster with unfailing regularity. The company which presented itself for patronage in the first week of April in one year was almost certain to present itself again in the corresponding week of the next year. Sometimes new faces came with it, but as a rule the same old favourites showed themselves for a good many years in succession. And every actor and actress who came to Norcaster knew Jerramy. He was the first official person encountered on entering upon the business of the week. He it was who handed out the little bundles of letters and papers, who exchanged the first greetings, of whom one could make useful inquiries, who always knew exactly what advice to give about lodgings and landladies. From noon onwards of Mondays, when the newcomers began to arrive at the theatre for the customary one o'clock call for rehearsal, Jerramy was invariably employed in hearing that he didn't look a day older, and was as blooming as ever, and sure to last another thirty years, and his reception always culminated in a hearty handshake and genial greeting from the great man of the company, who, of course, after the fashion of magnates, always turned up at the end of the irregular procession, and was not seldom late for the fixture which he himself had made.

At a quarter past one of a certain Monday afternoon in the course of a sunny October, Jerramy leaned over the half-door of his sanctum in conversation with an anxious-eyed man who for the past ten minutes had hung about in the restless fashion peculiar to those who are waiting for somebody. He had looked up the street and down the street a dozen times; he had pulled out his watch and compared it with the clock of a neighbouring church almost as often; he had several times gone up the dark passage which led to the dressing-rooms, and had come back again looking more perplexed than ever.

The fact was that he was the business manager of the great Mr. Bassett Oliver, who was opening for the week at Norcaster in his latest success, and who, not quite satisfied with the way in which a particular bit of it was being played called a special rehearsal for a quarter to one. Everything and everybody was ready for that rehearsal, but the great man himself had not arrived. Now Mr. Bassett Oliver, as every man well knew who ever had dealings with him, was not one of the irregular and unpunctual order; on the contrary, he was a very martinet as regarded rule, precision and system; moreover, he always did what he expected each member of his company to do. Therefore his non-arrival, his half hour of irregularity, seemed all the more extraordinary.

"Never knew him to be late before—never!" exclaimed the business manager, impatiently pulling out his watch for the twentieth time. "Not in all my ten years' experience of him—not once."

"I suppose you've seen him this morning, Mr. Stafford?" inquired Jerramy.
"He's in the town, of course?"
"I suppose he's in the town," answered Mr. Stafford. "I suppose he's at his old quarters—the 'Angel.' But I haven't seen him; neither had Rothwell—we've both been too busy to call there. I expect he came on to the 'Angel' from Northborough yesterday."

Jerramy opened the half-door, and going out to the end of the passage, looked up and down the street.

"There's a taxi-cab coming round the corner now," he announced presently.
"Coming quick, too—I should think he's in it."
The business manager bustled out to the pavement as the cab came to a halt. But instead of the fine face and distinguished presence of Mr. Bassett Oliver, he found himself confronting a young man who looked like a well-set-up subaltern, or a cricket-and-football loving undergraduate; a somewhat shy, rather nervous young man, scrupulously groomed, and neatly attired in tweeds, who, at sight of the two men on the pavement, immediately produced a card-case.

2

"Mr. Bassett Oliver?" he said inquiringly. "Is he here? I—I've got an appointment with him for one o'clock, and I'm sorry I'm late—my train—"

"Mr. Oliver is not here yet," broke in Stafford. "He's late, too—unaccountably late, for him. An appointment, you say?"

He was looking the stranger over as he spoke, taking him for some stage-struck youth who had probably persuaded the good-natured actor to give him an interview. His expression changed, however; as he glanced at the card which the young man handed over, and he started a little and held out his hand with a smile.

"Oh!—Mr. Copplestone?" he exclaimed. "How do you do? My name's Stafford—I'm Mr. Oliver's business manager. So he made an appointment with you, did he—here, today? Wants to see you about your play, of course."

Again he looked at the newcomer with a smiling interest, thinking secretly that he was a very youthful and ingenuous being to have written a play which Bassett Oliver, a shrewd critic, and by no means easy to please, had been eager to accept, and was about to produce. Mr. Richard Copplestone, seen in the flesh, looked very young indeed, and very unlike anything in the shape of a professional author. In fact he very much reminded Stafford of the fine and healthy young man whom one sees on the playing fields, and certainly does not associate with pen and ink. That he was not much used to the world on whose edge he just then stood Stafford gathered from a boyish trick of blushing through the tan of his cheeks.

"I got a wire from Mr. Oliver yesterday—Sunday," replied Mr. Copplestone. "I ought to have had it in the morning, I suppose, but I'd
gone out for the day, you know—gone out early. So I didn't find it until
I got back to my rooms late at night. I got the next train I could from

King's Cross, and it was late getting in here."

"Then you've practically been travelling all night?" remarked
Stafford. "Well, Mr. Oliver hasn't turned up—most unusual for him.
I don't know where—" Just then another man came hurrying down
the passage from the dressing-rooms, calling the business manager
by name.

"I say, Stafford!" he exclaimed, as he emerged on the street. "This is a
queer thing!—I'm sure there's something wrong. I've just rung up the
'Angel' hotel. Oliver hasn't turned up there! His rooms were all
ready for him as usual yesterday, but he never came. They've neither
seen nor heard of him. Did you see him yesterday?"

"No!" replied Stafford. "I didn't. Never seen him since last thing
Saturday night at Northborough. He ordered this rehearsal for one—
no, a
quarter to one, here, today. But somebody must have seen him
yesterday.
Where's his dresser—where's Hackett?"
"Hackett's inside," said the other man. "He hasn't seen him either,
since Saturday night. Hackett has friends living in these parts—he
went off to see them early yesterday morning, from Northborough,
and he's only just come. So he hasn't seen Oliver, and doesn't know
anything about him; he expected, of course, to find him here."

Stafford turned with a wave of the hand towards Copplestone.

"So did this gentleman," he said. "Mr. Copplestone, this is our stage-
manager, Mr. Rothwell. Rothwell, this is Mr. Richard Copplestone,
author of the new play that Mr. Oliver's going to produce next
month. Mr. Copplestone got a wire from him yesterday, asking him
to come here today at one o'clock, He's travelled all night to get
here."

"Where was the wire sent from?" asked Rothwell, a sharp-eyed,
keen-looking man, who, like Stafford, was obviously interested in
the new author's boyish appearance. "And when?"

Copplestone drew some letters and papers from his pocket and selected one. "That's it," he said. "There you are—sent off from Northborough at nine-thirty, yesterday morning—Sunday."

"Well, then he was at Northborough at that time," remarked Rothwell. "Look here, Stafford, we'd better telephone to Northborough, to his hotel. The 'Golden Apple,' wasn't it?"

"No good," replied Stafford, shaking his head. "The 'Golden Apple' isn't on the 'phone—old-fashioned place. We'd better wire."

"Too slow," said Rothwell. "We'll telephone to the theatre there, and ask them to step across and make inquiries. Come on!—let's do it at once."

He hurried inside again, and Stafford turned to Copplestone.

"Better send your cab away and come inside until we get some news," he said. "Let Jerramy take your things into his sanctum—he'll keep an eye on them till you want them—I suppose you'll stop at the 'Angel' with Oliver. Look here!" he went on, turning to the cab driver, "just you wait a bit—I might want you; wait ten minutes, anyway. Come in, Mr. Copplestone."

Copplestone followed the business manager up the passage to a dressing-room, in which a little elderly man was engaged in unpacking trunks and dress-baskets. He looked up expectantly at the sound of footsteps; then looked down again at the work in hand and went silently on with it.

"This is Hackett, Mr. Oliver's dresser," said Stafford. "Been with him—how long, Hackett?"

"Twenty years next January, Mr. Stafford," answered the dresser quietly.

"Ever known Mr. Oliver late like this?" inquired Stafford.

"Never, sir! There's something wrong," replied Hackett. "I'm sure of it.
I feel it! You ought to go and look for him, some of you gentlemen."
"Where?" asked Stafford. "We don't know anything about him. He's not come to the 'Angel,' as he ought to have done, yesterday. I believe you're the last person who saw him, Hackett. Aren't you, now?"

"I saw him at the 'Golden Apple' at Northborough at twelve o'clock Saturday night, sir," answered Hackett. "I took a bag of his to his rooms there. He was all right then. He knew I was going off first thing next morning to see an uncle of mine who's a farmer on the coast between here and Northborough, and he told me he shouldn't want me until one o'clock today. So of course, I came straight here to the theatre—I didn't call in at the 'Angel' at all this morning."

"Did he say anything about his own movements yesterday?" asked Stafford.
"Did he tell you that he was going anywhere?"
"Not a word, Mr. Stafford," replied Hackett. "But you know his habits as well as I do."

"Just so," agreed Stafford. "Mr. Oliver," he continued, turning to Copplestone, "is a great lover of outdoor life. On Sundays, when we're travelling from one town to another, he likes to do the journey by motor—alone. In a case like this, where the two towns are not very far apart, it's his practice to find out if there's any particular beauty spot or place of interest between them, and to spend his Sunday there. I daresay that's what he did yesterday. You see, all last week we were at Northborough. That, like Norcaster, is a coast town—there's fifty miles between them. If he followed out his usual plan he'd probably hire a motor-car and follow the coast-road, and if he came to any place that was of special interest, he'd stop there. But—in the usual way of things—he'd have turned up at his rooms at the 'Angel' hotel here last night. He didn't—and he hasn't turned up here, either. So where is he?"

"Have you made inquiries of the company, Mr. Stafford?" asked Hackett.

"Most of 'em wander about a bit of a Sunday—they might have seen him."

"Good idea!" agreed Stafford. He beckoned Copplestone to follow him on to the stage, where the members of the company sat or stood about in groups, each conscious that something unusual had occurred. "It's really a queer, and perhaps a serious thing," he whispered as he steered his companion through a maze of scenery. "And if Oliver doesn't turn up, we shall be in a fine mess. Of course, there's an understudy for his part, but—I say!" he went on, as they stepped upon the stage, "Have any of you seen Mr. Oliver, anywhere, since Saturday night? Can anybody tell anything about him—anything at all? Because—it's useless to deny the fact—he's not come here, and he's not come to town at all, so far as we know. So—"

Rothwell came hurrying on to the stage from the opposite wings. He hastened across to Stafford and drew him and Copplestone a little aside.

"I've heard from Northborough," he said. "I 'phoned Waters, the manager there, to run across to the 'Golden Apple' and make inquiries. The 'Golden Apple' people say that Oliver left there at eleven o'clock yesterday morning. He was alone. He simply walked out of the hotel. And they know nothing more."

CHAPTER II
GREY ROCK AND GREY SEA

The three men stood for a while silently looking at each other. Copplestone, as a stranger, secretly wondered why the two managers seemed so concerned; to him a delay of half an hour in keeping an appointment did not appear to be quite as serious as they evidently considered it. But he had never met Bassett Oliver, and knew nothing of his ways; he only began to comprehend matters when Rothwell turned to Stafford with an air of decision.

"Look here!" he said. "You'd better go and make inquiry at Northborough. See if you can track him. Something must be wrong—perhaps seriously wrong. You don't quite understand, do you, Mr. Copplestone?" he went on, giving the younger man a sharp glance. "You see, we know Mr. Oliver so well—we've both been with him a good many years. He's a model of system, regularity, punctuality, and all the rest of it. In the ordinary course of events, wherever he spent yesterday, he'd have been sure to turn up at his rooms at the 'Angel' hotel last night, and he'd have walked in here this morning at half-past twelve. As he hasn't done either, why, then, something unusual has happened. Stafford, you'd better get a move on."

"Wait a minute," said Stafford. He turned again to the groups behind him, repeating his question.

"Has anybody anything to tell?" he asked anxiously. "We've just heard that Mr. Oliver left his hotel at Northborough yesterday morning at eleven o'clock, alone, walking. Has anybody any idea of any project, any excursion, that he had in mind?"

An elderly man who had been in conversation with the leading lady stepped forward.

"I was talking to Oliver about the coast scenery between here and Northborough the other day—Friday," he remarked. "He'd never seen it—I told him I used to know it pretty well once. He said he'd try and see something of it on Sunday —yesterday, you know. And, I say—" here he came closer to the two managers and lowered his voice—"that coast is very wild, lonely, and a good bit dangerous — sharp and precipitous cliffs. Eh?"

Rothwell clapped a hand on Stafford's arm.

"You'd really better be off to Northborough," he said with decision. "You're sure to come across traces of him. Go to the 'Golden Apple' — then the station. Wire or telephone me—here. Of course, this rehearsal's off. About this evening—oh, well, a lot may happen before then. But go at once—I believe you can get expresses from here to Northborough pretty often."

"I'll go with you—if I may," said Copplestone suddenly. "I might be of use. There's that cab still at the door, you know—shall we run up to the station?"

"Good!" assented Stafford. "Yes, come by all means." He turned to Rothwell for a moment. "If he should turn up here, 'phone to Waters at the Northborough theatre, won't you?" he said. "We'll look in there as soon as we arrive."

He hurried out with Copplestone and together they drove up to the station, where an express was just leaving for the south. Once on their way to Northborough, Stafford turned to his companion with a grave shake of the head.

"I daresay you don't quite see the reason of our anxiety," he observed. "You see, we know Oliver. He's a trick of wandering about by himself on Sundays—when he gets the chance. Of course when there's a long journey between two towns, he doesn't get the chance, and then he's all right. But when, as in this case, the town of one week is fairly close to the town of the next, he invariably spots some place of interest, an old castle, or a ruined abbey, or some famous house, and goes looking round it. And if he's been exploring some spot on this coast yesterday, and it's as that chap Rutherford said, wild and dangerous, why, then—"

"You think he may have had an accident—fallen over the cliffs or something?" suggested Copplestone.

"I don't like to think anything," replied Stafford. "But I shall be a good deal relieved if we can get some definite news about him."

The first half-hour at Northborough yielded nothing definite. A telephone message from Rothwell had just come to the theatre when they drove up to it—nothing had so far been heard of the missing man at Norcaster—either at theatre or hotel. Stafford and Copplestone hurried across to the "Golden Apple" and interviewed its proprietor; he, keenly interested in the affair, could tell no more than that Mr. Bassett Oliver, having sent his luggage forward to Norcaster, had left the house on foot at eleven o'clock the previous morning, and had been seen to walk across the market-place in the direction of the railway station. But an old head-waiter, who had served the famous actor's breakfast, was able to give some information; Mr. Oliver, he said, had talked a little to him about the coast scenery between Northborough and Norcaster, and had asked him which stretch of it was worth seeing. It was his impression that Mr. Oliver meant to break his journey somewhere along the coast.

"Of course, that's it," said Stafford, as he and Copplestone drove off again. "He's gone to some place between the two towns. But where? Anyhow, nobody's likely to forget Oliver if they've once seen him, and wherever he went, he'd have to take a ticket. Therefore—the booking-office."

Here at last, was light. One of the clerks in the booking-office came forward at once with news. Mr. Bassett Oliver, whom he knew well enough, having seen him on and off the stage regularly for the past five years, had come there the previous morning, and had taken a first-class single ticket for Scarhaven. He would travel to Scarhaven by the 11.35 train, which arrived at Scarhaven at 12.10. Where was Scarhaven? On the coast, twenty miles off, on the way to Norcaster; you changed for it at Tilmouth Junction. Was there a train leaving soon for Scarhaven? There was—in five minutes.

Stafford and Copplestone presently found themselves travelling back along the main line. A run of twenty minutes brought them to the junction, where, at an adjacent siding they found a sort of train in miniature which ran over a narrow-gauge railway towards the sea. Its course lay through a romantic valley hidden between high heather-clad moorland; they saw nothing of their destination nor of the coast until, coming to a stop in a little station perched high on the side of a hill they emerged to see shore and sea lying far beneath them. With a mutual consent they passed outside the grey walls of the station-yard to take a comprehensive view of the scene.

"Just the place to attract Oliver!" muttered Stafford, as he gazed around him. "He'd revel in it—fairly revel!"

Copplestone gazed at the scene in silence. That was the first time he had ever seen the Northern coast, and the strange glamour and romance of this stretch of it appealed strongly to his artistic senses. He found himself standing high above the landward extremity of a narrow bay or creek, much resembling a Norwegian fiord in its general outlines; it ran in from the sea between high shelving cliffs, the slopes of which were thickly wooded with the hardier varieties of tree and shrub, through which at intervals great, gaunt masses of grey rock cropped out. On the edge of the water at either side of the bay were lines of ancient houses and cottages of grey walls and red roofs, built and grouped with the irregularity of individual liking; on the north side rose the square tower and low nave of a venerable church; amidst a mass of wood on the opposite side stood a great Norman keep, half ruinous, which looked down on a picturesque house at its foot. Quays, primitive and quaint, ran along between the old cottages and the water's edge; in the bay itself or nestling against the worn timbers of the quays, were small craft whose red sails hung idly against their tall masts and spars. And at the end of the quays and the wooded promontories which terminated the land view, lay the North Sea, cold, grey, and mysterious in the waning October light, and out of its bosom rose, close to the shore, great masses of high grey rocks, strong and fantastic of shape, and further away, almost indistinct in the distance, an island, on the highest point of

11

which the ruins of some old religious house were silhouetted against the horizon.

"Just the place!" repeated Stafford. "He'd have cheerfully travelled a thousand miles to see this. And now—we know he came here—what we next want to know is, what he did when he got here?"

Copplestone, who had been taking in every detail of the scene before him, pointed to a house of many gables and queer chimneys which stood a little way beneath them at the point where the waters of a narrow stream ran into the bay.

"That looks like an inn," he said. "I think I can make out a sign on the gable-end. Let's go down there and inquire. He would get here just about time for lunch, wouldn't he, and he'd probably turn in there. Also—they may have a telephone there, and you can call up the theatre at Norcaster and find out if anything's been heard yet."

Stafford smiled approvingly and started out in the direction of the buildings towards which Copplestone had pointed.

"Excellent notion!" he said. "You're quite a business man—an unusual thing in authors, isn't it? Come on, then—and that is an inn, too—I can make out the sign now—The 'Admiral's Arms'—Mary Wooler. Let's hope Mary Wooler, who's presumably the landlady, can give us some useful news!"

The "Admiral's Arms" proved to be an old-fashioned, capacious hostelry, eminently promising and comfortable in appearance, which stood on the edge of a broad shelf of headland, and commanded a fine view of the little village and the bay. Stafford and Copplestone, turning in at the front door, found themselves in a deep, stone-paved hall, on one side of which, behind a bar window, a pleasant-faced, buxom woman, silk-aproned and smartly-capped, was busily engaged in adding up columns of figures in a big account-book. At sight of strangers she threw open a door and smilingly invited them to walk into a snugly furnished bar-parlour where a bright fire burned in an open hearth. Stafford gave his companion a look—this

12

again was just the sort of old-world place which would appeal to Basset Oliver, supposing he had come across it.

"I wonder if you can give me some information?" he asked presently, when the good-looking landlady had attended to their requests for refreshment. "I suppose you are the landlady—Mrs. Wooler? Well, now, Mrs. Wooler, did you have a tall, handsome, slightly grey-haired gentleman in here to lunch yesterday—say about one o'clock?"

The landlady turned on her questioner with an intelligent smile.

"You mean Mr. Oliver, the actor?" she said.

"Good!" exclaimed Stafford, with a hearty sigh of relief. "I do! You know him, then?"

"I've often seen him, both at Northborough and at Norcaster," replied Mrs. Wooler. "But I never saw him here before yesterday. Oh, yes! of course I knew him as soon as he walked in, and I had a bit of chat with him before he went out, and he remarked that though he'd been coming into these parts for some years, he'd never been to Scarhaven before—usually, he said, he'd gone inland of a Sunday, amongst the hills. Oh, yes, he was here—he had lunch here."

"We're seeking him," said Stafford, going directly to the question. "He ought to have turned up at the 'Angel Hotel' at Norcaster last night, and at the theatre today at noon—he did neither. I'm his business manager, Mrs. Wooler. Now can you tell us anything— more than you've already told, I mean?"

The landlady, whose face expressed more and more concern as Stafford spoke, shook her head.

"I can't!" she answered. "I don't know any more. He was here perhaps an hour or so. Then he went away, saying he was going to have a look round the place. I expected he'd come in again on his way to the station, but he never did. Dear, dear! I hope nothing's happened to him—such a fine, pleasant man. And—"

"And—what?" asked Stafford.

"These cliffs and rocks are so dangerous," murmured Mrs. Wooler. "I often say that no stranger ought to go alone here. They aren't safe, these cliffs."

Stafford set down his glass and rose.

"I think you've got a telephone in your hall," he said. "I'll just call up Norcaster and find out if they've heard anything. If they haven't—"

He shook his head and went out, and Copplestone glanced at the landlady.

"You say the cliffs are dangerous," he said. "Are they particularly so?"

"To people who don't know them, yes," she replied. "They ought to be protected, but then, of course, we don't get many tourists here, and the Scarhaven people know the danger spots well enough. Then again at the end of the south promontory there, beyond the Keep—"

"Is the Keep that high square tower amongst the woods?" asked Copplestone.
"That's it—it's all that's left of the old castle," answered Mrs. Wooler. "Well, off the point beneath that, there's a group of rocks—you'd perhaps noticed them as you came down from the station? They've various names—there's the King, the Queen, the Sugar-Loaf, and so on. At low tide you can walk across to them. And of course, some people like to climb them. Now, they're particularly dangerous! On the Queen rock there's a great hole called the Devil's Spout, up which the sea rushes. Everybody wants to look over it, you know, and if a man was there alone, and his foot slipped, and he fell, why—"

14

Stafford came back, looking more cast down than ever.

"They've heard nothing there," he announced. "Come on—we'll go
down and see if we can hear anything from any of the people. We'll
call in and see you later, Mrs. Wooler, and if you can make any
inquiries in the meantime, do. Look here," he went on, when he and
Copplestone had got outside, "you take this south side of the bay,
and I'll take the north. Ask anybody you see—any likely person—
fishermen and so on. Then come back here. And if we've heard
nothing—"

He shook his head significantly, as he turned away, and
Copplestone, taking the other direction, felt that the manager's
despondency was influencing himself. A sudden disappearance of
this sort was surely not to be explained easily—nothing but
exceptional happenings could have kept Bassett Oliver from the
scene of his week's labours. There must have been an accident—it
needed little imagination to conjure up its easy occurrence. A too
careless step, a too near approach, a loose stone, a sudden giving
way of crumbling soil, the shifting of an already detached rock—any
of these things might happen, and then—but the thought of what
might follow cast a greyer tint over the already cold and grey sea.

He went on amongst the old cottages and fishing huts which lay at
the foot of the wooded heights on the tops of whose pines and firs
the gaunt ruins of the old Keep seemed to stand sentinel. He made
inquiry at open doors and of little groups of men gathered on the
quay and by the drawn-up boats—nobody knew anything.
According to what they told him, most of these people had been out
and about all the previous afternoon; it had been a particularly fine
day, that Sunday, and they had all been out of doors, on the quay
and the shore, in the sunshine. But nobody had any recollection of
the man described, and Copplestone came to the conclusion that
Oliver had not chosen that side of the bay. There was, however, one
objection to that theory—so far as he could judge, that side was
certainly the more attractive. And he himself went on to the end of
it—on until he had left quay and village far behind, and had come to
a spit of sand which ran out into the sea exactly opposite the group

15

of rocks of which Mrs. Wooler had spoken. There they lay, rising out of the surf like great monsters, a half-mile from where he stood. The tide was out at that time, and between him and them stretched a shining expanse of glittering wet sand. And, coming straight towards him across it, Copplestone saw the slim and graceful figure of a girl.

CHAPTER III
THE MAN WHO KNEW SOMETHING

It was not from any idle curiosity that Copplestone made up his mind to await the girl's nearer approach. There was no other human being in view, and he was anxious to get some information about the rocks whose grim outlines were rapidly becoming faint and indistinct in the gathering darkness. And so as the girl came towards him, picking her way across the pools which lay amidst the brown ribs of sand, he went forward, throwing away all formality and reserve in his eagerness.

"Forgive me for speaking so unceremoniously," he said as they met. "I'm looking for a friend who has disappeared—mysteriously. Can you tell me if, any time yesterday, afternoon or evening, you saw anywhere about here a tall, distinguished-looking man—the actor type. In fact, he is an actor—perhaps you've heard of him? Mr. Bassett Oliver."

He was looking narrowly at the girl as he spoke, and she, too, looked narrowly at him out of a pair of grey eyes of more than ordinary intelligence and perception. And at the famous actor's name she started a little and a faint colour stole over her cheeks.

"Mr. Bassett Oliver!" she exclaimed in a clear, cultured voice. "My mother and I saw Mr. Oliver at the Northborough Theatre on Friday evening. Do you mean that he—"

"I mean—to put it bluntly—that Bassett Oliver is lost," answered Copplestone. "He came to this place yesterday, Sunday, morning, to look round; he lunched at the 'Admiral's Arms,' he went out, after a chat with the landlady, and he's never been seen since. He should have turned up at the 'Angel' at Norcaster last night, and at a rehearsal at the Theatre Royal there today at noon—but he didn't. His manager and I have tracked him here—and so far I can't hear of him. I've asked people all through the village—this side, anyway—nobody knows anything."

He and the girl still looked attentively at each other; Copplestone, indeed, was quietly inspecting her while he talked. He judged her to be twenty-one or two; she was a little above medium height, slim, graceful, pretty, and he was quick to notice that her entire air and appearance suggested their present surroundings. Her fair hair escaped from a knitted cap such as fisher-folk wear; her slender figure was shown to advantage by a rough blue jersey; her skirt of blue serge was short and practical; she was shod in brogues which showed more acquaintance with sand and salt water than with polish. And her face was tanned with the strong northern winds, and the ungloved hands, small and shapely as they were, were brown as the beach across which she had come.

"I have not seen—nor heard—of Mr. Bassett Oliver—here," she answered. "I was out and about all yesterday afternoon and evening, too—not on this side of the bay, though. Have you been to the police-station?"

"The manager may have been there," replied Copplestone. "He's gone along the other shore. But—I don't think he'll get any help there. I'm afraid Mr. Oliver must have met with an accident. I wanted to ask you a question—I saw you coming from the direction of those rocks just now. Could he have got out there across those sands, yesterday afternoon?"

"Between three o'clock and evening—yes," said the girl.

"And—is it dangerous out there?"

"Very dangerous indeed—to any one who doesn't know them."

"There's something there called the Devil's Spout?"

"Yes—a deep fissure up which the sea boils. Oh! it seems dreadful to think of—I hope he didn't fall in there. If he did—"

"Well?" asked Copplestone bluntly, "what if he did?"

"Nothing ever came out that once went in," she answered. "It's a sort of whirlpool that's sucked right away into the sea. The people hereabouts say it's bottomless."

Copplestone turned his face towards the village.

"Oh, well," he said, with an accent of hopelessness. "I can't do any more down here, it's growing dusk. I must go back and meet the manager."

The girl walked along at his side as he turned towards the village.

"I suppose you are one of Mr. Oliver's company?" she observed presently.
"You must all be much concerned."
"They're all greatly concerned," answered Copplestone. "But I don't belong to the company. No—I came to Norcaster this morning to meet Mr. Oliver—he's going—I hope I oughtn't to say was going!— to produce a play of mine next month, and he wanted to talk about the rehearsals. Everything, of course, was at a standstill when I reached Norcaster at one o'clock, so I came with Stafford, the business manager, to see what we could do about tracking Mr. Oliver. And I'm afraid, I'm very much afraid—"

He paused, as a gate, set in the thick hedge of a garden at this point of the village, suddenly opened to let out a man, who at sight of the girl stopped, hesitated, and then waited for her approach. He was a tall, well-built man of apparently thirty years, dressed in a rough tweed knickerbocker suit, but the dusk had now so much increased that Copplestone could only gather an impression of ordinary good-lookingness from the face that was turned inquiringly on his companion. The girl turned to him and spoke hurriedly.

"This is my cousin, Mr. Greyle, of Scarhaven Keep," she murmured. "He may be able to help. Marston!" she went on, raising her voice, "can you give any help here? This gentleman—" she paused, looking at Copplestone.

"My name is Richard Copplestone," he said.

"Mr. Copplestone is looking for Mr. Bassett Oliver, the famous actor," she continued, as the three met. "Mr. Oliver has mysteriously disappeared. Mr. Copplestone has traced him here, to Scarhaven— he was here yesterday, lunching at the inn—but he can't get any further news. Did you see anything, or hear anything of him?"

Marston Greyle, who had been inspecting the stranger narrowly in the fading light, shook his head.

"Bassett Oliver, the actor," he said. "Oh, yes, I saw his name on the bills in Norcaster the other day. Came here, and has disappeared, you say? Under what circumstances?"

Copplestone had listened carefully to the newcomer's voice; more particularly to his accent. He had already gathered sufficient knowledge of Scarhaven to know that this man was the Squire, the master of the old house and grey ruin in the wood above the cliff; he also happened to know, being something of an archaeologist and well acquainted with family histories, that there had been Greyles of Scarhaven for many hundred years. And he wondered how it was that though this Greyle's voice was pleasant and cultured enough, its accent was decidedly American.

"Perhaps I'd better explain," said Copplestone. "I've already told most of it to this lady, but you will both understand more fully if I tell you more. It's this way—" and he went on to tell everything that had happened and come to light since one o'clock that day. "So you see, it's here," he concluded; "we're absolutely certain that Oliver went out of the 'Admiral's Arms' up there about half-past two yesterday, but—where? From that moment, no one seems to have seen him. Yet how he could come along this village street, this quay, without being seen—"

"He need not have come along the quayside," interrupted the girl. "There is a cliff path just below the inn which leads up to the Keep."

"Also, he mayn't have taken this side of the bay, either." remarked Greyle. "He may have chosen the other. You didn't see or hear of him on your side, Audrey?"

"Nothing!" replied the girl. "Nothing!"

Marston Greyle had fallen into line with the other two, and they were now walking along the quay in the direction of the "Admiral's Arms." And presently Stafford, accompanied by a policeman, came hurriedly round a corner and quickened his steps at sight of Copplestone. The policeman, evidently much puzzled and interested, saluted the Squire obsequiously as the two groups met.

"No news at all!" exclaimed Stafford, glancing at Copplestone's companions. "You got any?"

"None," replied Copplestone. "Not a word. This is Mr. Greyle, of the Keep—he has heard nothing. This lady—Miss Greyle?—was out a good deal yesterday afternoon; she knows Oliver quite well by sight, but she did not see him. So if you've no news—"

Marston Greyle interrupted, turning to the policeman.

"What ought to be done, Haskett?" he asked. "You've had cases of disappearance to deal with before, eh?"

"Can't say as I have, sir, in my time," answered the policeman. "Leastways, not of this sort. Of course, we can get search parties together, and one of 'em can go along the coast north'ards, and the other can go south'ards, and we might have a look round the rocks out yonder, tomorrow, as soon as it's light. But if the gentleman went out there, and had the bad luck to fall into that Devil's Spout, why, then, sir, I'm afraid all the searching in the world'll do no good. And the queer thing is, gentlemen, if I may express an opinion, that nobody ever saw the gentleman after he had left Mrs. Wooler's! That seems—"

A fisherman came lounging across the quay from the shadow of one of the neighbouring cottages. He touched his cap to Marston Greyle, and looked inquiringly at the two strangers.

"Are you the gentlemen as is asking after another gentleman?" he said. "'Cause if so, I make no doubt as how I had a word or two with him yesterday afternoon."

Stafford and Copplestone turned sharply on the newcomer—an elderly man of plain and homely aspect who responded frankly to their questioning glances. He went on at once, before they could put their questions into words.

"It 'ud be about half-past two, or maybe a bit nearer three o'clock," he said. "Up yonder it was, about a hundred yards this side of the 'Admiral's Arms.' I was sitting on a baulk o' timber there, doing nothing, when he comes along—a tall, fine-looking man. He gives me a pleasant sort o' nod, and said it was a grand day, and we got talking a bit, about the scenery and such-like, and he said he'd never been here before. Then he pointed up to the big house and the old Keep yonder, and asked whose place that might be, and I said that was the Squire's. 'And who may the Squire be?' says he. 'Mr. Marston Greyle,' says I, 'Recent come into the property.' 'Marston Greyle!' he says, sharp-like. 'Why, I used to know a young man of that very name in America!' he says. 'Very like,' says I, 'I have heard as how the Squire had been in them parts before he came here.' 'Bless me!' he says, 'I've a good mind to call on him. How do you get up there?' he says. So I showed him that side path that runs up through the plantation to near the top, and I told him that if he followed that till he came to the Keep, he'd find another path there as would take him to the door of the house. And he gave me a shilling to drink his health, and off he went, the way as I'd pointed out. D'ye think that'll be the same gentleman, now?"

Nobody answered this question. Everybody there was looking at Marston Greyle. The little group had drawn near to the light of one of the three gas-lamps which feebly illuminated the quay; it seemed to Copplestone that the Squire's face had paled when the fisherman arrived at the middle of his story. But it flushed as his companion turned to him, and he laughed, a little uneasily.

"Said he knew me—in America?" he exclaimed. "I don't remember meeting Mr. Bassett Oliver out there. But then I met so many Englishmen in one place or another that I may have been introduced to him somewhere, at some time, and—forgotten all about it."

Stafford spoke—with unnecessary abruptness, in Copplestone's opinion.

"I don't think it very likely that any one would forget Bassett Oliver," he said. "He isn't—or wasn't—the sort of man anybody could forget, once they'd met him. Anyhow—did he come to your house yesterday afternoon as this man suggests?"

Marston Greyle drew himself up. He looked Stafford up and down. Then he made a slight gesture to the girl, whose face had already assumed a troubled expression.

"If I had seen Mr. Bassett Oliver yesterday, sir, we should not be discussing his possible whereabouts now," said Greyle, icily. "Are you coming, Audrey?"

The girl hesitated, glanced at Copplestone, and then walked away with her cousin. Stafford sniffed contemptuously.

"Ass!" he muttered. "Couldn't he see that what I meant was that Oliver must either have been mistaken, or have referred to some other Greyle whom he met? Hang his pride! Well, now," he went on, turning to the fisherman, "you're dead certain about what you've told us?"

"As certain as mortal man can be of aught there is!" answered the informant. "Sure certain, mister."

"Make a note of it, constable," said Stafford. "Mr. Oliver was last seen going up the path to the Keep, having said he meant to call on Mr.

Marston Greyle. I'll call on you again tomorrow morning.
Copplestone!" he went on, drawing his companion away, "I'm off to
Norcaster—I shall see the police there and get detectives. There's
something seriously wrong here—and by heaven, we've got to get to
the bottom of it! Now, look here—will you stay here for the night, so
as to be on the spot? I'll come back first thing in the morning and
bring your luggage—I can't come sooner, for there are heaps of
business matters to deal with. You will—good! Now I can just catch
a train. Copplestone!—keep your eyes and ears open. It's my firm
belief—I don't know why—that there's been foul play. Foul play!"

Stafford hurried away up hill to the station, and Copplestone, after
waiting a minute or two, turned along the quay on the north of the
bay—following Audrey Greyle, who was in front, alone.

CHAPTER IV
THE ESTATE AGENT

Copplestone had kept a sharp watch on Marston Greyle and his cousin when they walked off, and he had seen that they had parted at a point a little farther along the shore road—the man turning up into the wood, the girl going forward along the quay which led to the other half of the village. He quickened his pace and followed her, catching her up as she came to a path which led towards the old church. At the sound of his hurrying steps she turned and faced him, and he saw in the light of a cottage lamp that she still looked troubled and perplexed.

"Forgive me for running after you," said Copplestone as he went up to her. "I just wanted to say that I'm sorry about—about that little scene down there, you know. Your cousin misunderstood Mr. Stafford—what Stafford meant was that—"

"I saw what Mr. Stafford meant," she broke in quickly. "I'm sorry my cousin didn't see it. It was—obvious."

"All the same, Stafford put it rather—shall we say, brusquely," remarked Copplestone. "Of course, he's terribly upset about Oliver's disappearance, and he didn't consider the effect of his words. And it was rather a surprise to hear that Oliver had known some man of your cousin's name over there in America, wasn't it?"

"And that Mr. Oliver should mysteriously disappear just after making such an announcement," said Audrey. "That certainly seems very surprising."

The two looked at each other, a question in the eyes of each, and Copplestone knew that the trouble in the girl's eyes arose from inability to understand what was already a suspicious circumstance.

"But after all, that may have been a mere coincidence," he hastened to say. "Let's hope things may be cleared. I only hope that Oliver hasn't met with an accident and is lying somewhere without help.

I'm going to remain here for the night, however, and Stafford will come back early in the morning and go more thoroughly into things—I suppose there'll have to be a search of the neighbourhood."

They had walked slowly up a path on the side of the cliff as they talked, and now the girl stopped before a small cottage which stood at the end of the churchyard, set in a tree-shaded garden, and looking out on the bay. She laid her hand on the gate, glancing at Copplestone, and suddenly she spoke, a little impulsively.

"Will you come in and speak to my mother?" she said. "She was a great admirer of Mr. Oliver's acting—and she knew him at one time. She will be interested—and grieved."

Copplestone followed her up the garden and into the house, where she led the way into a small old-fashioned parlour in which a grey-haired woman, who had once been strikingly handsome, and whose face seemed to the visitor to bear traces of great trouble, sat writing at a bureau. She turned in surprise as her daughter led Copplestone in, but her manner became remarkably calm and collected as Audrey explained who he was and why he was there. And Copplestone, watching her narrowly, fancied that he saw interest flash into her eyes when she heard of Bassett Oliver's remark to the fisherman. But she made no comment, and when Audrey had finished the story, she turned to Copplestone as if she had already summed up the situation.

"We know this place so well—having lived here so long, you know," she said, "that we can make a fairly accurate guess at what Mr. Oliver might do. There seems no doubt that he went up the path to the Keep. According to Mr. Marston Greyle's statement, he certainly did not go to the house. Well, he might have done one of two other things. There is a path which leads from the Keep down to the beach, immediately opposite the big rocks which you have no doubt seen. There is another path which turns out of the woods and follows the cliffs towards Lenwick, a village along the coast, a mile away. But— at that time, on a Sunday afternoon, both paths would be frequented. Speaking from knowledge, I should say that Mr. Oliver cannot have left the woods—he must have been seen had he done so. It's impossible that he could have gone down to the shore or along the cliffs without being seen, too—impossible!"

There was a certain amount of insistence in the last few words which puzzled Copplestone—also they conveyed to him a queer suggestion which repulsed him; it was almost as if the speaker was appealing to him to use his own common-sense about a difficult question. And before he could make any reply Mrs. Greyle put a direct inquiry to him.

"What is going to be done?"

"I don't know, exactly," answered Copplestone. "I'm going to stay here for the night, anyway, on the chance of hearing something. Stafford is coming back in the morning—he spoke of detectives."

He looked a little doubtfully at his questioner as he uttered the last word, and again he saw the sudden strange flash of unusual interest in her eyes, and she nodded her head emphatically.

"Precisely!—the proper thing to do," she said. "There must have been foul play—must!"

"Mother!" exclaimed Audrey, half doubtfully. "Do you really think—that?"

"I don't think anything else," replied Mrs. Greyle. "I certainly don't believe that Bassett Oliver would put himself into any position of danger which would result in his breaking his neck. Bassett Oliver never left Scarhaven Wood!"

Copplestone made no comment on this direct assertion.

Instead, after a brief silence, he asked Mrs. Greyle a question.

"You knew Mr. Oliver—personally?"

"Five and twenty years ago—yes," she answered. "I was on the stage myself before my marriage. But I have never met him since then. I have seen him, of course, at the local theatres."

"He—you won't mind my asking?" said Copplestone, diffidently, "he didn't know that you lived here?"

Mrs. Greyle smiled, somewhat mysteriously.

"Not at all—my name wouldn't have conveyed anything to him," she answered. "He never knew whom I married. Otherwise, if he met some one named Marston Greyle in America he would have connected him with me, and have made inquiry about me, and had he known I lived here, he would have called. It is odd, Audrey, that if your cousin met Mr. Oliver over there he should have forgotten him. For one doesn't easily forget a man of reputation—and Mr. Oliver was that of course!—and on the other hand, Marston Greyle is not a common name. Did you ever hear the name before, Mr. Copplestone?"

"Only in connection with your own family—I have read of the Greyles of Scarhaven," replied Copplestone. "But, after all, I suppose it is not confined to your family. There may be Greyles in America. Well—it's all very queer," he went on, as he rose to leave. "May I come in tomorrow and tell you what's being done?—I'm sure Stafford means to leave no stone unturned—he's tremendously keen about it."

"Do!" said Mrs. Greyle, heartily. "But the probability is that you'll see us out and about in the morning—we spend most of our time out of doors, having little else to do."

Copplestone went away feeling more puzzled than ever.

Now that he was alone, for the first time since meeting Audrey Greyle on the beach, he was able to reflect on certain events of the afternoon in uninterrupted fashion. He thought over them as he walked back towards the "Admiral's Arms." It was certainly a strange thing that Bassett Oliver, after remarking to the fisherman that he had known a Mr. Marston Greyle in America, and hearing that the Squire of Scarhaven had been in that country, should have gone up to the house saying that he would call on the Squire and should never have been seen again. It was certainly strange that if this Marston Greyle, of Scarhaven, had met Bassett Oliver in America he should have completely forgotten the fact. Bassett Oliver had a considerable reputation in the United States—he was, in fact, more popular in that country than in his own, and he had toured in the principal towns and cities across there regularly for several years. To meet him there was to meet a most popular celebrity—could any man forget it? Therefore, were there two men of the name of Marston Greyle?

That was one problem—closely affecting Oliver's disappearance. The other had nothing to do with Oliver's disappearance—nevertheless, it interested Richard Copplestone. He was a young man of quick perception and accurate observation, and his alert eyes had seen that the Squire of Scarhaven occupied a position suggestive of power and wealth. The house which stood beneath the old Keep was one of size and importance, the sort of place which could only be kept up by a rich man—Copplestone's glances at its grounds, its gardens, its entrance lodge, its entire surroundings had shown him that only a well-to-do man could live there. How came it, then, that the Squire's relations—his cousin and her mother—lived in a small and unpretentious cottage, and were obviously not well off as regards material goods? Copplestone had the faculty of seeing things at a glance, and refined and cultivated as the atmosphere of Mrs. Greyle's parlour was, it had taken no more than a glance from his perceptive eyes to see that he was there confronted with what folk call genteel poverty. Mrs. Greyle's almost nun-like attire of black had done duty for a long time; the carpet was threadbare; there was an absence of those little touches of comfort with which refined women of even modest means love to surround themselves; a sure instinct told him that here were two women who had to carefully count their pence, and lay out their shillings with caution. Genteel, quiet poverty, without doubt—and yet, on the other side of the little bay, a near kinsman whose rent-roll must run to a few thousands a year!

And yet one more curious occasion of perplexity—to add to the
other two. Copplestone had felt instinctively attracted to Audrey
Greyle when he met her on the sands, and the attraction increased as
he walked at her side towards the village. In his quiet unobtrusive
fashion he had watched her closely when they encountered the man
whom she introduced as her cousin; and he had fancied that her
manner underwent a curious change when Marston Greyle came on
the scene—she had seemed to become constrained, chilled, distant,
aloof—not with the stranger, himself, but with her kinsman. This
fancy had become assurance during the conversation which had
abruptly ended when Greyle took offence at Stafford's brusque
remark. Copplestone had seen a sudden look in the girl's eyes when
the fisherman repeated what Oliver had said about meeting a Mr.
Marston Greyle in America; it was a look of sharply awakened—
what? Suspicion? apprehension?—he could not decide. But it was
the same look which had come into her mother's eyes later on.
Moreover, when the Squire turned huffily away, taking his cousin
with him, Copplestone had noticed that there was evidently a smart
passage of words between them after leaving the little group on the
quay, and they had parted unceremoniously, the man turning on his
heel up a side path into his own grounds and the girl going forward
with a sudden acceleration of pace. All this made Copplestone draw
a conclusion.

"There's no great love lost between the gentleman at the big house
and his lady relatives in the little cottage," he mused. "Also, around
the gentleman there appears to be some cloud of mystery. What?—
and has it anything to do with the Oliver mystery?"

He went back to the inn and made his arrangements with its
landlady, who by that time was full to overflowing with interest and
amazement at the strange affair which had brought her this guest.
But Mrs. Wooler had eyes as well as ears, and noticing that
Copplestone was already looking weary and harassed, she hastened
to provide a hot dinner for him, and to recommend a certain claret
which in her opinion possessed remarkable revivifying qualities.
Copplestone, who had eaten nothing for several hours, accepted her

hospitable attentions with gratitude, and he was enjoying himself greatly in a quaint old-world parlour, in close proximity to a bright fire, when Mrs. Wooler entered with a countenance which betokened mystery in every feature.

"There's the estate agent, Mr. Chatfield, outside, very anxious to have a word with you about this affair," she said. "Would you be for having him in? He's the sort of man," she went on, sinking her tones to a whisper, "who must know everything that's going on, and, of course, having the position he has, he might be useful. Mr. Peter Chatfield, Mr. Greyle's agent, and his uncle's before him — that's who he is — Peeping Peter, they call him hereabouts, because he's fond of knowing everybody's business."

"Bring him in," said Copplestone. He was by no means averse to having a companion, and Mrs. Wooler's graphic characterization had awakened his curiosity. "Tell him I shall be glad to see him."

Mrs. Wooler presently ushered in a figure which Copplestone's dramatic sense immediately seized on. He saw before him a tall, heavily-built man, with a large, solemn, deeply-lined face, out of which looked a pair of the smallest and slyest eyes ever seen in a human being — queer, almost hidden eyes, set beneath thick bushy eyebrows above which rose the dome of an unusually high forehead and a bald head. As for the rest of him, Mr. Peter Chatfield had a snub nose, a wide slit of a mouth, and a flabby hand; his garments were of a Quaker kind in cut and hue; he wore old-fashioned stand-up collars and a voluminous black stock; in one hand he carried a stout oaken staff, in the other a square-crowned beaver hat; altogether, his mere outward appearance would have gained notice for him anywhere, and Copplestone rejoiced in him as a character. He rose, greeted his visitor cordially, and invited him to a seat by the fire. The estate agent settled his heavy figure comfortably, and made a careful inspection of the young stranger before he spoke. At last he leaned forward.

"Sir!" he whispered in a confidential tone. "Do you consider this here a matter of murder?"

31

CHAPTER V
THE GREYLE HISTORY

If Copplestone had followed his first natural impulse, he would have laughed aloud at this solemnly propounded question: as it was, he found it difficult to content himself with a smile.

"Isn't it a little early to arrive at any conclusion, of any sort, Mr. Chatfield?" he asked. "You haven't made up your own mind, surely?"
Chatfield pursed up his long thin lips and shook his head, continuing to
stare fixedly at Copplestone.
"Now I may have, and I may not have, mister," he said at last, suddenly relaxing. "What I was asking of was—what might you consider?"

"I don't consider at all—yet," answered Copplestone. "It's too soon. Let me offer you a glass of claret."

"Many thanks to you, sir, but it's too cold for my stomach," responded the visitor. "A drop of gin, now, is more in my line, since you're so kind. Ah, well, in any case, sir, this here is a very unfortunate affair. I'm a deal upset by it—I am indeed!"

Copplestone rang the bell, gave orders for Mr. Chatfield's suitable entertainment with gin and cigars, and making an end of his dinner, drew up a chair to the fire opposite his visitor.

"You are upset, Mr. Chatfield?" he remarked. "Now, why?"

Chatfield sipped his gin and water, and flourished a cigar with a comprehensive wave of his big fat hand.

"Oh, in general, sir!" he said. "Things like this here are not pleasant to have in a quiet, respectable community like ours. There's very wicked people in this world, mister, and they will not control what's termed the unruly member. They will talk. You'll excuse me, but I doubt not that I'm a good deal more than twice your age, and I've learnt experience. My experience, sir, is that a wise man holds his tongue until he's called upon to use it. Now, in my opinion, it was a very unwise thing of yon there sea-going man, Ewbank, to say that this unfortunate play-actor told him that he'd met our Squire in America—very unfortunate!"

Copplestone pricked his ears. Had the estate agent come there to tell him that? And if so, why?

"Oh!" he said. "You've heard that, have you? Now who told you that, Mr.
Chatfield? For I don't think that's generally known."
"If you knew this here village, mister, as well as what I do," replied Chatfield coolly, "you'd know that there is known all over the place by this time. The constable told me, and of course yon there man, Ewbank, he'll have told it all round since he had that bit of talk with you and your friend. He'll have been in to every public there is in Scarhaven, repeating of it. And a very, very serious complexion, of course, could be put on them words, sir."

"How?" asked Copplestone.

"Put it to yourself, sir," replied Chatfield. "The unfortunate man comes here, tells Ewbank he knew Mr. Greyle in that far-away land, says he'll call on him, is seen going towards the big house—and is never seen no more! Why, sir, what does human nature—which is wicked—say?"

"What does your human nature—which I'm sure is not wicked, say?" suggested Copplestone. "Come, now!"

"What I say, sir, is neither here nor there," answered the agent. "It's what evil-disposed tongues says."

"But they haven't said anything yet," said Copplestone.

"I should say they've said a deal, sir," responded Chatfield, lugubriously. "I know Scarhaven tongues. They'll have thrown out a deal of suspicious talk about the Squire."

"Have you seen Mr. Greyle?" asked Copplestone. He was already sure that the agent was there with a purpose, and he wanted to know its precise nature. "Is he concerned about this?"

"I have seen Mr. Greyle, mister, and he is concerned about what yon man, Ewbank, related," replied Chatfield. "Mr. Greyle, sir, came straight to me—I reside in a residence within the park. Mr. Greyle, mister, says that he has no recollection whatever of meeting this play-actor person in America—he may have done and he mayn't. But he doesn't remember him, and it isn't likely he should—him, an English landlord and a gentleman wouldn't be very like to remember a play-actor person that's here today and gone tomorrow! I hope I give no offence, sir—maybe you're a play-actor yourself."

"I am not," answered Copplestone. He sat staring at his visitor for awhile, and when he spoke again his voice had lost its cordial tone. "Well," he said, "and what have you called on me about?"

Chatfield looked up sharply, noticing the altered tone.

"To tell you—and them as you no doubt represent—that Mr. Greyle will be glad to help in any possible way towards finding out something in this here affair," he answered. "He'll welcome any inquiry that's opened."

"Oh!" said Copplestone. "I see! But you're making a mistake, Mr. Chatfield. I don't represent anybody. I'm not even a relation of Mr. Bassett Oliver. In fact, I never met Mr. Oliver in my life: never spoke to him. So—I'm not here in any representative or official sense." Chatfield's small eyes grew smaller with suspicious curiosity.

"Oh?" he said questioningly. "Then—what might you be here for, mister?"

Copplestone stood up and rang the bell.

"That's my business." he answered. "Sorry I can't give you any more time," he went on as Mrs. Wooler opened the door. "I'm engaged now. If you or Mr. Greyle want to see Mr. Oliver's friends I believe his brother, Sir Cresswell Oliver, will be here tomorrow—he's been wired for anyhow."

Chatfield's mouth opened as he picked up his hat. He stared at this self-assured young man as if he were something quite new to him.

"Sir Cresswell Oliver!" he exclaimed. "Did you say, sir?"

"I said Sir Cresswell Oliver—quite plainly," answered Copplestone.

Chatfield's mouth grew wider.

"You don't mean to tell me that a play-actor's own brother to a titled gentleman!" he said.

"Good-night!" replied Copplestone, motioning his visitor towards the door. "I can't give you any more time, really. However, as you seem anxious, Mr. Bassett Oliver is the younger brother of Rear-Admiral Sir Cresswell Oliver, Baronet, and I should imagine that Sir Cresswell will want to know a lot about what's become of him. So you'd better—or Mr. Greyle had better—speak to him. Now once more—good-night."

When Chatfield had gone, Copplestone laughed and flung himself into an easy chair before the fire. Of course, the stupid, ignorant, self-sufficient old fool had come fishing for news—he and his master wanted to know what was going to be done in the way of making inquiry. But why?—why so much anxiety if they knew nothing whatever about Bassett Oliver's strange disappearance? "Why this profession of eager willingness to welcome any inquiry that might be made? Nobody had accused Marston Greyle of having anything to do with Bassett Oliver's strange exit—if it was an exit—why, then—

"But it's useless speculating," he mused. "I can't do anything—and here
I am, with nothing to do!"
He had pleaded an engagement, but he had none, of course. There
was a shelf of old books in the room, but he did not care to read. And
presently, hands in pockets, he lounged out into the hall and saw
Mrs. Wooler standing at the door of the little parlour into which she
had shown him and Stafford earlier in the day.

"There's nobody in here, sir," she said, invitingly; "if you'd like to
smoke your pipe here—"

"Thank you—I will," answered Copplestone. "I got rid of that old
fellow," he observed confidentially when he had followed the
landlady within, and had dropped into a chair near her own. "I think
he had come—fishing."

"That's his usual occupation," said Mrs. Wooler, with a meaning
smile. "I told you he was called Peeping Peter. He's the sort of man
who will have his nose in everybody's affairs. But," she added, with
a shake of the head which seemed to mean a good deal more than
the smile, "he doesn't often come here. This is almost the only house
in Scarhaven that doesn't belong to the Greyle estate. This house, and
the land round it, have belonged to the Wooler family as long as the
rest of the place has belonged to the Greyles. And many a Greyle has
wanted to buy it, and every Wooler has refused to sell it—and
always will!"

"That's very interesting," said Copplestone. "Does the present Greyle
want to buy?"

The landlady picked up a piece of sewing and sat down in a chair
which seemed to be purposely placed so that she could keep an eye
on the adjacent bar-parlour on one side and the hall on the other.

"I don't know much about what the present Squire would like," she
said. "Nobody does. He's a newcomer, and nobody knows anything
about him. You saw him this afternoon?"

36

"I met a young lady on the sands who turned out to be his cousin, and he came up while I was talking to her," replied Copplestone. "Yes, I saw him. I'm afraid Mr. Stafford, who came in here with me, you know, offended him," he continued, and gave Mrs. Wooler an account of what had happened. "Is he rather—touchy?" he concluded.

"I don't know that he is," she said. "No one sees much of him. You see he's a stranger: although he's a Greyle, he's not a Scarhaven man. Of course, I know all his family history—I'm Scarhaven born and bred. In my time there have been three generations of Greyles. The first one I knew was this Squire's grandfather, old Mr. Stephen Greyle: he died when I was a girl in my 'teens. He had three sons and no daughters. The three sons were all different in their tastes and ideas; the eldest, Stephen John, who came into the estates on his father's death, was a real home bird—he never left Scarhaven for more than a day or two at a time all his life. And he never married— he was a real old bachelor, almost a woman-hater. The next one, Marcus, went out to America and settled there—he was the father of this present Squire, Mr. Marston Greyle. Then there was the third son, Valentine—he went to live in London. And years after he came back here, very poor, and settled down in a little house near Scarhaven Church with his wife and daughter—that was the daughter you met this afternoon, Miss Audrey. I don't know why, and nobody else knows, either, but the last Squire, Stephen John, never had anything to do with Valentine and his family; what's more, when Valentine died and left the widow and daughter very poorly off, Stephen John did nothing for them. But he himself died very soon after Valentine, and then of course, as Marcus had already died in America, everything came to this Mr. Marston. And, as I said, he's a stranger to Scarhaven folk and Scarhaven ways. Indeed, you might say to England and English ways, for I understand he'd never been in England until he came to take up the family property."

"Is he more friendly with the mother and daughter than the last Squire was?" asked Copplestone, who had been much interested in this chapter of family history.

Mrs. Wooler made several stitches in her sewing before she answered this direct question, and when, she spoke it was in lower tones and with a glance of caution.

"He would be, if he could!" she said. "There are those in the village who say that he wants to marry his cousin. But the truth is—so far as one can see or learn it—that for some reason or other, neither Mrs. Valentine Greyle nor Miss Audrey can bear him! They took some queer dislike to the young man when he first came, and they've kept it up. Of course, they're outwardly friendly, and he occasionally, I believe, goes to the cottage, but they rarely go to the big house, and it's very seldom they're ever seen together. I have heard—one does hear things in villages—that he'd be very glad to do something handsome for them, but they're both as proud as they're poor, and not the sort to accept aught from anybody. I believe they've just enough to live on, but it can't be a great deal, for everybody knows that Valentine Greyle made ducks and drakes of his fortune long before he came back to Scarhaven, and old Stephen John only left them a few hundreds of pounds. However—there it is. However much the new Squire wants to marry his cousin, it's very flat she'll not have anything to say to him. I've once or twice had an opportunity of seeing those two together, and it's my private opinion that Miss Audrey dislikes that young man just about as heartily as she possibly could!"

"What does Mr. Marston Greyle find to do with himself in this place?" asked Copplestone, turning the conversation. "Can't be very lively for him if he's a man of any activity."

"Oh, I don't know," replied Mrs. Wooler. "I think he's a good deal like his uncle, the last squire—he certainly never goes anywhere, except out to sea in his yacht. He shoots a bit, and fishes a bit, and so on, and spends a lot of time with Peeping Peter—he's a widower, is Chatfield, and lives alone, except when his daughter runs down to see him. And that daughter, bye-the-bye, Mr. Copplestone, is on the stage."

"Dear me!" said Copplestone. "That is surprising! Her father made several contemptuous references to play-actors when he was talking to me."

"Oh, he hates them, and all connected with them!" replied Mrs. Wooler, laughing. "All the same, his own daughter has been on the stage for a good five years, and I fancy she's doing well. A fine, handsome girl she is, too—she's been down here a good deal lately, and—"

The landlady suddenly paused, hearing a light step in the hall. She glanced through the window and then turned to Copplestone with an arch smile.

"Talk of the—you know," she exclaimed. "Here's Addie Chatfield herself!"

CHAPTER VI
THE LEADING LADY

Copplestone looked up with interest as the door of the private parlour was thrown open, and a tall, handsome young woman burst in with a briskness of movement which betokened unusual energy and vivacity. He got an impression of the old estate agent's daughter in one glance, and wondered how Chatfield came to have such a good-looking girl as his progeny. The impression was of dark, sparkling eyes, a mass of darker, highly-burnished hair, bright colour, a flashing vivacious smile, a fine figure, a general air of sprightliness and glowing health—this was certainly the sort of personality that would recommend itself to a considerable mass of theatre-goers, and Copplestone, as a budding dramatist, immediately began to cast Addie Chatfield for an appropriate part.

The newcomer stopped short on the threshold as she caught sight of a stranger, and she glanced with sharp inquisitiveness at Copplestone as he rose from his chair.

"Oh!—I supposed you were alone, Mrs. Wooler," she exclaimed. "You usually are, you know, so I came in anyhow—sorry!"

"Come in," said the landlady. "Don't go, Mr. Copplestone. This is Miss
Adela Chatfield. Your father has just been to see this gentleman, Addie—perhaps he told you?"
Addie Chatfield dropped into a chair at Mrs. Wooler's side, and looked the stranger over slowly and carefully.

"No," she answered. "My father didn't tell me—he doesn't tell me anything about his own affairs. All his talk is about mine—the iniquity of them, and so on."

She showed a fine set of even white teeth as she made this remark, and her eyes sought Copplestone's again with a direct challenge. Copplestone looked calmly at her, half-smiling; he was beginning, in his youthful innocence, to think that he already understood this type of young woman. And seeing him smile, Addie also smiled.

"Now I wonder whatever my father wanted to see you about?" she said, with a strong accent on the personal pronoun. "For you don't look his sort, and he certainly isn't yours—unless you're deceptive."

"Perhaps I am," responded Copplestone, still keeping his eyes on her. "Your father wanted to see me about the strange disappearance of Mr.
Bassett Oliver. That was all."
The girl's glance, bold and challenging, suddenly shifted before Copplestone's steady look. She half turned to Mrs. Wooler, and her colour rose a little.

"I've heard of that," she said, with an affectation of indifference. "And as I happen to know a bit of Bassett Oliver, I don't see what all this fuss is about. I should say Bassett Oliver took it into his head to go off somewhere yesterday on a little game of his own, and that he's turned up at Norcaster by this time, and is safe in his dressing-room, or on the stage. That's my notion."

"I wish I could think it the correct one," replied Copplestone. "But we can soon find out if it is—there's a telephone in the hall. Yet—I'm so sure that you're wrong, that I'm not even going to ring Norcaster up. Mr. Bassett Oliver has—disappeared here!"

"Are you a member of his company?" asked Addie, again looking Copplestone over with speculative glances.

"Not at all! I'm a humble person whose play Mr. Oliver was about to produce next month, in consequence of which I came down to see him, and to find this state of affairs. And—having nothing else to do—I'm now here to help to find him—alive or dead."

"Oh!" said Addie. "So—you're a writer?"

"I understand that you are an actress?" responded Copplestone. "I wonder if I've ever seen you anywhere?"

Addie bowed her head and gave him a sharp glance.

"Evidently not!" she retorted. "Or you wouldn't wonder! As if anybody could forget me, once they'd seen me! I believe you're pulling my leg, though. Do you live in town?"

"I live," replied Copplestone slowly and with affected solemnity, "in chambers in Jermyn Street."

"And do you mean to tell me that you didn't see me last year in The Clever Lady Hartletop?" she exclaimed.
Copplestone put the tips of his fingers together and his head on one side and regarded her critically.

"What part did you play?" he asked innocently.

"Part? Why, the part, of course!" she retorted. "Goodness! Why, I created it! And played it to crowded houses for nearly two hundred nights, too!"

"Ah!" said Copplestone. "But I'll make a confession to you. I rarely visit the theatre. I never saw Lady Hartletop. I haven't been in a theatre of any sort for two years. So you must forgive me. I congratulate you on your success."

Addie received this tribute with a mollified smile, which changed to a glance of surprised curiosity.

"You never go to the theatre?—and yet you write plays!" she exclaimed. "That's queer, isn't it? But I believe writing people are queer—they look it, anyhow. All the same, you don't look like a writer—what does he look like, Mrs. Wooler? Oh, I know—a sort of nice little officer boy, just washed and tidied up!"

The landlady, who had evidently enjoyed this passage at arms, laughed as she gave Copplestone a significant glance.

"And when did you come down home, Addie?" she asked quietly. "I didn't know you were here again."

"Came down Saturday night," said Addie. "I'm on my way to Edinburgh—business there on Wednesday. So I broke the journey here—just to pay my respects to my worshipful parent."

"I think I heard you say that you knew Mr. Bassett Oliver?" asked Copplestone. "You've met him?"
"Met him in this country and in America," replied Addie, calmly. "He was on tour over there when I was—three years ago. We were in two or three towns together at the same time—different houses, of course. I never saw much of him in London, though."

"You didn't see anything of him yesterday, here?" suggested Copplestone.

Addie stared and glanced at the landlady.

"Here?" she exclaimed. "Goodness, no! When I'm here of a Sunday, I lie in bed all day, or most of it. Otherwise, I'd have to walk with my parent to the family pew. No—my Sundays are days of rest! You really think this disappearance is serious?"

"Oliver's managers—who know him best, of course—think it most serious," replied Copplestone. "They say that nothing but an accident of a really serious nature would have kept him from his engagements."

"Then that settles it!" said Addie. "He's fallen down the Devil's Spout. Plain as plain can be, that! He's made his way there, been a bit too daring, and slipped over the edge. And whoever falls in there never comes out again!—isn't that it, Mrs. Wooler?"

"That's what they say," answered the landlady.

"But I don't remember any accident at the Devil's Spout in my time."

"Well, there's been one now, anyway—that's flat," remarked Addie. "Poor old Bassett—I'm sorry for him! Well, I'm off. Good-night, Mr. Copplestone—and perhaps you'll so far overcome your repugnance to the theatre as to come and see me in one some day?"

"Supposing I escort you homeward instead—now?" suggested Copplestone.
"That will at least show that I am ready to become your devoted—"
"Admirer, I suppose," said Addie. "I'm afraid he's not quite as innocent as he looks, Mrs. Wooler. Well—you can escort me as far as the gates of the park, then—I daren't take you further, because it's so dark in there that you'd surely lose your way, and then there'd be a second disappearance and all sorts of complications."

She went out of the inn, laughing and chattering, but once outside she suddenly became serious, and she involuntarily laid her hand on Copplestone's arm as they turned down the hillside towards the quay.

"I say!" she said in a low voice. "I wasn't going to ask questions in there, but—what's going to be done about this Oliver affair? Of course you're stopping here to do something. What?"

Copplestone hesitated before answering this direct question. He had not seen anything which would lead him to suppose that Miss Adela Chatfield was a disingenuous and designing young woman, but she was certainly Peeping Peter's daughter, and the old man, having failed to get anything out of Copplestone himself, might possibly have sent her to see what she could accomplish. He replied noncommittally.

"I'm not in a position to do anything," he said. "I'm not a relative—not even a personal friend. I daresay you know that Bassett Oliver was—one's already talking of him in the past tense!—the brother of Rear-Admiral Sir Cresswell Oliver, the famous seaman?"

"I knew he was a man of what they call family, but I didn't know that," she answered. "What of it?"

"Stafford's wired to Sir Cresswell," replied Copplestone. "He'll be down here some time tomorrow, no doubt. And of course he'll take everything into his own hands."

"And he'll do—what?" she asked.

"Oh, I don't know," replied Copplestone. "Set the police to work, I should think. They'll want to find out where Bassett Oliver went, where he got to, when he turned up to the Keep, saying he'd go and call on the Squire, as he'd met some man of that name in America. By-the-bye, you said you'd been in America. Did you meet anybody of the Squire's name there?"

They were passing along the quay by that time, and in the light of one of its feeble gas-lamps he turned and looked narrowly at his companion. He fancied that he saw her face change in expression at his question; if there was any change, however, it was so quick that it was gone in a second. She shook her head with emphatic decision.

"I?" she exclaimed. "Never! It's a most uncommon name, that. I never heard of anybody called Greyle except at Scarhaven."

"The present Mr. Greyle came from America," said Copplestone.

"I know, of course," she answered. "But I never met any Greyles out there. Bassett Oliver may have done, though. I know he toured in a lot of American towns—I only went to three—New York, Chicago, St. Louis. I suppose," she continued, turning to Copplestone with a suggestion of confidence in her manner, "I suppose you consider it a very damning thing that Bassett Oliver should disappear, after saying what he did to Ewbank."

It was very evident to Copplestone that whether Miss Chatfield had spoken the truth or not when she said that her father had not told her of his visit to the "Admiral's Arms," she was thoroughly conversant with all the facts relating to the Oliver mystery, and he was still doubtful as to whether she was not seeking information.

"Does it matter at all what I think," he answered evasively. "I've no part in this affair—I'm a mere spectator. I don't know how what you refer to might be considered by people who are accustomed to size things up. They might say all that was a mere coincidence."

"But what do you think?" she said with feminine persistence. "Come, now, between ourselves?"

Copplestone laughed. They had come to the edge of the wooded park in which the estate agent's house stood, and at a gate which led into it, he paused.

"Between ourselves, then, I don't think at all—yet," he answered. "I haven't sized anything up. All I should say at present is that if—or as, for I'm sure the fisherman repeated accurately what he heard—as Oliver said he met somebody called Marston Greyle in America, why—I conclude he did. That's all. Now, won't you please let me see you through these dark woods?"

But Addie said her farewell, and left him somewhat abruptly, and he watched her until she had passed out of the circle of light from the lamp which swung over the gate. She passed on into the shadows—and Copplestone, who had already memorized the chief geographical points of his new surroundings, noticed what she probably thought no stranger would notice—that instead of going towards her father's house, she turned up the drive to the Squire's.

CHAPTER VII
LEFT ON GUARD

Stafford was back at Scarhaven before breakfast time next morning, bringing with him a roll of copies of the Norcaster Daily Chronicle, one of which he immediately displayed to Copplestone and Mrs. Wooler, who met him at the inn door. He pointed with great pride to certain staring headlines.

"I engineered that!" he exclaimed. "Went round to the newspaper office last night and put them up to everything. Nothing like publicity in these cases. There you are!

MYSTERIOUS DISAPPEARANCE OF FAMOUS ACTOR! BASSETT OLIVER MISSING! INTERVIEW WITH MAN WHO SAW HIM LAST!
That's the style, Copplestone!—every human being along this coast'll be reading that by now!"

"So there was no news of him last night?" asked Copplestone.

"Neither last night nor this morning, my boy," replied Stafford. "Of course not! No—he never left here, not he! Now then, let Mrs. Wooler serve us that nice breakfast which I'm sure she has in readiness, and then we're going to plunge into business, hot and strong. There's a couple of detectives coming on by the nine o'clock train, and we're going to do the whole thing thoroughly."

"What about his brother?" inquired Copplestone.

"I wired him last night to his London address, and got a reply first thing this morning," said Stafford. "He's coming along by the 5:15 A.M. from King's Cross—he'll be here before noon. I want to get things to work before he arrives, though. And the first thing to do, of course, is to make sympathetic inquiry, and to search the shore, and the cliffs, and these woods—and that Keep. All that we'll attend to at once."

But on going round to the village police-station they found that Stafford's ideas had already been largely anticipated. The news of the strange gentleman's mysterious disappearance had spread like wild-fire through Scarhaven and the immediate district during the previous evening, and at daybreak parties of fisher-folk had begun a systematic search. These parties kept coming in to report progress all the morning: by noon they had all returned. They had searched the famous rocks, the woods, the park, the Keep, and its adjacent ruins, and the cliffs and shore for some considerable distance north and south of the bay, and there was no result. Not a trace, not a sign of the missing man was to be found anywhere. And when, at one o'clock, Stafford and Copplestone walked up to the little station to meet Sir Cresswell Oliver, it was with the disappointing consciousness that they had no news to give him.

Copplestone, who nourished a natural taste for celebrities of any sort, born of his artistic leanings and tendencies, had looked forward with interest to meeting Sir Cresswell Oliver, who, only a few months previously, had made himself famous by a remarkable feat of seamanship in which great personal bravery and courage had been displayed. He had a vague expectation of seeing a bluff, stalwart, sea-dog type of man; instead, he presently found himself shaking hands with a very quiet-looking, elderly gentleman, who might have been a barrister or a doctor, of pleasant and kindly manners. With him was another gentleman of a similar type, and of about the same age, whom he introduced as the family solicitor, Mr. Petherton. And to these two, in a private sitting-room at the "Admiral's Arms," Stafford, as Bassett Oliver's business representative, and Copplestone, as having remained on the spot since the day before, told all and every detail of what had transpired since it was definitely established that the famous actor was missing. Both listened in silence and with deep attention; when all the facts had been put before them, they went aside and talked together; then they returned and Sir Cresswell besought Stafford and Copplestone's attention.

"I want to tell you young gentlemen precisely what Mr. Petherton and I think it best to do," he said in the mild and bland accents which had so much astonished Copplestone. "We have listened, as you will admit, with our best attention. Mr. Petherton, as you know, is a man of law; I myself, when I have the good luck to be ashore, am a Chairman of Quarter Sessions, so I'm accustomed to hearing and weighing evidence. We don't think there's any doubt that my poor brother has met with some curious mishap which has resulted in his death. It seems impossible, going on what you tell us from the evidence you've collected, that he could ever have approached that Devil's Spout place unseen; it also seems impossible that he could have had a fatal fall over the cliffs, since his body has not been found. No—we think something befell him in the neighbourhood of Scarhaven Keep. But what? Foul play? Possibly! If it was—why? And there are three people Mr. Petherton and I would like to speak to, privately—the fisherman, Ewbank, Mr. Marston Greyle, and Mrs. Valentine Greyle. We should like to hear Ewbank's story for ourselves; we certainly want to see the Squire; and I, personally, wish to see Mrs. Greyle because, from what Mr. Copplestone there has told us, I am quite sure that I, too, knew her a good many years ago, when she was acquainted with my brother Bassett. So we propose, Mr. Stafford, to go and see these three people—and when we have seen them, I will tell you and Mr. Copplestone exactly what I, as my brother's representative, wish to be done."

The two younger men waited impatiently in and about the hotel while their elders went on their self-appointed mission. Stafford, essentially a man of activity, speculated on their reasons for seeing the three people whom Sir Cresswell Oliver had specifically mentioned: Copplestone was meanwhile wondering if he could with propriety pay another visit to Mrs. Greyle's cottage that night. It was drawing near to dusk when the two quiet-looking, elderly gentlemen returned and summoned the younger ones to another conference. Both looked as reserved and bland as when they had set out, and the old seaman's voice was just as suave as ever when he addressed them.

"Well, gentlemen," he said, "we have paid our visits, and I suppose I had better tell you at once that we are no wiser as to actual facts than we were when we left you earlier in the afternoon. The man Ewbank stands emphatically by his story; Mr. Marston Greyle says that he cannot remember any meeting with my brother in America, and that he certainly did not call on him here on Sunday: Mrs. Valentine Greyle has not met Bassett for a great many years. Now—there the matter stands. Of course, it cannot rest there. Further inquiries will have to be made. Mr. Petherton and I are going on to Norcaster this evening, and we shall have a very substantial reward offered to any person who can give any information about my brother. That may result in something—or in nothing. As to my brother's business arrangements, I will go fully into that matter with you, Mr. Stafford, at Norcaster, tomorrow. Now, Mr. Copplestone, will you have a word or two with me in private?"

Copplestone followed the old seaman into a quiet corner of the room, where Sir Cresswell turned on him with a smile.

"I take it," he said, "that you are a young gentleman of leisure, and that you can abide wherever you like, eh?"

"Yes, you may take that as granted," answered Copplestone, wondering what was coming.

"Doesn't much matter if you write your plays in Jermyn Street or—anywhere else, eh?" questioned Sir Cresswell with a humorous smile.

"Practically, no," replied Copplestone.

Sir Cresswell tapped him on the shoulder.

"I want you to do me a favour," he said. "I shall take it as a kindness if you will. I don't want to talk about certain ideas which Petherton and I have about this affair, yet, anyway—not even to you—but we have formed some ideas this afternoon. Now, do you think you could manage to stay where you are for a week or two?"

"Here?" exclaimed Copplestone.

"This seems very comfortable," said Sir Cresswell, looking round. "The landlady is a nice, motherly person; she gave me a very well-cooked lunch; this is a quiet room in which to do your writing, eh?"

"Of course I can stay here," answered Copplestone, who was a good deal bewildered. "But—mayn't I know why—and in what capacity?"

"Just to keep your eyes and your ears open," said Sir Cresswell. "Don't seem to make inquiries—in fact, don't make any inquiry—do nothing. I don't want you to do any private detective work—not I! Just stop here a bit—amuse yourself—write—read—and watch things quietly. And—don't be cross—I've an elderly man's privilege, you know—you'll send your bills to me."

"Oh, that's all right, thanks!" said Copplestone, hurriedly. "I'm pretty well off as regards this world's goods."

"So I guessed when I found that you lived in the expensive atmosphere of Jermyn Street," said Sir Cresswell, with a sly laugh. "But all the same, you'll let me be paymaster here, you know—that's only fair."

"All right—certainly, if you wish it," agreed Copplestone. "But look here—won't you trust me? I assure you I'm to be trusted. You suspect somebody! Hadn't you better give me your confidence? I won't tell a soul—and when I say that, I mean it literally. I won't tell one single soul!"

Sir Cresswell waited a moment or two, looking quietly at Copplestone.
Then he clapped a hand on the young man's shoulder.
"All right, my lad," he said. "Yes!—we do suspect somebody. Marston
Greyle! Now you know it."
"I expected that," answered Copplestone. "All right, sir. And my orders are—just what you said."

"Just what I said," agreed Sir Cresswell. "Carry on at that—eyes and ears open; no fuss; everything quiet, unobtrusive, silent. Meanwhile—Petherton will be at work. And I say—if you want company, you know—I think you'll find it across the bay there at Mrs. Greyle's—eh?"

"I was there last night," said Copplestone. "I liked both of them very much. You knew Mrs. Greyle once upon a time, I think; you and your brother?"

"We did!" replied Sir Cresswell, with a sigh. "Um!—the fact is, both Bassett and I were in love with her at that time. She married another man instead. That's all!"

He gave Copplestone a squeeze of the elbow, laughed, and went across to the solicitor, who was chatting to Stafford in one of the bow windows. Ten minutes later all three were off to Norcaster, and Copplestone was alone, ruminating over this sudden and extraordinary change in the hitherto even tenor of his life. Little more than twenty-four hours previously, all he had been concerned about was the production of his play by Bassett Oliver—here he was now, mixed up in a drama of real life, with Bassett Oliver as its main figure, and the plot as yet unrevealed. And he himself was already committed to play in it—but what part?

Now that the others had gone, Copplestone began to feel strangely alone. He had accepted Sir Cresswell Oliver's commission readily, feeling genuinely interested in the affair, and being secretly conscious that he would be glad of the opportunity of further improving his acquaintance with Audrey Greyle. But now that he considered things quietly, he began to see that his position was a somewhat curious and possibly invidious one. He was to watch— and to seem not to watch. He was to listen—and appear not to listen. The task would be difficult—and perhaps unpleasant. For he was very certain that Marston Greyle would resent his presence in the village, and that Chatfield would be suspicious of it. What reason could he, an utter stranger, have for taking up his quarters at the "Admiral's Arms?" The tourist season was over: Autumn was well set in; with Autumn, on that coast, came weather which would send most southerners flying homewards. Of course, these people would say that he was left there to peep and pry—and they would all know that the Squire was the object of suspicion. It was all very well, his telling Mrs. Wooler that being an idle man he had taken a fancy to Scarhaven, and would stay in her inn for a few weeks, but Mrs. Wooler, like everybody else, would see through that. However, the promise had been given, and he would keep it—literally. He would do nothing in the way of active detective work—he would just wait and see what, if anything, turned up.

But upon one thing Copplestone had made up his mind determinedly before that second evening came—he would make no pretence to Audrey Greyle and her mother. And availing himself of their permission to call again, he went round to the cottage, and before he had been in it five minutes told them bluntly that he was going to stay at Scarhaven awhile, on the chance of learning any further news of Bassett Oliver.

"Which," he added, with a grim smile, "seems about as likely as that I should hear that I am to be Lord Chancellor when the Woolsack is next vacant!"

"You don't know," remarked Mrs. Greyle. "A reward for information is to be offered, isn't it?"

"Do you think that will do much good?" asked Copplestone.

"It depends upon the amount," replied Mrs. Greyle. "We know these people. They are close and reserved—no people could keep secrets better. For all one knows, somebody in this village may know something, and may at present feel it wisest to keep the knowledge to himself. But if money—what would seem a lot of money—comes into question—ah!"

"Especially if the information could be given in secret," said Audrey. "Scarhaven folk love secrecy—it's the salt of life to them: it's in their very blood. Chatfield is an excellent specimen. He'll watch you as a cat watches a mouse when he finds you're going to stay here."

"I shall be quite open," said Copplestone. "I'm not going to indulge in any secret investigations. But I mean to have a thorough look round the place. That Keep, now?—may one look round that?"

"There's a path which leads close by the Keep, from which you can get a good outside view of it," replied Audrey. "But the Keep itself, and the rest of the ruins round about it are in private ground."

"But you have a key, Audrey, and you can take Mr. Copplestone in there," said Mrs. Greyle. "And you would show him more than he would find out for himself—Audrey," she continued, turning to Copplestone, "knows every inch of the place and every stone of the walls."

Copplestone made no attempt to conceal his delight at this suggestion. He turned to the girl with almost boyish eagerness.

"Will you?" he exclaimed. "Do! When?"

"Tomorrow morning, if you like," replied Audrey. "Meet me on the south quay, soon after ten."

Copplestone was down on the quay by ten o'clock. He became aware as he descended the road from the inn that the fisher-folk, who were always lounging about the sea-front, were being keenly interested in something that was going on there. Drawing nearer he found that an energetic bill-poster was attaching his bills to various walls and doors. Sir Cresswell and his solicitor had evidently lost no time, and had set a Norcaster printer to work immediately on their arrival the previous evening. And there the bill was, and it offered a thousand pounds reward to any person who should give information which would lead to the finding of Bassett Oliver, alive or dead.

Copplestone purposely refrained from mingling with the groups of men and lads who thronged about the bills, eagerly discussing the great affair of the moment. He sauntered along the quay, waiting for Audrey. She came at last with an enigmatic smile on her lips.

"Our particular excursion is off, Mr. Copplestone," she said. "Extraordinary events seem to be happening. Mr. Chatfield called on us an
hour ago, took my key away from me, and solemnly informed us that
Scarhaven Keep is strictly closed until further notice!"

CHAPTER VIII
RIGHT OF WAY

The look of blank astonishment which spread over Copplestone's face on hearing this announcement seemed to afford his companion great amusement, and she laughed merrily as she signed to him to turn back towards the woods.

"All the same," she observed, "I know how to steal a countermarch on
Master Chatfield. Come along!—you shan't be disappointed."
"Does your cousin know of that?" asked Copplestone. "Are those his orders?"

Audrey's lips curled a little, and she laughed again—but this time the laughter was cynical.

"I don't think it much matters whether my cousin knows or not," she said. "He's the nominal Squire of Scarhaven, but everybody knows that the real over-lord is Peter Chatfield. Peter Chatfield does—everything. And—he hates me! He won't have had such a pleasant moment for a long time as he had this morning when he took my key away from me and warned me off."

"But why you?" asked Copplestone.

"Oh—Peter is deep!" she said. "Peter, no doubt, knew that you came to see us last night—Peter knows all that goes on in Scarhaven. And he put things together, and decided that I might act as your cicerone over the Keep and the ruins, and so—there you are!"

"Why should he object to my visiting the Keep?" demanded Copplestone.

"That's obvious! He considers you a spy," replied Audrey. "And—there may be reasons why he doesn't desire your presence in those ancient regions. But—we'll go there, all the same, if you don't mind breaking rules and defying Peter."

"Not I!" said Copplestone. "Hang Peter!"

"There are people who firmly believe that Peter Chatfield should have been hanged long since," she remarked quietly. "I'm one of them. Chatfield is a bad old man—thoroughly bad! But I'll circumvent him in this, anyhow. I know how to get into the Keep in spite of him and of his locks and bolts. There's a big curtain wall, twenty feet high, all round the Keep, but I know where there's a hole in it, behind some bushes, and we'll get in there. Come along!"

She led him up the same path through the woods along which Bassett Oliver had gone, according to Ewbank's account. It wound through groves of fir and pine until it came out on a plateau, in the midst of which, surrounded by a high irregular wall, towered at the angles and buttressed all along its length, stood Scarhaven Keep. And there, at the head of a path which evidently led up from the big house, stood Chatfield, angry and threatening. Beyond him, distributed at intervals about the other paths which converged on the plateau were other men, obviously estate labourers, who appeared to be mounting guard over the forbidden spot.

"Now there's going to be a row!—between me and Chatfield," murmured Audrey. "You play spectator—don't say a word. Leave it to me. We are on our rights along this path—take no notice of Peter."

But Chatfield was already bearing down on them, his solemn-featured face dark with displeasure. He raised his voice while he was yet a dozen yards away.

"I thought I'd told you as you wasn't to come near these here ruins!" he said, addressing Audrey in a fashion which made Copplestone's fingers itch to snatch the oak staff from the agent and lay it freely about his person. "My orders was to that there effect! And when I give orders I mean 'em to be obeyed. You'll turn straight back where you came from, miss, and in future do as I instruct—d'ye hear that, now?"

"If you expect me to keep quiet or dumb under that sort of thing," whispered Copplestone, bending towards Audrey, "you're very much mistaken in me! I shall give this fellow a lesson in another minute if—"

"Well, wait another minute, then," said Audrey, who had continued to walk forward, steadily regarding the agent's threatening figure. "Let me talk a little, first—I'm enjoying it. Are you addressing me, Mr. Chatfield?" she went on in her sweetest accents. "I hear you speaking, but I don't know if you are speaking to me. If so, you needn't shout."

"You know very well who I'm a-speaking to," growled Chatfield. "I told you you wasn't to come near these ruins—it's forbidden, by order. You'll take yourself off, and that there young man with you— we want no paid spies hereabouts!"

"If you speak to me like that again I'll knock you down!" exclaimed Copplestone, stepping forward before Audrey could stop him. "Or to this lady, either. Stand aside, will you?"

Chatfield twisted on his heel with a surprising agility—not to stand aside, but to wave his arm to the men who stood here and there, behind him.

"Here, you!" he shouted. "Here, this way, all of you! This here fellow's threatening me with assault. You lay a finger on me, you young snapper, and I'll have you in the lock-up in ten minutes. Stand between us, you men!—he's for knocking me down. Now then!" he went on, as the bodyguard got between him and Copplestone, "off you go, out o' these grounds, both of you—quick! I'll have no defiance of my orders from neither gel nor boy, man nor woman. Out you go, now—or you'll be put out."

But Audrey continued to advance, still watching the agent. "You're under a mistake, Mr. Chatfield," she said calmly. "You will observe that Mr. Copplestone and I are on this path. You know very well that this is a public foot-path, with a proper and legal right-of-way from

58

time immemorial. You can't turn us off it, you know—without exposing yourself to all sorts of pains and penalties. You men know that, too," she continued, turning to the labourers and dropping her bantering tone. "You all know this is a public footpath. So stand out of our way, or I'll summon every one of you!"

The last words were spoken with so much force and decision that the three labourers involuntarily moved aside. But Chatfield hastened to oppose Audrey's progress, planting himself in front of a wicket-gate which there stood across the path, and he laughed sneeringly.

"And where would you find money to take summonses out?" he said, with a look of contempt, "I should think you and your mother's something better to do with your bit o' money than that. Now then, no more words!—back you turn!"

Copplestone's temper had been gradually rising during the last few minutes. Now, at the man's carefully measured taunts, he let it go. Before Chatfield or the labourers saw what he was at, he sprang on the agent's big form, grasped him by the neck with one hand, twisted his oak staff away from him with the other, flung him headlong on the turf, and raised the staff threateningly.

"Now!" he said, "beg Miss Greyle's pardon, instantly, or I'll split your wicked old head for you. Quick, man—I mean it!"

Before Chatfield, moaning and groaning, could find his voice capable of words, Marston Greyle, pale and excited, came round a corner of the ruins.

"What's this, what's all this?" he demanded. "Here, yon sir, what are you doing with that stick! What—"

"I'm about to chastise your agent for his scoundrelly insolence to your cousin," retorted Copplestone with cheerful determination. "Now then, my man, quick—I always keep my word!"

"Hand the stick to Mr. Marston Greyle, Mr. Copplestone," said Audrey in her demurest manner. "I'm sure he would beat Chatfield soundly if he had heard what he said to me—his cousin."

"Thank you, but I'm in possession," said Copplestone, grimly. "Mr. Marston Greyle can kick him when I've thrashed him. Now, then— are you going to beg Miss Greyle's pardon, you hoary sinner?"

"What on earth is it all about?" exclaimed Greyle, obviously upset and afraid. "Chatfield, what have you been saying? Go away, you men—go away, all of you, at once. Mr. Copplestone, don't hit him. Audrey, what is it? Hang it all!—I seem to have nothing but bother— it's most annoying. What is it, I say?"

"It is merely, Marston, that your agent there, after trying to turn Mr. Copplestone and myself off this public foot-path, insulted me with shameful taunts about my mother's poverty," replied Audrey. "That's all! Whereupon—as you were not here to do it—Mr. Copplestone promptly and very properly knocked him down. And now—is Mr. Copplestone to punish him or—will you?"

Copplestone, keeping a sharp eye on the groaning and sputtering agent, contrived at the same time to turn a corner of it on Marston Greyle. That momentary glance showed him much. The Squire was mortally afraid of his man. That was certain—as certain as that they were there. He stood, a picture of vexation and indecision, glancing furtively at Chatfield, then at Audrey, and evidently hating to be asked to take a side.

"Confound it all, Chatfield!" he suddenly burst out. "Why don't you mind what you're saying? It's all very well, Audrey, but you shouldn't have come along here—especially with strangers. The fact is, I'm so upset about this Oliver affair that I'm going to have a thorough search and examination of the Keep and the ruins, and, of course, we can't allow any one inside the grounds while it's going on. You should have kept to Chatfield's orders—"

"And since when has a Greyle of Scarhaven kept to a servant's orders?" interrupted Audrey, with a sneer that sent the blood rushing to the Squire's face. "Never!—until this present régime, I should think. Orders, indeed!—from an agent! I wonder what the last Squire of Scarhaven would have said to a proposition like that? Mr. Copplestone—you've punished that bad old man quite sufficiently. Will you open the gate for me—and we'll go on our way."

The girl spoke with so much decision that Copplestone moved away from Chatfield, who struggled to his feet, muttering words that sounded very much like smothered curses.

"I'll have the law on you!" he growled, shaking his fist at Copplestone.
"Before this day's out, I'll have the law!"
"Sooner the better," retorted Copplestone. "Nothing will please me so much as to tell the local magistrates precisely what you said to your master's kinswoman. You know where I'm to be found—and there," he added, throwing a card at the agent's feet, "there you'll find my permanent address."

"Give me my walking-stick!" demanded Chatfield.

"Not I!" exclaimed Copplestone. "That's mine, my good man, by right of conquest. You can summon me, or arrest me, if you like, for stealing it."

He opened the wicket-gate for Audrey, and together they passed through, skirted the walls of the ruins, and went away into the higher portion of the woods. Once there the girl laughed.

"Now there'll be another row!" she said. "Between master and man this time."

"I think not!" observed Copplestone, with unusual emphasis. "For the master is afraid of the man."

"Ah!—but which is master and which is man?" asked Audrey in a low voice.

Copplestone stopped and looked narrowly at her.

"Oh?" he said quietly, "so you've seen that?"

"Does it need much observation?" she replied. "My mother and I have known for some time that Marston Greyle is entirely under Peter Chatfield's thumb. He daren't do anything—save by Chatfield's permission."

Copplestone walked on a few yards, ruminating.

"Why!" he asked suddenly.

"How do we know?" retorted Audrey.

"Well, in cases like that," said Copplestone, "it generally means that one man has a hold on the other. What hold can Chatfield have on your cousin? I understand Mr. Marston Greyle came straight to his inheritance from America. So what could Chatfield know of him—to have any hold?"

"Oh, I don't know—and I don't care—much," replied Audrey, as they passed out of the woods on to the headlands beyond. "Never mind all that—here's the sea and the open sky—hang Chatfield, and Marston, too! As we can't see the Keep, let's enjoy ourselves some other way. What shall we do?"

"You're the guide, conductress, general boss!" answered Copplestone. "Shall I suggest something that sounds very material, though? Well, then, can't we go along these cliffs to some village where we can find a nice old fishing inn and get a simple lunch of some sort?"

"That's certainly material and eminently practical," laughed Audrey. "We can—that place, along there to the south—Lenwick. And so, come on—and no more talk of Squire and agent. I've a remarkable facility in throwing away unpleasant things."

"It's a grand faculty—and I'll try to imitate you," said Copplestone. "So—today's our own, eh? Is that it?"
"Say until the middle of this afternoon," responded Audrey. "Don't forget that I have a mother at home."

It was, however, well past the middle of the afternoon when these two returned to Scarhaven, very well satisfied with themselves. They had found plenty to talk about without falling back on Marston Greyle, or Peter Chatfield, or the event of the morning, and Copplestone suddenly remembered, almost with compunction, that he had been so engrossed in his companion that he had almost forgotten the Oliver mystery. But that was sharply recalled to him as he entered the "Admiral's Arms." Mrs. Wooler came forward from her parlour with a mysterious smile on her good-looking face.

"Here's a billet-doux for you, Mr. Copplestone," she said. "And I can't tell you who left it. One of the girls found it lying on the hall table an hour ago." With that she handed Copplestone a much thumbed, very grimy, heavily-sealed envelope.

CHAPTER IX
HOBKIN'S HOLE

Copplestone carried the queer-looking missive into his private
sitting-room and carefully examined it, back and front, before slitting
it open. The envelope was of the cheapest kind, the big splotch of red
wax at the flap had been pressed into flatness by the summary
method of forcing a coarse-grained thumb upon it; the address was
inscribed in ill-formed characters only too evidently made with
difficulty by a bad pen, which seemed to have been dipped into
watery ink at every third or fourth letter. And it read thus:—

"THE YOUNG GENTLEMAN STAYING AT 'THE ADMIRAL'—
PRIVATE"
The envelope contained nothing but a scrap of paper obviously torn
from a penny cash book. No ink had been used in transcribing the
two or three lines which were scrawled across this scrap—the vehicle
this time was an indelible pencil, which the writer appeared to have
moistened with his tongue every now and then, some letters being
thicker and darker than others. The message, if mysterious, was
straightforward enough. "Sir," it ran, "if so be as you'd like to have a
bit of news from one as has it, take a walk through Hobkin's Hole
tomorrow morning and look out for Yours truly—Him as writes
this."

Like most very young men Copplestone on arriving at what he
called manhood (by which he meant the age of twenty-one years),
had drawn up for himself a code of ethics, wherein he had mentally
scheduled certain things to be done and certain things not to be
done. One of the things which he had firmly resolved never to do
was to take any notice of an anonymous letter. Here was an
anonymous letter, and with it a conflict between his principles and
his inclinations. In five minutes he learnt that cut-and-dried codes
are no good when the hard facts of every-day life have to be faced
and that expediency is a factor in human existence which has its
moral values. In plain English, he made up his mind to visit
Hobkin's Hole next morning and find out who the unknown
correspondent was.

He was half tempted to go round to the cottage and show the queer scrawl to Audrey Greyle, of whom, having passed six delightful hours in her company—he was beginning to think much more than was good for him, unless he intended to begin thinking of her always. But he was still young enough to have a spice of bashfulness about him, and he did not want to seem too pushing or forward. Again, it seemed to him that the anonymous letter conveyed, in some subtle fashion, a hint that it was to be regarded as sacred and secret, and Copplestone had a strong sense of honour. He knew that Mrs. Wooler was femininely curious to hear all about that letter, but he took care not to mention it to her. Instead he quietly consulted an ordnance map of the district which hung framed and glazed in the hall of the inn, and discovering that Hobkin's Hole was marked on it as being something or other a mile or two out of Scarhaven on the inland side, he set out in its direction next morning after breakfast, without a word to anyone as to where he was going. And that he might not be entirely defenceless he carried Peter Chatfield's oaken staff with him—that would certainly serve to crack any ordinary skull, if need arose for measure of defence.

The road which Copplestone followed out of the village soon turned off into the heart of the moorlands that lay, rising and falling in irregular undulations, between the sea and the hills. He was quickly out of sight of Scarhaven, and in the midst of a solitude. All round him stretched wide expanses of heather and gorse, broken up by great masses of rock: from a rise in the road he looked about him and saw no sign of a human habitation and heard nothing but the rush of the wind across the moors and the plaintive cry of the sea-birds flapping their way to the cultivated land beyond the barrier of hills. And from that point he saw no sign of any fall or depression in the landscape to suggest the place which he sought. But at the next turn he found himself at the mouth of a narrow ravine, which cut deep into the heart of the hill, and was dark and sombre enough to seem a likely place for secret meetings, if for nothing more serious and sinister. It wound away from a little bridge which carried the road over a brawling stream; along the side of that stream were faint indications of a path which might have been made by human feet, but was more likely to have been trodden out by the mountain sheep. This path was quickly obscured by dwarf oaks and alder bushes, which completely roofed in the narrow valley, and about everything hung a suggestion of solitude that would have caused any timid or suspicious soul to have turned back. But Copplestone was neither timid nor suspicious, and he was already intensely curious about this adventure; wherefore, grasping Peter Chatfield's oaken cudgel firmly in his right hand, he jumped over the bridge and followed the narrow path into the gloom of the trees.

He soon found that the valley resolved itself into a narrow and rocky defile. The stream, level at first, soon came tumbling down amongst huge boulders; the path disappeared; out of the oaks and alder high cliffs of limestones began to lift themselves. The morning was unusually dark and grey, even for October, and as leaves, brown and sere though they were, still clustered thickly on the trees, Copplestone quickly found himself in a gloom that would have made a nervous person frightened. He also found that his forward progress became increasingly difficult. At the foot of a tall cliff which suddenly rose up before him he was obliged to pause; on that side of the stream it seemed impossible to go further. But as he hesitated, peering here and there under the branches of the dwarf oaks, he heard a voice, so suddenly, that he started in spite of himself.

"Guv'nor!"

Copplestone looked around and saw nothing. Then came a low laugh, as if the unseen person was enjoying his perplexity.

"Look overhead, guv'nor," said the voice. "Look aloft!"

Copplestone glanced upward, and saw a man's head and face, framed in a screen of bushes which grew on a shelf of the limestone cliff. The head was crowned by a much worn fur cap; the face, very brown and seamed and wrinkled, was ornamented by a short, well-blackened clay pipe, from the bowl of which a wisp of blue smoke curled upward. And as he grew accustomed to the gloom he was aware of a pair of shrewd, twinkling eyes, and a set of very white teeth which gleamed like an animal's.

"Hullo!" said Copplestone. "Come out of that!"

The white teeth showed themselves still more; their owner laughed again.

"You come up, guv'nor," he said. "There's a natural staircase round the corner. Come up and make yourself at home. I've a nice little parlour here, and a matter of refreshment in it, too."

"Not till you show yourself," answered Copplestone. "I want to see what
I'm dealing with. Come out, now!"
The unseen laughed again, moved away from his screen, and presently showed himself on the edge of the shelf of rock. And Copplestone found himself staring at a queer figure of a man—an under-sized, quaint-looking fellow, clad in dirty velveteens, a once red waistcoat, and leather breeches and gaiters, a sort of compound between a poacher, a game-keeper, and an ostler. But quainter than figure or garments was the man's face—a gnarled, weather-beaten, sea-and-wind stained face, which, in Copplestone's opinion, was honest enough and not without abundant traces of a sense of humour.

Copplestone at once trusted that face. He swung himself up by the nooks and crannies of the rock, and joined the man on his ledge.

"Well?" he said. "You're the chap who sent me that letter? Why?"

"Come this way, guv'nor," replied the brown-faced one. "Well talk more comfortable, like, in my parlour. Here you are!"

He led Copplestone along the ridge behind the bushes, and presently revealed a cave in the face of the overhanging limestone, mostly natural, but partly due to artifice, wherein were rude seats, covered over with old sacking, a box or two which evidently served for pantry and larder, and a shelf on which stood a wicker-covered bottle in company with a row of bottles of ale.

The lord of this retreat waved a hospitable hand towards his cellar.

"You'll not refuse a poor man's hospitality, guv'nor?" he said politely. "I can give you a clean glass, and if you'll try a drop of rum, there's fresh water from the stream to mix it with—good as you'll find in England. Or, maybe, it being the forepart of the day, you'd prefer ale, now? Say the word!"

"A bottle of ale, then, thank you," responded Copplestone, who saw that he had to deal with an original, and did not wish to appear stand-offish. "And whom am I going to drink with, may I ask?"

The man carefully drew the cork of a bottle, poured out its contents with the discrimination of a bartender, handed the glass to his visitor with a bow, helped himself to a measure of rum, and bowed again as he drank.

"My best respects to you, guv'nor," he said. "Glad to see you in Hobkin's
Hole Castle—that's here. Queer place for gentlemen to meet in, ain't it?
Who are you talking to, says you? My name, guv'-nor—well-known hereabouts—is Zachary Spurge!"
"You sent me that note last night?" asked Copplestone, taking a seat and filling his pipe. "How did you get it there—unseen?"

"Got a cousin as is odd-job man at the 'Admiral's Arms,'" replied Spurge. "He slipped it in for me. You may ha' seen him there, guv'nor—chap with one eye, and queer-looking, but to be trusted. As I am!—down to the ground."

"And what do you want to see me about?" inquired Copplestone. "What's this bit of news you've got to tell?"

Zachary Spurge thrust a hand inside his velveteen jacket and drew out a much folded and creased paper, which, on being unwrapped, proved to be the bill which offered a reward for the finding of Bassett Oliver. He held it up before his visitor.

"This!" he said. "A thousand pound is a vast lot o' money, guv'nor! Now, if I was to tell something as I knows of, what chances should I have of getting that there money?"

"That depends," replied Copplestone. "The reward is to be given to — but you see the plain wording of it. Can you give information of that sort?"

"I can give a certain piece of information, guv'nor," said Spurge. "Whether it'll lead to the finding of that there gentleman or not I can't say. But something I do know — certain sure!"

Copplestone reflected awhile.

"Ill tell you what, Spurge," he said. "I'll promise you this much. If you can give any information I'll give you my word that — whether what you can tell is worth much or little — you shall be well paid. That do?"

"That'll do, guv'nor," responded Spurge. "I take your word as between gentlemen! Well, now, it's this here — you see me as I am, here in a cave, like one o' them old eremites that used to be in the ancient days. Why am I here! 'Cause just now it ain't quite convenient for me to show my face in Scarhaven. I'm wanted for poaching, guv'nor — that's the fact! This here is a safe retreat. If I was tracked here, I could make my way out at the back of this hole — there's a passage here — before anybody could climb that rock. However, nobody suspects I'm here. They think — that is, that old devil Chatfield and the police — they think I'm off to sea. However, here I am — and last Sunday afternoon as ever was, I was in Scarhaven! In the wood I was, guv'nor, at the back of the Keep. Never mind what for — I was there. And at precisely ten minutes to three o'clock I saw Bassett Oliver."

"How did you know him?" demanded Copplestone.

"Cause I've had many a sixpenn'orth of him at both Northborough and Norcaster," answered Spurge. "Seen him a dozen times, I have, and knew him well enough, even if I'd only viewed him from the the-ayter gallery. Well, he come along up the path from the south quay. He passed within a dozen yards of me, and went up to the door in the wall of the ruins, right opposite where I was lying doggo amongst some bushes. He poked the door with the point of his stick—it was ajar, that door, and it went open. And so he walks in—and disappears. Guv'nor!—I reckon that'ud be the last time as he was seen alive!—unless—unless—"

"Unless—what?" asked Copplestone eagerly.

"Unless one other man saw him," replied Spurge solemnly. "For there was another man there, guv'nor. Squire Greyle!"

Copplestone looked hard at Spurge; Spurge returned the stare, and nodded two or three times.

"Gospel truth!" he said. "I kept where I was—I'd reasons of my own. May be eight minutes or so—certainly not ten—after Bassett Oliver walked in there, Squire Greyle walked out. In a hurry, guv'nor. He come out quick. He looked a bit queer. Dazed, like. You know how quick a man can think, guv'nor, under certain circumstances? I thought quicker'n lightning. I says to myself 'Squire's seen somebody or something he hadn't no taste for!' Why, you could read it on his face! plain as print. It was there!"

"Well?" said Copplestone. "And then?"

"Then," continued Spurge. "Then he stood for just a second or two, looking right and left, up and down. There wasn't a soul in sight—nobody! But—he slunk off—sneaked off—same as a fox sneaks away from a farm-yard. He went down the side of the curtain-wall that shuts in the ruins, taking as much cover as ever he could find—at the

70

end of the wall, he popped into the wood that stands between the ruins and his house. And then, of course, I lost all sight of him."

"And—Mr. Oliver?" said Copplestone. "Did you see him again?"

Spurge took a pull at his rum and water, and relighted his pipe.

"I did not," he answered. "I was there until a quarter-past three— then I went away. And no Oliver had come out o' that door when I left."

CHAPTER X
THE INVALID CURATE

Spurge and his visitor sat staring at each other in silence for a few minutes; the silence was eventually broken by Copplestone.

"Of course," he said reflectively, "if Mr. Oliver was looking round those ruins he could easily spend half an hour there."

"Just so," agreed Spurge. "He could spend an hour. If so be as he was one of these here antiquarian-minded gents, as loves to potter about old places like that, he could spend two hours, three hours, profitable-like. But he'd have come out in the end, and the evidence is, guv'nor, that he never did come out! Even if I am just now lying up, as it were, I'm fully what they term o-fay with matters, and, by all accounts, after Bassett Oliver went up that there path, subsequent to his bit of talk with Ewbank, he was never seen no more 'cepting by me, and possibly by Squire Greyle. Them as lives a good deal alone, like me guv'nor, develops what you may call logical faculties—they thinks—and thinks deep. I've thought. B.O.—that's Oliver—didn't go back by the way he'd come, or he'd ha' been seen. B.O. didn't go forward or through the woods to the headlands, or he'd ha' been seen, B.O. didn't go down to the shore, or he'd ha' been seen. 'Twixt you and me, guv'nor, B.O.'s dead body is in that there Keep!"

"Are you suggesting anything?" asked Copplestone.

"Nothing, guv'nor—no more than that," answered Spurge. "I'm making no suggestion and no accusation against nobody. I've seen a bit too much of life to do that. I've known more than one innocent man hanged there at Norcaster Gaol in my time all through what they call circumstantial evidence. Appearances is all very well—but appearances may be against a man to the very last degree, and yet him be as innocent as a new born baby! No—I make no suggestions. 'Cepting this here—which has no doubt occurred to you, or to B.O.'s brother. If I were the missing gentleman's friends I should want to know a lot! I should want to know precisely what he meant when he said to Dan'l Ewbank as how he'd known a man called Marston Greyle in America. 'Taint a common name, that, guv'nor."

Copplestone made no answer to these observations. His own train of thought was somewhat similar to his host's. And presently he turned to a different track.

"You saw no one else about there that afternoon?" he asked.

"No one, guv'nor," replied Spurge.

"And where did you go when you left the place?" inquired Copplestone.

"To tell you the truth, guv'nor, I was waiting there for that cousin o' mine—him as carried you the letter," answered Spurge. "It was a fixture between us—he was to meet me there about three o'clock that day. If he wasn't there, or in sight, by a quarter-past three I was to know he wasn't able to get away. So as he didn't come, I slipped back into the woods, and made my way back here, round by the moors."

"Are you going to stay in this place?" asked Copplestone.

"For a bit, guv'nor—till I see how things are," replied Spurge. "As I say, I'm wanted for poaching, and Chatfield's been watching to get his knife into me this long while. All the same, if more serious things drew his attention off, he might let it slide. What do you ask for, guv'nor?"

"I wanted to know where you could be found in case you were required to give evidence about seeing Mr. Oliver," replied Copplestone. "That evidence may be wanted."

"I've thought of that," observed Spurge. "And you can always find that much out from my cousin at the 'Admiral.' He keeps in touch with me—if it got too hot for me here, I should clear out to Norcaster—there's a spot there where I've laid low many a time. You can trust my cousin—Jim Spurge, that's his name. One eye, no mistaking of him—he's always about the yard there at Mrs. Wooler's."

"All right," said Copplestone. "If I want you, I'll tell him. By-the-bye, have you told this to anybody?"

"Not to a soul, guv'nor," replied Spurge. "Not even to Jim. No—I kept it dark till I could see you. Considering, of course, that you are left in charge of things, like."

Copplestone presently went away and returned slowly to Scarhaven, meditating deeply on what he had heard. He saw no reason to doubt the truth of Zachary Spurge's tale—it bore the marks of credibility. But what did it amount to? That Spurge saw Bassett Oliver enter the ruins of the Keep, by the one point of ingress; that a few moments later he saw Marston Greyle come away from the same place, evidently considerably upset, and sneak off in a manner which showed that he dreaded observation. That was all very suspicious, to say the least of it, taken in relation to Oliver's undoubted disappearance—but it was only suspicion; it afforded no direct proof. However, it gave material for a report to Sir Cresswell Oliver, and he determined to write out an account of his dealings with Spurge that afternoon, and to send it off at once by registered letter.

He was busily engaged in this task when Mrs. Wooler came into his sitting-room to lay the table for his lunch. Copplestone saw at once that she was full of news.

"Never rains but it pours!" she said with a smile. "Though, to be sure, it isn't a very heavy shower. I've got another visitor now, Mr. Copplestone."

"Oh?" responded Copplestone, not particularly interested. "Indeed!"

"A young clergyman from London—the Reverend Gilling," continued the landlady. "Been ill for some time, and his doctor has recommended him to try the north coast air. So he came down here, and he's going to stop awhile to see how it suits him."

"I should have thought the air of the north coast was a bit strong for an invalid," remarked Copplestone. "I'm not delicate, but I find it quite strong enough for me."

"I daresay it's a case of kill or cure," replied Mrs. Wooler. "Chest complaint, I should think. Not that the young gentleman looks particularly delicate, either, and he tells me that he's a very good appetite and that his doctor says he's to live well and to eat as much as ever he can."

Copplestone got a view of his fellow-visitor that afternoon in the hall of the inn, and agreed with the landlady that he showed no evident signs of delicacy of health. He was a good type of the conventional curate, with a rather pale, good-humoured face set between his round collar and wide brimmed hat, and he glanced at Copplestone with friendly curiosity and something of a question in his eyes. And Copplestone, out of good neighbourliness, stopped and spoke to him.

"Mrs. Wooler tells me you're come here to pick up," he remarked. "Pretty strong air round this quarter of the globe!"

"Oh, that's all right!" said the new arrival. "The air of Scarhaven will do me good—it's full of just what I want." He gave Copplestone another look and then glanced at the letters which he held in his hand. "Are you going to the post-office?" he asked. "May I come?—I want to go there, too."

The two young men walked out of the inn, and Copplestone led the way down the road towards the northern quay. And once they were well out of earshot of the "Admiral's Arms," and the two or three men who lounged near the wall in front of it, the curate turned to his companion with a sly look.

"Of course you're Mr. Copplestone?" he remarked. "You can't be anybody else—besides, I heard the landlady call you so."

"Yes," replied Copplestone, distinctly puzzled by the other's manner. "What then?"
The curate laughed quietly, and putting his fingers inside his heavy overcoat, produced a card which he handed over.

"My credentials!" he said.

Copplestone glanced at the card and read "Sir Cresswell Oliver," He turned wonderingly to his companion, who laughed again.

"Sir Cresswell told me to give you that as soon as I conveniently could," he said. "The fact is, I'm not a clergyman at all—not I! I'm a private detective, sent down here by him and Petherton. See?"

Copplestone stared for a moment at the wide-brimmed hat, the round collar, the eminently clerical countenance. Then he burst into laughter. "I congratulate you on your make-up, anyway!" he exclaimed. "Capital!"

"Oh, I've been on the stage in my time," responded the private detective. "I'm a good hand at fitting myself to various parts; besides I've played the conventional curate a score of times. Yes, I don't think anybody would see through me, and I'm very particular to avoid the clergy."

"And you left the stage—for this?" asked Copplestone. "Why, now?"

"Pays better—heaps better," replied the other calmly. "Also, it's more exciting—there's much more variety in it. Well, now you know who I am—my name, by-the-bye is Gilling, though I'm not the Reverend Gilling, as Mrs. Wooler will call me. And so—as I've made things plain—how's this matter going so far?"

Copplestone shook his head.

"My orders," he said, with a significant look, "are—to say nothing to any one."

"Except to me," responded Gilling. "Sir Cresswell Oliver's card is my passport. You can tell me anything."

"Tell me something first," replied Copplestone. "Precisely what are you here for? If I'm to talk confidentially to you, you must talk in the same fashion to me."

He stopped at a deserted stretch of the quay, and leaning against the wall which separated it from the sand, signed to Gilling to stop also.

"If we're going to have a quiet talk," he went on, "we'd better have it now—no one's about, and if any one sees us from a distance they'll only think we're, what we look to be—casual acquaintances. Now—what is your job?"

Gilling looked about him and then perched himself on the wall.

"To watch Marston Greyle," he replied.

"They suspect him?" asked Copplestone.

"Undoubtedly!"

"Sir Cresswell Oliver said as much to me—but no more. Have they said more to you?"

"The suspicion seemed to have originated with Petherton. Petherton, in spite of his meek old-fashioned manners, is as sharp an old bird as you'll find in London! He fastened at once on what Bassett Oliver said to that fisherman, Ewbank. A keen nose for a scent, Petherton's! And he 's determined to find out who it was that Bassett Oliver met in the United States under the name of Marston Greyle. He's already set the machinery in motion. And in the meantime, I'm to keep my eye on this Squire—as I shall!"

"Why watch him particularly?"

"To see that he doesn't depart for unknown regions—or, if he does, to follow in his track. He's not to be lost sight of until this mystery is cleared. Because—something is wrong."

Copplestone considered matters in silence for a few moments, and decided not to reveal the story of Zachary Spurge to Gilling—yet awhile at any rate. However, he had news which there was no harm in communicating.

"Marston Greyle," he said, presently, "or his agent, Peter Chatfield, or both, in common agreement, are already doing something to solve the mystery—so far as Greyle's property is concerned. They've closed the Keep and its surrounding ruins to the people who used to be permitted to go in, and they're conducting an exhaustive search— for Bassett Oliver, of course."

Gilling made a grimace.

"Of course!" he said, cynically. "Just so! I expected something of that sort. That's all part of a clever scheme."

"I don't understand you," remarked Copplestone. "How—a clever scheme?"

"Whitewash!" answered Gilling. "Sheer whitewash! You don't suppose that either Greyle or Chatfield are fools?—I should say they're far from it, from what little I've heard of 'em. Well—don't they know very well that Marston Greyle is under suspicion? All right—they want to clear him. So they close their ruins and make a search—a private search, mind you—and at the end they announce that nothing's been found—and there you are! And—supposing they did find something—supposing they found Bassett Oliver's body— What is it?" he asked suddenly, seeing Copplestone staring hard across the sands at the opposite quay. "Something happened?"

"By Gad!—I believe something has happened!" exclaimed Copplestone. "Look there—men running down the hillside from the Keep. And listen—they're shouting to those fellows on the other quay. Come on across! Will it be out of keeping with your invalid pose if you run?"

Gilling answered that question by lightly vaulting the wall and dropping to the sands beneath.

"I'm not an invalid in my legs, anyhow," he answered, as they began to splash across the pools left by the recently retreated tide. "By George!—I believe something has happened, too! Look at those people, running out of their cottages!"

All along the south quay the fisher-folk, men, women, and children, were crowding eagerly towards the gate of the path by which Bassett Oliver had gone up towards the Keep. When Copplestone and his companion gained the quay and climbed up its wall they were pouring in at this gate, and swarming up to the woods, all talking at the top of their voices. Copplestone suddenly recognized Ewbank on the fringe of the crowd and called to him.

"What is it?" he demanded. "What's happened?"

Ewbank, a man of leisurely movement, paused and waited for the two young men to come up. At their approach he took his pipe out of his mouth, and inclined his head towards the Keep.

"They're saying something's been found up there." he replied. "I don't know what. But Chatfield, he's sent two men down here to the village. One of 'em's gone for the police and the doctor, and t'other's gone to the 'Admiral,' looking for you. You're wanted up there—partiklar!"

CHAPTER XI
BENEATH THE BRAMBLES

By the time Copplestone and the pseudo-curate had reached the plateau of open ground surrounding the ruins it seemed as if half the population of Scarhaven had gathered there. Men, women and children were swarming about the door in the curtain wall, all manifesting an eager desire to pass through. But the door was strictly guarded. Chatfield, armed with a new oak cudgel stood there, masterful and lowering; behind him were several estate labourers, all keeping the people back. And within the door stood Marston Greyle, evidently considerably restless and perturbed, and every now and then looking out on the mob which the fast-spreading rumour had called together. In one of these inspections he caught sight of Copplestone, and spoke to Chatfield, who immediately sent one of his body-guard through the throng.

"Mr. Greyle says will you go forward, sir?" said the man. "Your friend can go in too, if he likes."

"That's your clerical garb," whispered Copplestone as he and Gilling made their way to the door. "But why this sudden politeness?"

"Oh, that's easy to reckon up," answered Gilling. "I see through it. They want creditable and respectable witnesses to something or other. This big, heavy-jowled man is Chatfield, of course?"

"That's Chatfield," responded Copplestone. "What's he after?"

For the agent, as the two young men approached, ostentiously turned away from them, moving a few steps from the door. He muttered a word or two to the men who guarded it and they stood aside and allowed Copplestone and the curate to enter. Marston Greyle came forward, eyeing Gilling with a sharp glance of inspection. He turned from him to Copplestone.

"Will you come in?" he asked, not impolitely and with a certain anxiety of manner. "I want you to—to be present, in fact. This gentleman is a friend of yours?"

"An acquaintance of an hour," interposed Gilling, with ready wit. "I have just come to stay at the inn—for my health's sake."

"Perhaps you'll be kind enough to accompany us?" said Greyle. "The fact is, Mr. Copplestone, we've found Mr. Bassett Oliver's body."

"I thought so," remarked Copplestone.

"And as soon as the police come up," continued Greyle, "I want you all to see exactly where it is. No one's touched it—no one's been near it. Of course, he's dead!"

He lifted his hand with a nervous gesture, and the two others, who were watching him closely, saw that he was trembling a good deal, and that his face was very pale.

"Dead!—of course," he went on. "He—he must have been killed instantaneously. And you'll see in a minute or two why the body wasn't found before—when we made that first search. It's quite explainable. The fact is—"

A sudden bustle at the door in the wall heralded the entrance of two policemen. The Squire went forward to meet them. The prospect of immediate action seemed to pull him together and his manner changed to one of assertive superintendence of things.

"Now, Mr. Chatfield!" he called out. "Keep all these people away! Close the door and let no one enter on any excuse. Stay there yourself and see that we are not interrupted. Come this way now," he went on, addressing the policemen and the two favoured spectators.

"You've found him, then, sir?" asked the police-sergeant in a thick whisper, as Greyle led his party across the grass to the foot of the

Keep. "I suppose it's all up with the poor gentleman; of course? The doctor, he wasn't in, but they'll send him up as soon—"

"Mr. Bassett Oliver is dead," interrupted Greyle, almost harshly. "No doctors can do any good. Now, look here," he continued, pulling them to a sudden halt, "I want all of you to take particular notice of this old tower—the Keep. I believe you have not been in here before, Mr. Copplestone—just pay particular attention to this place. Here you see is the Keep, standing in the middle of what I suppose was the courtyard of the old castle. It's a square tower, with a stair-turret at one angle. The stair in that turret is in a very good state of preservation—in fact, it is quite easy to climb to the top, and from the top there's a fine view of land and sea: the Keep itself is nearly a hundred feet in height. Now the inside of the Keep is completely gutted, as you'll presently see—there isn't a floor left of the five or six which were once there. And I'm sorry to say there's very little protection when one's at the top—merely a narrow ledge with a very low parapet, which in places is badly broken. Consequently, any one who climbs to the top must be very careful, or there's the danger of slipping off that ledge and falling to the bottom. Now in my opinion that's precisely what happened on Sunday afternoon. Oliver evidently got in here, climbed the stairs in the turret to enjoy the view and fell from the parapet. And why his body hasn't been found before I'll now show you."

He led the way to the extreme foot of the Keep, and to a very low-arched door, at which stood a couple of the estate labourers, one of whom carried a lighted lantern. To this man the Squire made a sign.

"Show the way," he said, in a low voice.

The man turned and descended several steps of worn and moss-covered stone which led through the archway into a dark, cellar-like place smelling strongly of damp and age. Greyle drew the attention of his companions to a heap of earth and rubbish at the entrance.

"We had to clear all that out before we could get in here," he said. "This archway hadn't been opened for ages. This, of course, is the very lowest story of the Keep, and half beneath the level of the ground outside. Its roof has gone, like all the rest, but as you see, something else has supplied its place. Hold up your lantern, Marris!"

The other men looked up and saw what the Squire meant. Across the tower, at a height of some fifteen or twenty feet from the floor, Nature, left unchecked, had thrown a ceiling of green stuff. Bramble, ivy, and other spreading and climbing plants had, in the course of years, made a complete network from wall to wall. In places it was so thick that no light could be seen through it from beneath; in other places it was thin and glimpses of the sky could be seen from above the grey, tunnel-like walls. And in one of those places, close to the walls, there was a distinct gap, jagged and irregular, as if some heavy mass had recently plunged through the screen of leaf and branch from the heights above, and beneath this the startled searchers saw the body, lying beside a heap of stones and earth in the unmistakable stillness of death.

"You see how it must have happened," whispered Greyle, as they all bent round the dead man. "He must have fallen from the very top of the Keep—from the parapet, in fact—and plunged through this mass of green stuff above us. If he had hit that where it's so thick— there!—it might have broken his fall, but, you see, he struck it at the very thinnest part, and being a big and heavyish man, of course, he'd crash right through it. Now of course, when we examined the Keep on Monday morning, it never struck us that there might be something down here—if you go up the turret stairs to the top and look down on this mass of green stuff from the very top, you'll see that it looks undisturbed; there's scarcely anything to show that he fell through it, from up there. But—he did!"

"Whose notion was it that he might be found here?" asked Copplestone.

"Chatfield's," replied the Squire. "Chatfield's. He and I were up at the top there, and he suddenly suggested that Oliver might have fallen from the parapet and be lying embedded in that mass of green stuff beneath. We didn't know then—even Chatfield didn't know—that there was this empty space beneath the green stuff. But when we came to go into it, we found there was, so we had that archway cleared of all the stone and rubbish and of course we found him."

"The body'll have to be removed, sir," whispered the police-sergeant. "It'll have to be taken down to the inn, to wait the inquest."
Marston Greyle started.

"Inquest!" he said. "Oh! — will that have to be held? I suppose so — yes.
But we'd better wait until the doctor comes, hadn't we? I want him — "

The doctor came into the gloomy vault at that moment, escorted by Chatfield, who, however, immediately retired. He was an elderly, old-fashioned somewhat fussy-mannered person, who evidently attached much more importance to the living Squire than to the dead man, and he listened to all Marston Greyle's explanations and theories with great deference and accepted each without demur. "Ah yes, to be sure!" he said, after a perfunctory examination of the body. "The affair is easily understood. It is precisely as you suggest, Squire. The unfortunate man evidently climbed to the top of the tower, missed his footing, and fell headlong. That slight mass of branch and leaf would make little difference — he was, you see, a heavy man — some fourteen or fifteen stone, I should think. Oh, instantaneous death, without a doubt! Well, well, these constables must see to the removal of the body, and we must let my friend the coroner know — he will hold the inquest tomorrow, no doubt. Quite a mere formality, my dear sir! — the whole thing is as plain as a pikestaff. It will be a relief to know that the mystery is now satisfactorily solved."

Outside in the welcome freshness, Copplestone turned to the doctor.

"You say the inquest will be held tomorrow?" he asked. The doctor looked his questioner up and down with an inquiry which signified doubt as to Copplestone's right to demand information.

"In the usual course," he replied stiffly.

"Then his brother, Sir Cresswell Oliver, and his solicitor, Mr. Petherton, must be wired for from London," observed Copplestone, turning to Greyle. "I'll communicate with them at once. I suppose we may go up the tower?" he continued as Greyle nodded his assent. "I'd like to see the stairs and the parapet."

Greyle looked a little doubtful and uneasy.

"Well, I had meant that no one should go up until all this was gone into," he answered. "I don't want any more accidents. You'll be careful?"

"We're both young and agile," responded Copplestone.

"There's no need for alarm. Do you care to go up, Mr. Gilling?"

The pseudo-curate accepted the invitation readily, and he and Copplestone entered the turret. They had climbed half its height before
Copplestone spoke.
"Well?" he whispered. "What do you think?"

"It may be accident," muttered Gilling. "It—mayn't."

"You think he might have been—what?—thrown down?"

"Might have been caught unawares, and pushed over. Let's see what there is up above, anyway."

The stair in the turret, much worn, but comparatively safe, and lighted by loopholes and arrow-slits, terminated in a low arched doorway, through which egress was afforded to a parapet which ran completely round the inner wall of the Keep. It was in no place more than a yard wide; the balustrading which fenced it in was in some places completely gone, a mere glance was sufficient to show that only a very cool-headed and extremely sure-footed person ought to traverse it. Copplestone contented himself with an inspection from the archway; he looked down and saw at once that a fall from that height must mean sure and swift death: he saw, too, that Greyle had been quite right in saying that the sudden plunge of Oliver's body through the leafy screen far beneath had made little difference to the appearance of that screen as seen from above. And now that he saw everything it seemed to him that the real truth might well lie in one word—accident.

"Coming round this parapet?" asked Gilling, who was looking narrowly about him.

"No!" replied Copplestone. "I can't stand looking down from great heights. It makes my head swim. Are you?"

"Sure!" answered Gilling. He took off his heavy overcoat and handed it to his companion. "Mind holding it?" he asked. "I want to have a good look at the exact spot from which Oliver must have fallen. There's the gap—such as it is, and it doesn't look much from here, does it?—in the green stuff, down below, so he must have been here on the parapet exactly above it. Gad! it's very narrow, and a bit risky, this, when all's said and done!"

Copplestone watched his companion make his way round to the place from which it was only too evident Oliver must have fallen. Gilling went slowly, carefully inspecting every yard of the moss and lichen-covered stones. Once he paused some time and seemed to be examining a part of the parapet with unusual attention. When he reached the precise spot at which he had aimed, he instantly called across to Copplestone.

"There's no doubt about his having fallen from here!" he said. "Some of the masonry on the very edge of this parapet is loose. I could dislodge it with a touch."

"Then be careful," answered Copplestone. "Don't cross that bit!"

But Gilling quietly continued his progress and returned to his companion by the opposite side from which he had set out, having thus accomplished the entire round. He quietly reassumed his overcoat.

"No doubt about the fall," he said as they turned down the stair. "The next thing is—was it accidental?"

"And—as regards that—what's to be done next?" asked Copplestone.

"That's easy. We must go at once and wire for Sir Cresswell and old Petherton," replied Gilling. "It's now four-thirty. If they catch an evening express at King's Cross they'll get here early in the morning. If they like to motor from Norcaster they can get here in the small hours. But—they must be here for that inquest."

Greyle was talking to Chatfield at the foot of the Keep when they got down. The agent turned surlily away, but the Squire looked at both with an unmistakable eagerness.

"There's no doubt whatever that Oliver fell from the parapet," said Copplestone. "The marks of a fall are there—quite unmistakably." Greyle nodded, but made no remark, and the two made their way through the still eager crowd and went down to the village post-office. Both were wondering, as they went, about the same thing—the evident anxiety and mental uneasiness of Marston Greyle.

CHAPTER XII
GOOD MEN AND TRUE

Copplestone saw little of his bed that night. At seven o'clock in the evening came a telegram from Sir Cresswell Oliver, saying that he and Petherton were leaving at once, would reach Norcaster soon after midnight, and would motor out to Scarhaven immediately on arrival. Copplestone made all arrangements for their reception, and after snatching a couple of hours' sleep was up to receive them. By two o'clock in the morning Sir Cresswell and the old solicitor and Gilling—smuggled into their sitting-room—had heard all he had to tell about Zachary Spurge and his story.

"We must have that fellow at the inquest," said Petherton. "At any cost we must have him! That's flat!"

"You think it wise?" asked Sir Cresswell. "Won't it be a bit previous? Wouldn't it be better to wait until we know more?"
"No—we must have his evidence," declared Petherton. "It will serve as an opening. Besides, this inquest will have to be adjourned—I shall ask for that. No—Spurge must be produced."

"If Spurge comes into Scarhaven," observed Copplestone, "he'll be promptly collared by the police. They want him for poaching."

"Then they can get him when the proceedings are over," retorted the old lawyer, dryly. "They daren't touch him while he's giving evidence and that's all we want. Perhaps he won't come?—Oh he'll come all right if we make it worth his while. A month in Norcaster gaol will mean nothing to him if he knows there's a chance of that reward or something substantial out of it at the end of his sentence. You must go out to this retreat of his and bring him in—we must have him. Better go very early in the morning."

"I'll go now," said Copplestone. "It's as easy to go by night as by day." He left the other three to seek their beds, and himself slipped quietly out of the hotel by one of the ground-floor windows and set off in a pitch-black night to seek Spurge in his lair. And after sundry barkings of his shins against the rocks and scratchings of his hands and cheeks by the undergrowth of Hobkin's Hole he rounded the poacher out and delivered his message.

Spurge, blinking at his visitor in the pale light of a guttering candle, shook his head.

"I'll come, guv'nor," he said. "Of course. I'll come—and I'll trust to luck to get away, and it don't matter a deal if the luck's agen me—I've done a month in Norcaster before today, and it ain't half a bad rest-cure, if you only take it that way. But guv'nor—that old lawyer's making a mistake! You didn't ought to have my bit of evidence at this stage. It's too soon. You want to work up the case a bit. There's such a thing, guv'nor, in this world as being a bit previous. This here's too previous—you want to be surer of your facts. Because you know, guv'nor nobody'll believe my word agen Squire Greyle's. Guv'nor—this here inquest'll be naught but a blooming farce! Mark me! You ain't a native o' this part—I am. D'you think as how a Scarhaven jury's going to say aught agen its own Squire and landlord? Not it! I say, guv'nor—all a blooming farce! Mark my words!"

"All the same, you'll come?" asked Copplestone, who was secretly of Spurge's opinion. "You won't lose by it in the long run."
"Oh, I'll be there," responded Spurge. "Out of curiosity, if for nothing else. You mayn't see me at first, but, let the lawyer from London call my name out, and Zachary Spurge'll step forward."

There was abundant cover for Zachary Spurge and for half-a-dozen like him in the village school-house when the inquest was opened at ten o'clock that morning. It seemed to Copplestone that it would have been a physical impossibility to crowd more people within the walls than had assembled when the coroner, a local solicitor, who was obviously testy, irritable, self-important and afflicted with deafness, took his seat and looked sourly on the crowd of faces. Copplestone had already seen him in conversation with the village doctor, the village police, Chatfield, and Marston Greyle's solicitor, and he began to see the force of Spurge's shrewd remarks. What, of ff f fff f ff f ff fff fff f f f ff f ff f ffff ff f f f f f fff f fff f f f f f f f f f f f f f ff f f f

"I don't know if you notice that Greyle isn't here?" he whispered grimly.

"In my opinion, he doesn't intend to show! We'll see!"

Certainly the Squire was not in the place. And there were soon signs that those who conducted the proceedings evidently did not consider his presence necessary. The witnesses were few; their examinations was perfunctory; they were out of the extemporised witness-box as soon as they were in it. Sir Cresswell Oliver—to give formal identification. Mrs. Wooler—to prove that the deceased man came to her house. One of the foremen of the estate—to prove the great care with which the Squire had searched for traces of the missing man. One of the estate labourers—to prove the actual finding of the body. The doctor—to prove, beyond all doubt, that the deceased had broken his neck.

The coroner, an elderly man, obviously well satisfied with the trend of things, took off his spectacles and turned to the jury.

"You have heard everything there is to be heard, gentlemen," said he. "As I remarked at the opening of this inquest, the case is one of great simplicity. You will have no difficulty in deciding that the deceased came to his death by accident—as to the exact wording of your verdict, you had better put it in this way:—that the deceased Bassett Oliver died as the result—"

Petherton, who, noticing the coroner's deafness, had contrived to seat himself as close to his chair of office as possible, quietly rose.

"Before the jury consider any verdict," he said in his loudest tones, "they must hear certain evidence which I wish to call. And first of all—is Mr. Marston Greyle present in this room?"

The coroner frowned, and the Squire's solicitor turned to Petherton.

"Mr. Greyle is not present," he said. "He is not at all well. There is no need for his presence—he has no evidence to give."

"If you don't have Mr. Greyle down here at once," said Petherton, quietly, "this inquest will have to be adjourned for his attendance. You had better send for him—or I'll get the authorities to do so. In the meantime, we'll call one or two witnesses,—Daniel Ewbank!—to begin with."

There was a brief and evidently anxious consultation between Greyle's solicitor and the coroner; there were dark looks at Petherton and his companions. Then the foreman of the jury spoke, sullenly.

"We don't want to hear no Ewbanks!" he said. "We're quite satisfied, us as sits here. Our verdict is—"

"You'll have to bear Ewbank and anybody I like to call, my good sir," retorted Petherton quietly. "I am better acquainted with the law than you are." He turned to the coroner's officer. "I warned you this morning to produce Ewbank," he said. "Now, where is he?"

Out of a deep silence a shrill voice came from the rear of the crowd.

"Knows better than to be here, does Dan'l Ewbank, mister! He's off!"

"Very good—or bad—for somebody," remarked Petherton, quietly. "Then—until Mr. Marston Greyle comes—we will call Zachary Spurge."
The assemblage, jurymen included, broke into derisive laughter as Spurge suddenly appeared from the most densely packed corner of the room, and it was at once evident to Copplestone that whatever the poacher might say, no one there would attach any importance to it. The laughter continued and increased while Spurge was under examination. Petherton appealed to the coroner; the coroner affected not to hear. And once more the foreman of the jury interrupted.

"We don't want to hear no more o' this stuff!" he said. "It's an insult to us to put a fellow like that before us. We don't believe a word o' what he says. We don't believe he was within a mile o' them ruins on Sunday afternoon. It's all a put-up job!"

Petherton leaned towards the reporters.

"I hope you gentlemen of the press will make a full note of these proceedings," he observed suavely. "You at any rate are not biassed or prejudiced."

The coroner heard that in spite of his deafness, and he grew purple.

"Sir!" he exclaimed. "That is a most improper observation! It's a reflection on my position, sir, and I've a great mind—"

"Mr. Coroner," observed Petherton, leaning towards him, "I shall hand in a full report concerning your conduct of these proceedings to the Home Office tomorrow. If you attempt to interfere with my duty here, all the worse for you. Now, Spurge, you can stand down. And as I see Mr. Greyle there—call Marston Greyle!"

The Squire had appeared while Spurge was giving his evidence, and had heard what the poacher alleged. He entered the box very pale, angry, and disturbed, and the glances which he cast on Sir Cresswell Oliver and his party were distinctly those of displeasure.

"Swear him!" commanded Petherton. "Now, Mr. Greyle—"

But Greyle's own solicitor was on his legs, insisting on his right to put a first question. In spite of Petherton, he put it.

"You heard the evidence of the last witness?—Spurge. Is there a word of truth in it?"

Marston Greyle—who certainly looked very unwell—moistened his lips.

"Not one word!" he answered. "It's a lie!"

The solicitor glanced triumphantly at the Coroner and the jury, and the crowd raised unchecked murmurs of approval. Again the foreman endeavoured to stop the proceedings.

"We regard all this here as very rude conduct to Mr. Greyle," he said angrily. "We're not concerned—"

"Mr. Foreman!" said Petherton. "You are a foolish man—you are interfering with justice. Be warned!—I warn you, if the Coroner doesn't.
Mr. Greyle, I must ask you certain questions. Did you see the deceased
Bassett Oliver on Sunday last?"
"No!"

"I needn't remind you that you are on your oath. Have you ever met the deceased man in your life?"

"Never!"

"You never met him in America?"

"I may have met him—but not to my recollection. If I did, it was in such a casual fashion that I have completely forgotten all about it."

"Very well—you are on your oath, mind. Where did you live in America, before you succeeded to this estate?"

The Squire's solicitor intervened.

"Don't answer that question!" he said sharply. "Don't answer any more. I object altogether to your line," he went on, angrily, turning to Petherton. "I claim the Coroner's protection for the witness."

"I quite agree," said the Coroner. "All this is absolutely irrelevant. You can stand down," he continued, turning to the Squire. "I will have no more of this—and I will take the full responsibility!"

"And the consequences, Mr. Coroner," replied Petherton calmly. "And the first consequence is that I now formally demand an adjournment of this inquest, sine die."

"On what grounds, sir?" demanded the Coroner.

"To permit me to bring evidence from America," replied Petherton, with a side glance at Marston Greyle. "Evidence already being prepared."

The Coroner hesitated, looked at Greyle's solicitor, and then turned sharply to the jury.

"I refuse that application!" he said. "You have heard all I have to say, gentlemen," he went on, "and you can return your verdict."

Petherton quietly gathered up his papers and motioned to his friends to follow him out of the schoolroom. The foreman of the jury was returning a verdict of accidental death as they passed through the door, and they emerged into the street to an accompaniment of loud cheers for the Squire and groans for themselves.

"What a travesty of justice!" exclaimed Sir Cresswell. "That fellow Spurge was right, you see, Copplestone. I wish we hadn't brought him into danger."

Copplestone suddenly laughed and touched Sir Cresswell's arm. He pointed to the edge of the moorland just outside the school-yard. Spurge was disappearing over that edge, and in a moment had vanished.

CHAPTER XIII
MR. DENNIE

Amongst the little group of actors and actresses who had come over from Norcaster to hear all that was to be told concerning their late manager, sat an old gentleman who, hands folded on the head of his walking cane, and chin settled on his hands, watched the proceedings with silent and concentrated attention. He was a striking figure of an old gentleman—tall, distinguished-looking, handsome, with a face full of character, the strong lines and features of which were further accentuated by his silvery hair. He was a smart old gentleman, too, well and scrupulously attired and groomed, and his blue bird's-eye necktie, worn at a rakish angle, gave him the air of something of a sporting man rather than of a follower of Thespis. His fellow members of the Oliver company seemed to pay him great attention, and at various points of the proceedings whispered questions to him as to an acknowledged authority.

This old gentleman, when the inquest came to its extraordinary end and the crowd went out murmuring and disputing, separated himself from his companions and made his way towards Mrs. Greyle and her daughter, who were quietly setting out homewards. To Audrey's surprise the two elders shook hands in silence, and inspected each other with a palpable wistfulness of look.

"And yet it's twenty-five years since we met, isn't it?" said the old gentleman, almost as if he were talking to himself. "But I knew you at once—I was wondering if you remembered me?"

"Why, of course," responded Mrs. Greyle. "Besides, I've had an advantage over you. I've seen you, you know, several times—at Norcaster. We go to the theatre now and then. Audrey—this is Mr. Dennie—you've seen him, too."
"On the stage—on the stage!" murmured the old actor, as he shook hands with the girl. "Um!—I wonder if any of us are ever really off it! This affair, for instance—there's a drama for you! By the-bye—this young Squire—he's your relation, of course?"

"My nephew-in-law, and Audrey's cousin," replied Mrs. Greyle. Mr. Dennie, who had walked along with them towards their cottage, stopped in a quiet stretch of the quay, and looked meditatively at Audrey.

"Then this young lady," he said, "is next heir to the Greyle estates, eh?
For I understand this present Squire isn't married. Therefore—"
"Oh, that's something that isn't worth thinking about," replied Mrs. Greyle hastily. "Don't put such notions into the girl's head, Mr. Dennie.
Besides, the Greyle estates are not entailed, you know. The present owner
can do what he pleases with them—besides that, he's sure to marry."
"All the same," observed Mr. Dennie, imperturbably, "if this young man had not been in existence, this child would have succeeded, eh?"

"Why, of course," agreed Mrs. Greyle a little impatiently. "But what's the use of talking about that, my old friend! The young man is in possession—and there you are!"

"Do you like the young man?" asked Mr. Dennie. "I take an old fellow's privilege in asking direct questions, you know. And—though we haven't seen each other for all these years—you can say anything to me."

"No, we don't," replied Mrs. Greyle. "And we don't know why we don't—so there's a woman's answer for you. Kinsfolk though we are, we see little of each other."

Mr. Dennie made no remark on this. He walked along at Audrey's side, apparently in deep thought, and suddenly he looked across at her mother.

"What do you think about this extraordinary story of Bassett Oliver's having met a Marston Greyle over there in America?" he asked abruptly. "What do people here think about it?"

"We're not in a position to hear much of what other people think," answered Mrs. Greyle. "What I think is that if this Marston Greyle ever did meet such a very notable and noticeable man as Bassett Oliver it's a very, very strange thing that he's forgotten all about it!"

Mr. Dennie laughed quietly.

"Aye, aye!" he said. "But—don't you think we folk of the profession are a little bit apt to magnify our own importance? You say 'Bless me, how could anybody ever forget an introduction to Bassett Oliver!' But we must remember that to some people even a famous actor is of no more importance than—shall we say a respectable grocer? Marston Greyle may be one of those people—it's quite possible he may have been introduced, quite casually, to Oliver at some club, or gathering, something-or-other, over there and have quite forgotten all about it. Quite possible, I think."

"I agree with you as to the possibility, but certainly not as to the probability," said Mrs. Greyle, dryly. "Bassett Oliver was the sort of man whom nobody would forget. But here we are at our cottage—you'll come in, Mr. Dennie?"

"It will only have to be for a little time, my dear lady," said the old actor, pulling out his watch. "Our people are going back very soon, and I must join them at the station."

"I'll give you a glass of good old wine," said Mrs. Greyle as they went into the cottage. "I have some that belonged to my father-in-law, the old Squire. You must taste it—for old times' sake."

Mr. Dennie followed Audrey into the little parlour as Mrs. Greyle disappeared to another part of the house. And the instant they were alone, he tapped the girl's arm and gave her a curiously warning look.

"Hush, my dear!" he whispered. "Not a word—don't want your mother to know! Listen—have you a specimen—letter—anything—of your cousin, the Squire's handwriting? Anything so long as it's his. You have? Give it to me—say nothing to your mother. Wait until tomorrow morning. I'll run over to see you again—about noon. It's important—but silence!"

Audrey, scarcely understanding the old man's meaning, opened a desk and drew out one or two letters. She selected one and handed it to Mr. Dennie, who made haste to put it away before Mrs. Greyle returned. He gave Audrey another warning look.

"That was what I wanted!" he said mysteriously. "I thought of it during the inquest. Never mind why, just now—you shall know tomorrow."

He lingered a few minutes, chatting to his hostess about old times as he sipped the old Squire's famous port; then he went off to the little station, joined Stafford and his fellow actors and actresses, and returned with them to Norcaster. And at Norcaster Mr. Dennie separated himself from the rest and repaired to his quiet lodgings—rooms which he had occupied for many years in succession whenever he went that way on tour—and once safely bestowed in them he pulled out a certain old-fashioned trunk, which he had owned since boyhood and lugged about wherever he went in two continents, and from it, after much methodical unpacking, he disinterred a brown paper parcel, neatly tied up with green ribbon. From this parcel he drew a thin packet of typed matter and a couple of letters—the type script he laid aside, the letters he opened out on his table. Then he took from his pocket the letter which Audrey Greyle had given him and put it side by side with those taken from the parcel. And after one brief glance at all three Mr. Dennie made typescript and letters up again into a neat packet, restored them to his trunk, locked them up, and turned to the two hours' rest which he always took before going to the theatre for his evening's work.

He was back at Scarhaven by eleven o'clock the next morning, with his neat packet under his arm and he held it up significantly to Audrey who opened the door of the cottage to him.

"Something to show you," he said with a quiet smile as he walked in. "To show you and your mother." He stopped short on the threshold of the little parlour, where Copplestone was just then talking to Mrs. Greyle. "Oh!" he said, a little disappointedly, "I hoped to find you alone—I'll wait."

Mrs. Greyle explained who Copplestone was, and Mr. Dennie immediately brightened. "Of course—of course!" he explained. "I know! Glad to meet you, Mr. Copplestone—you don't know me, but I know you—or your work—well enough. It was I who read and recommended your play to our poor dear friend. It's a little secret, you know," continued Mr. Dennie, laying his packet on the table, "but I have acted for a great many years as Bassett Oliver's literary adviser—taster, you might say. You know, he had a great number of plays sent to him, of course, and he was a very busy man, and he used to hand them over to me in the first place, to take a look at, a taste of, you know, and if I liked the taste, why, then he took a mouthful himself, eh? And that brings me to the very point, my dear ladies and my dear young gentleman, that I have come specially to Scarhaven this morning to discuss. It's a very, very serious matter indeed," he went on as he untied his packet of papers, "and I fear that it's only the beginning of something more serious. Come round me here at this table, all of you, if you please."

The other three drew up chairs, each wondering what was coming, and the old actor resumed his eyeglasses and gave obvious signs of making a speech.

"Now I want you all to attend to me, very closely," he said. "I shall have to go into a detailed explanation, and you will very soon see what I am after. As you may be aware, I have been a personal friend of Bassett Oliver for some years, and a member of his company without break for the last eight years. I accompanied Bassett Oliver on his two trips to the United States—therefore, I was with him when he was last there, years ago.

"Now, while we were at Chicago that time, Bassett came to me one day with the typescript of a one-act play and told me that it had been sent to him by a correspondent signing himself Marston Greyle; who in a covering letter, said that he sprang from an old English family, and that the play dealt with a historic, romantic episode in its history. The principal part, he believed, was one which would suit Bassett—therefore he begged him to consider the matter. Bassett asked me to read the play, and I took it away, with the writer's letter, for that purpose. But we were just then very busy, and I had no opportunity of reading anything for a time. Later on, we went to St. Louis, and there, of course, Bassett, as usual, was much fêted and went out a great deal, lunching with people and so on. One day he came to me, 'By-the-bye, Dennie!' he said, 'I met that Mr. Marston Greyle today who sent me that romantic one-act thing. He wanted to know if I'd read it, and I had to confess that it was in your hands. Have you looked at it?' I, too, had to confess—I hadn't. 'Well,' said he, 'read it and let me know what you think—will it suit me?' I made time to read the little play during the following week, and I told Bassett that I didn't think it would suit him, but I felt sure it might suit Montagu Gaines, who plays just such parts. Bassett thereupon wrote to the author and said what I, his reader, thought, and kindly offered, as he knew Gaines intimately, to show the little work to him on his return to England. And this Mr. Marston Greyle wrote back, thanking Bassett warmly and accepting his kind offer. Accordingly, I brought the play with me to England. Montagu Gaines, however, had just set off on a two years' tour to Australia—consequently, the play and the author's two letters have remained in my possession ever since. And—here they are!"

Mr. Dennie laid his hand dramatically on his packet, looked significantly at his audience, and went on.

"Now, when I heard all that I did hear at that inquest yesterday," he said, "I naturally remembered that I had in my possession two letters which were undoubtedly written to Bassett Oliver by a young man named Marston Greyle, whom Oliver—just as undoubtedly!—had personally met in St. Louis. And so when the inquest was over, Mr. Copplestone, I recalled myself to Mrs. Greyle here, whom I had known many years ago, and I walked back to this house with her and her charming daughter, and—don't be angry, Mrs. Greyle—while the mother's back was turned—on hospitable thoughts intent—I got the daughter to lend me—secretly—a letter written by the present Squire of Scarhaven. Armed with that, I went home to my lodgings in Norcaster, found the letter written by the American Marston Greyle, and compared it with them. And—here is the result!"

The old actor selected the two American letters from his papers, laid them out on the table, and placed the letter which Audrey had given him beside them.

"Now!" he said, as his three companions bent eagerly over these exhibits,
"Look at those three letters. All bear the same signature, Marston Greyle—but the hand-writing of those two is as different from that of
this one as chalk is from cheese!"

CHAPTER XIV
BY PRIVATE TREATY

There was little need for the three deeply interested listeners to look long at the letters—one glance was sufficient to show even a careless eye that the hand which had written one of them had certainly not written the other two. The letter which Audrey had handed to Mr. Dennie was penned in the style commonly known as commercial—plain, commonplace, utterly lacking in the characteristics which are supposed to denote imagination and a sense of artistry. It was the sort of caligraphy which one comes across every day in shops and offices and banks—there was nothing in any upstroke, downstroke or letter which lifted it from the very ordinary. But the other two letters were evidently written by a man of literary and artistic sense, possessing imagination and a liking for effect. It needed no expert in handwriting to declare that two totally different individuals had written those letters.

"And now," observed Mr. Dennie, breaking the silence and putting into words what each of the others was vaguely feeling, "the question is—what does all this mean? To start with, Marston Greyle is a most uncommon name. Is it possible there can be two persons of that name? That, at any rate, is the first thing that strikes me."

"It is not the first thing that strikes me," said Mrs. Greyle. She took up the typescript which the old actor had brought in his packet, and held its title-page significantly before him. "That is the first thing that strikes me!" she exclaimed. "The Marston Greyle who sent this to Bassett Oliver said according to your story—that he sprang from a very old family in England, and that this is a dramatization of a romantic episode in its annals. Now there is no other old family in England named Greyle, and this episode is of course, the famous legend of how Prince Rupert once sought refuge in the Keep yonder and had a love-passage with a lady of the house. Am I right, Mr. Dennie?"

"Quite right, ma'am, quite correct," replied the old actor. "It is so—you have guessed correctly!"

"Very well, then—the Marston Greyle who wrote this, and those letters, and who met Bassett Oliver was without doubt the son of Marcus Greyle, who went to America many years ago. He was the same Marston Greyle, who, his father being dead, of course succeeded his uncle, Stephen John Greyle—that seems an absolute certainty. And in that case," continued Mrs. Greyle, looking earnestly from one to the other, "in that case—who is the man now at Scarhaven Keep?"

A dead silence fell on the little room. Audrey started and flushed at her mother's eager, pregnant question; Mr. Dennie sat up very erect and took a pinch of snuff from his old-fashioned box. Copplestone pushed his chair away from the table and began to walk about. And Mrs. Greyle continued to look from one face to the other as if demanding a reply to her question.

"Mother!" said Audrey in a low voice. "You aren't suggesting—"

"Ahem!" interrupted Mr. Dennie. "A moment, my dear. There is nothing, I believe," he continued, waxing a little oracular, "nothing like plain speech. We are all friends—we have a common cause— justice! It may be that justice demands our best endeavours not only as regards our deceased friend, Bassett Oliver, but in the interests of—this young lady. So—"

"I wish you wouldn't, Mr. Dennie!" exclaimed Audrey. "I don't like this at all. Please don't!"

She turned, almost instinctively, to seek Copplestone's aid in repressing the old man. But Copplestone was standing by the window, staring moodily at the wind-swept quay beyond the garden, and Mr. Dennie waved his snuff-box and went on.

"An old man's privilege!" he said. "In your interests, my dear. Allow me." He turned again to Mrs. Greyle. "In plain words, ma'am, you are wondering if the present holder of the estates is really what he claims to be. Plain English, eh?"

"I am!" answered Mrs. Greyle with a distinct ring of challenge and defiance. "And now that it comes to the truth, I have wondered that ever since he came here. There!"

"Why, mother?" asked Audrey, wonderingly.

"Because he doesn't possess a single Greyle characteristic," replied Mrs. Greyle, readily enough, "I ought to know—I married Valentine Greyle, and I knew Stephen John, and I saw plenty of both, and something of their father, too, and a little of Marcus before he emigrated. This man does not possess one single scrap of the Greyle temperament!"

Mr. Dennie put away his snuff-box and drumming on the table with his fingers looked out of his eye corners at Copplestone who still stood with his back to the rest, staring out of the window.

"And what," said Mr. Dennie, softly, "what—er, does our good friend Mr.
Copplestone say?"
Copplestone turned swiftly, and gave Audrey a quick glance.

"I say," he answered in a sharp, business-like fashion, "that Gilling, who's stopping at the inn, you know, is walking up and down outside here, evidently looking out for me, and very anxious to see me, and with your permission, Mrs. Greyle, I'd like to have him in. Now that things have got to this pitch, I'd better tell you something—I don't see any good in concealing it longer. Gilling isn't an invalid curate at all!—he's a private detective. Sir Cresswell Oliver and Petherton, the solicitor, sent him down here to watch Greyle— the Squire, you know—that's Gilling's job. They suspect Greyle— have suspected him from the very first—but of what I don't know. Not—not of this, I think. Anyway, they do suspect him, and Gilling's had his eye on him ever since he came here. And I'd like to fetch Gilling in here, and I'd like him to know all that Mr. Dennie's told us. Because, don't you see, Sir Cresswell and Petherton ought to know all that, immediately, and Gilling's their man."

Audrey's brows had been gathering in lines of dismay and perplexity all the time Copplestone was talking, but her mother showed no signs of anything but complete composure, crowned by something very like satisfaction, and she nodded a ready acquiescence in Copplestone's proposal.

"By all means!" she responded. "Bring Mr. Gilling in at once."

Copplestone hurried out into the garden and signalled to the pseudo-curate, who came hurrying across from the quay. One glance at him showed Copplestone that something had happened.

"Gad! — I thought I should never attract your attention!" said Gilling hastily. "Been making eyes at you for ten minutes. I say — Greyle's off!"

"Off!" exclaimed Copplestone. "How do you mean — off?"

"Left Scarhaven, anyhow — for London," replied Gilling. "An hour ago I happened to be at the station, buying a paper, when he drove up — luggage and man with him, so I knew he was off for some time. And I took good care to dodge round by the booking-office when the man took the tickets. King's Cross. So that's all right, for the time being."

"How do you mean — all right?" asked Copplestone. "I thought you were to keep him in sight?"

"All right," repeated Gilling. "I have more eyes than these, my boy! I've a particularly smart partner in London — name of Swallow — and he and I have a cypher code. So soon as the gentleman had left, I repaired to the nearest post office and wired a code message to Swallow. Swallow will meet that train when it strikes King's Cross. And it doesn't matter if Greyle hides himself in one of the spikes on top of the Monument or inside the lion house at the Zoo — Swallow will be there! No man ever got away from Swallow — once Swallow had set eyes on him."

106

Copplestone looked, listened, and laughed.

"Professional pride!" he said. "All right. I want you to come in here with me—to Mrs. Greyle's. Something's happened here, too. And of such a serious nature that I've taken the liberty of telling them who and what you really are. You'll forgive me when you hear what it is that we've learnt here this morning."

Gilling had looked rather doubtful at Copplestone's announcement, but he immediately turned towards the cottage.

"Oh, well!" he said good-naturedly. "I'm sure you wouldn't have told if you hadn't felt there was good reason. What is this fresh news?—something about—him?"

"Very much about him," answered Copplestone. "Come in."

He himself, at Mrs. Greyle's request, gave Gilling a brief account of Mr. Dennie's revelations, the old actor supplementing it with a shrewd remark or two. And then all four turned to Gilling as to an expert in these matters.

"Queer!" observed Gilling. "Decidedly queer! There may be some explanation, you know: I've known stranger things than that turn out to be perfectly straight and plain when they were gone into. But—putting all the facts together—I don't think there's much doubt that there's something considerably wrong in this case. I should like to repeat it to my principals—I must go up to town in any event this afternoon. Better let me have all those documents, Mr. Dennie—I'll give you a proper receipt for them. There's something very valuable in them, anyhow."

"What?" asked Copplestone.

"The address in St. Louis from which that Marston Greyle wrote to Bassett Oliver." replied Gilling. "We can communicate with that address—at once. We may learn something there. But," he went on, turning to Mrs. Greyle, "I want to learn something here—and now. I want to know where and under what circumstances the Squire came to Scarhaven. You were here then, of course, Mrs. Greyle? You can tell me?"

"He came very quietly," replied Mrs. Greyle. "Nobody in Scarhaven—unless it was Peter Chatfield—knew of his coming. In fact, nobody in these parts, at any rate—knew he was in England. The family solicitors in London may have known. But nothing was ever said or written to me, though my daughter, failing this man, is the next in succession."

"I do wish you'd leave all that out, mother!" exclaimed Audrey. "I don't like it."

"Whether you like it or not, it's the fact," said Mrs. Greyle imperturbably, "and it can't be left out. Well, as I say, no one knew the Squire had come to England, until one day Chatfield calmly walked down the quay with him, introducing him right and left. He brought him here."

"Ah!" said Gilling. "That's interesting. Now I wonder if you found out if he was well up in the family history?"

"Not then, but afterwards," answered Mrs. Greyle. "He is particularly well up in the Greyle records—suspiciously well up."

"Why suspiciously?" asked Cobblestone.

"He knows more—in a sort of antiquarian and historian fashion—than you'd suppose a young man of his age would," said Mrs. Greyle. "He gives you the impression of having read it up—studied it deeply. And—his usual tastes don't lie in that direction."

"Ah!" observed Mr. Dennie, musingly. "Bad sign, ma'am,—bad sign! Looks as if he had been—shall we say put up to overstudying his part. That's possible! I have known men who were so anxious to be what one calls letter-perfect, Mr. Copplestone, that though they knew their parts, they didn't know how to play them. Fact, sir!"

While the old actor was chuckling over this reminiscence, Gilling turned quietly to Mrs. Greyle.

"I think you suspect this man?" he said.

"Frankly—yes," replied Mrs. Greyle. "I always have done, though I have said so little—"

"Mother!" interrupted Audrey. "Is it really worth while saying so much now! After all, we know nothing, and if this is all mere supposition—however," she broke off, rising and going away from the group, "perhaps I had better say nothing."

Copplestone too rose and followed her into the window recess.

"I say!" he said entreatingly. "I hope you don't think me interfering? I assure you—"

"You!" she exclaimed. "Oh, no!—of course. I think you're anxious to clear things up about Mr. Oliver. But I don't want my mother dragged into it—for a simple reason. We've got to live here—and Chatfield is a vindictive man."

"You're frightened of him?" said Copplestone incredulously. "You!"

"Not for myself," she answered, giving him a warning look and glancing apprehensively at Mrs. Greyle, who was talking eagerly to Mr. Dennie and Gilling. "But my mother is not as strong as she looks and it would be a blow to her to leave this place and we are the Squire's tenants, and therefore at Chatfield's mercy. And you know that Chatfield does as he likes! Now do you understand?"

"It maddens me to think that you should be at Chatfield's mercy!" muttered Copplestone. "But do you really mean to say that if—if

Chatfield thought you—that is, your mother—were mixed up in anything relating to the clearing up of this affair he would—"

"Drive us out without mercy," replied Audrey. "That's dead certain."

"And that your cousin would let him?" exclaimed Copplestone. "Surely not!"
"I don't think the Squire has any control over Chatfield," she answered.
"You have seen them together."
"If that's so," said Copplestone, "I shall begin to think there is something queer about the Squire in the way your mother suggests. It looks as if Chatfield had a hold on him. And in that case—"

He suddenly broke off as a smart automobile drove up to the cottage door and set down a tall, distinguished-looking man who after a glance at the little house walked quickly up the garden. Audrey's face showed surprise.

"Mother!" she said, turning to Mrs. Greyle. "There's Lord Altmore here!
He must want you. Or shall I go?"
Mrs. Greyle quitted the room hastily. The others heard her welcome the visitor, lead him up the tiny hall; they heard a door shut. Audrey looked at Copplestone.

"You've heard of Lord Altmore, haven't you?" she said. "He's our biggest man in these parts—he owns all the country at the back, mountains, valleys, everything. The Greyle land shuts him off from the sea. In the old days, Greyles and Altmores used to fight over their boundaries, and—"

Mrs. Greyle suddenly showed herself again and looked at her daughter.

"Will you come here, Audrey?" she said. "You gentlemen will excuse both of us for a few minutes?"

110

Mother and daughter went away, and the two young men drew up their chairs to the table at which Mr. Dennie sat and exchanged views with him on the curious situation. Half-an-hour went by; then steps and voices were heard in the hall and the garden; Mrs. Greyle and Audrey were seeing their visitor out to his car. In a few minutes the car sped away, and they came back to the parlour. One glance at their faces showed Gilling that some new development had cropped up and he nudged Copplestone.

"Here is remarkable news!" said Mrs. Greyle as she went back to her chair. "Lord Altmore called to tell me of something that he thought I ought to know. It is almost unbelievable, yet it is a fact. Marston Greyle—if he is Marston Greyle!—has offered to sell Lord Altmore the entire Scarhaven estate, by private treaty. Imagine it!—the estate which has belonged to the Greyles for five hundred years!"

CHAPTER XV
THE CABLEGRAM FROM NEW YORK

The two younger men received this announcement with no more than looks of astonished inquiry, but the elder one coughed significantly, had further recourse to his snuff-box and turned to Mrs. Greyle with a knowing glance.

"My dear lady!" he said impressively. "Now this is a matter in which I believe I can be of service—real service! You may have forgotten the fact—it is all so long ago—and perhaps I never mentioned it in the old days—but the truth is that before I went on the stage, I was in the law. The fact is, I am a duly and fully qualified solicitor—though," he added, with a dry chuckle, "it is a good five and twenty years since I paid the six pounds for the necessary annual certificate. But I have not forgotten my law—or some of it—and no doubt I can furbish up a little more, if necessary. You say that Mr. Marston Greyle, the present owner of Scarhaven, has offered to sell his estate to Lord Altmore? But—is not the estate entailed?"

"No!" replied Mrs. Greyle. "It is not."

Mr. Dennie's face fell—unmistakably. He took another pinch of snuff and shook his head.

"Then in that case," he said dryly, "all the lawyers in the world can't help. It's his—absolutely—and he can do what he pleases with it. Five hundred years, you say? Remarkable!—that a man should want to sell land his forefathers have walked over for half a thousand years! Extraordinary!"

"Did Lord Altmore say if any reason had been given him as to why Mr.
Greyle wished to sell?" asked Gilling.
"Yes," replied Mrs. Greyle, who was obviously greatly upset by the recent news. "He did. Mr. Greyle gave as his reason that the north does not suit him, and that he wishes to buy an estate in the south of England. He approached Lord Altmore first because it is well-known

that the Altmores have always been anxious to extend their own borders to the coast."

"Does Lord Altmore want to buy?" asked Gilling.

"It is very evident that he would be quite willing to buy," said Mrs. Greyle.
"What made him come to you," continued Gilling. "He must have had some reason?"

"He had a reason," Mrs. Greyle answered, with a glance at Audrey. "He knows the family history, of course—he is very well aware that my daughter is at present the heir apparent. He therefore thought we ought to know of this offer. But that is not quite all. Lord Altmore has, of course, read the accounts of the inquest in this morning's paper. Also his steward was present at the inquest. And from what he has read, and from what his steward told him, Lord Altmore thinks there is something wrong—he thinks, for instance, that Marston Greyle should explain this mystery about the meeting with Bassett Oliver in America. At any rate, he will go no further in any negotiations until that mystery is properly cleared up. Shall I tell you what Lord Altmore said on that point? He said—"

"Is it worth while, mother?" interrupted Audrey. "It was only his opinion."

"It is worth while—amongst ourselves—" insisted Mrs. Greyle. "Why not? Lord Altmore said—in so many words—'I have a sort of uneasy feeling, after reading the evidence at that inquest, and hearing what my steward's impressions were, that this man calling himself Marston Greyle may not be Marston Greyle at all and I shall want good proof that he is before I even consider the proposal he has made to me.' There! So—what's to be done?"

"The law, ma'am," observed Mr. Dennie, solemnly, "the law must step in.
You must get an injunction, ma'am, to prevent Mr. Marston Greyle from

dealing with the property until his own title to it has been established.

That, at any rate, is my opinion."

"May I ask a question?" said Copplestone who had been listening and thinking intently. "Did Lord Altmore say when this offer was made to him?"

"Yes," replied Mrs. Greyle. "A week ago."

"A week ago!" exclaimed Copplestone. "That is, before last Sunday — before the Bassett Oliver episode. Then — the offer to sell is quite independent of that affair!"

"Strange — and significant!" muttered Gilling.

He rose from his chair and looked at his watch.

"Well," he went on, "I am going off to London. Will you give me leave,
Mrs. Greyle, to report all this to Sir Cresswell Oliver and Mr. Petherton? They ought to know."

"I'm going, too," declared Copplestone, also rising. "Mrs. Greyle, I'm sure will entrust the whole matter to us. And Mr. Dennie will trust us with those papers."

"Oh, certainly, certainly!" asserted Mr. Dennie, pushing his packet across the table. "Take care of 'em, my boy! — ye don't know how important they may turn out to be."

"And — Mrs. Greyle?" asked Copplestone.

"Tell whatever you think it best to tell," replied Mrs. Greyle. "My own opinion is that a lot will have to be told — and to come out, yet."

"We can catch a train in three-quarters of an hour, Copplestone," said Gilling. "Let's get back and settle up with Mrs. Wooler and be off."
Copplestone contrived to draw Audrey aside.

"This isn't good-bye," he whispered, with a meaning look. "You'll see me back here before many days are over. But listen—if anything happens here, if you want anybody's help—in any way—you know what I mean—promise you'll wire to me at this address. Promise!—or I won't go."

"Very well," said Audrey, "I promise. But—why shall you come back?"

"Tell you when I come," replied Copplestone with another look. "But—I shall come—and soon. I'm only going because I want to be of use—to you."

An hour later he and Gilling were on their way to London, and from opposite corners of a compartment which they had contrived to get to themselves, they exchanged looks.

"This is a queer business, Copplestone!" said Gilling. "It strikes me it's going to be a big one, too. And—it's coming to a point round Squire Greyle."

"Do you think your man will have tracked him?" asked Copplestone.

"It will be the first time Swallow's ever lost sight of anybody if he hasn't," answered Gilling. "He's a human ferret! However, I wired to him just before we left, telling him to meet me at King's Cross, so we'll get his report. Oh, he'll have followed him all right—I don't imagine for a moment that Greyle is trying to evade anybody, at this juncture, at any rate."

But when—four hours later—the train drew into King's Cross—and Gilling's partner, a young and sharp-looking man, presented himself, it was with a long and downcast face and a lugubrious shake of the head.

"Done!—for the first time in my life!" he growled in answer to Gilling's eager inquiry. "Lost him! Never failed before—as you know. Well, it had to come, I suppose—can't go on without an occasional defeat. But—I'm a bit licked as to the whole thing—unless your man is dodging somebody. Is he?"

"Tell your tale," commanded Gilling, motioning Copplestone to follow him and Swallow aside.

"I was up here in good time this afternoon to meet his train," reported Swallow. "I spotted him and his man at once; no difficulty, as your description of both was so full. They were together while the luggage was got out; then he, Greyle, gave some instructions to the man and left him. He himself got into a taxi-cab; I got into another close behind and gave its driver certain orders. Greyle drove straight to the Fragonard Club—you know."

"Ah!" exclaimed Gilling. "Did he, now? That's worth knowing."

"What's the Fragonard Club?" asked Copplestone. "Never heard of it."

"Club of folk connected with the stage and the music-halls," answered Gilling, testily. "In a side street, off Shaftesbury Avenue— tell you more of it, later. Go on, Swallow."

"He paid off his driver there, and went in," continued Swallow. "I paid mine and hung about—there's only one entrance and exit to that spot, as you know. He came out again within five minutes, stuffing some letters into his pocket. He walked away across Shaftesbury Avenue into Wardour Street—there he went into a tobacconist's shop. Of course, I hung about again. But this time he didn't come. So at last I walked in—to buy something. He wasn't there!"

"Pooh!—he'd slipped out—walked out—when you weren't looking!" said
Gilling. "Why didn't you keep your eye on the ball, man?—you!"
"You be hanged!" retorted Swallow. "Never had an eyelash off that shop door from the time he entered until I, too, entered."

"Then there's a side-door to that shop—into some alley or passage," said Gilling.

"Not that I could find," answered Swallow. "Might be at the rear of the premises perhaps, but I couldn't ascertain, of course. Remember!—there's another thing. He may have stopped on the premises. There's that in it. However, I know the shop and the name."

"Why didn't you bring somebody else with you, to follow the man and the luggage?" demanded Gilling, half-petulantly.

Swallow shook his head.

"There I made a mess of it, I confess," he admitted. "But it never struck me they'd separate. I thought, of course, they'd drive straight to some hotel, and—"

"And the long and the short of it is, Greyle's slipped you," said Gilling. "Well—there's no more to be done tonight. The only thing of value is that Greyle called at the Fragonard. What's a country squire—only recently come to England, too!—to do with the Fragonard? That is worth something. Well—Copplestone, we'd better meet in the morning at Petherton's. You be there at ten o'clock, and I'll get Sir Cresswell Oliver to be there, too."

Copplestone betook himself to his rooms in Jermyn Street; it seemed an age—several ages—since he had last seen the familiar things in them. During the few days which had elapsed since his hurried setting-off to meet Bassett Oliver so many things had happened that he felt as if he had lived a week in a totally different world. He had met death, and mystery, and what appeared to be sure evidence of deceit and cunning and perhaps worse—fraud and crime blacker than fraud. But he had also met Audrey Greyle. And it was only natural that he thought more about her than of the strange atmosphere of mystery which wrapped itself around Scarhaven. She, at any rate, was good to think upon, and he thought much as he looked over the letters that had accumulated, changed his clothes, and made ready to go and dine at his club, Already he was counting the hours which must elapse before he would go back to her.

Nevertheless, Copplestone's mind was not entirely absorbed by this pleasant subject; the events of the day and of the arrival in London kept presenting themselves. And coming across a fellow club-member whom he knew for a thorough man about town, he suddenly plumped him with a question.

"I say!" he said. "Do you know the Fragonard Club?"

"Of course!" replied the other man. "Don't you?"

"Never even heard of it till this evening," said Copplestone. "What is it?"
"Mixed lot!" answered his companion. "Theatrical and music-hall folk—men and women—both. Lively spot—sometimes. Like to have a look in when they have one of their nights?"

"Very much," assented Copplestone. "Are you a member?"

"No, but I know several men who are members," said the other. "I'll fix it all right. Worth going to when they've what they call a house-dinner—Sunday night, of course."

"Thanks," said Copplestone. "I suppose membership of that's confined to the profession, eh?"

"Strictly," replied his friend. "But they ain't at all particular about their guests—you'll meet all sorts of people there, from judges to jockeys, and millionairesses to milliners."

Copplestone was still wondering what the Squire of Scarhaven could have to do with the Fragonard Club when he went to Mr. Petherton's office the next morning. He was late for the appointment which Gilling had made, and when he arrived Gilling had already reported all that had taken place the day before to the solicitor and to Sir Cresswell Oliver. And on that Copplestone produced the papers entrusted to him by Mr. Dennie and they all compared the handwritings afresh.

"There is certainly something wrong, somewhere," remarked Petherton, after a time. "However, we are in a position to begin a systematic inquiry. Here," he went on, drawing a paper from his desk, "is a cablegram which arrived first thing this morning from New York—from an agent who has been making a search for me in the shipping lists. This is what he says: 'Marston Greyle, St. Louis, Missouri, booked first-class passenger from New York to Falmouth, England, by S.S. Araconda, September 28th, 1912.' There—that's something definite. And the next thing," concluded the old lawyer, with a shrewd glance at Sir Cresswell, "is to find out if the Marston Greyle who landed at Falmouth is the same man whom we have recently seen!"

CHAPTER XVI
IN TOUCH WITH THE MISSING

Sir Cresswell Oliver took the cablegram from Petherton and read it over slowly, muttering the precise and plain wording to himself.

"Don't you think, Petherton, that we had better get a clear notion of our exact bearings?" he said as he laid it back on the solicitor's desk. "Seems to me that the time's come when we ought to know exactly where we are. As I understand it, the case is this—rightly or wrongly we suspect the present holder of the Scarhaven estates. We suspect that he is not the rightful owner—that, in short, he is no more the real Marston Greyle than you are. We think that he's an impostor—posing as Marston Greyle. Other people—Mrs. Valentine Greyle, for example—evidently think so, too. Am I right?"

"Quite!" responded Petherton. "That's our position—exactly."

"Then—in that case, what I want to get at is this," continued Sir Cresswell. "How does this relate to my brother's death? What's the connection? That—to me at any rate—is the first thing of importance. Of course I have a theory. This, that the impostor did see my brother last Sunday afternoon. That he knew that my brother would at once know that he, the impostor, was not the real Marston Greyle, and that the discovery would lead to detection. And therefore he put him out of the way. He might accompany him to the top of the tower and fling him down. It's possible. Do you follow me?"

"Precisely," replied Petherton. "I, too, incline to that notion, though I've worked it out in a different fashion. My reconstruction of what took place at Scarhaven Keep is as follows—I think that Bassett Oliver met the Squire—we'll call this man that for the sake of clearness—when he entered the ruins. He probably introduced himself and mentioned that he had met a Marston Greyle in America. Then the Squire saw the probabilities of detection—and what subsequently took place was most likely what you suggest. It may have been that the Squire recognized Bassett Oliver, and knew that he'd met Marston Greyle; it may have been that he didn't know him and didn't know anything until Bassett Oliver enlightened him. But—either way—I firmly believe that Bassett Oliver came to his death by violence—that he was murdered. So—there's the case in a nutshell! Murdered!—to keep his tongue still."

"What's to be done, then?" asked Sir Cresswell as Petherton tapped the cablegram.

"The first thing," he answered, "is to make use of this. We now know that the real Marston Greyle—who certainly did live in St. Louis, where his father had settled—left New York for England to take up his inheritance, on September 28th, 1912, and booked a passage to Falmouth. He would land at Falmouth from the Araconda about October 5th. Probably there is some trace of him at Falmouth. He no doubt stayed a night there. Anyway, somebody must go to Falmouth and make inquiries. You'd better go, Gilling, and at once. While you're away your partner had better resume his search for the man we know as the Squire. You've two good clues—the fact that he visited the Fragonard Club and that particular tobacconist's shop. Urge Swallow to do his best—the man must be kept in sight. See to both these things immediately."

"Swallow is at work already," replied Gilling. "He's got good help, too, and his failure yesterday has put him on his mettle. As for me, I'll go to Falmouth by the next express. Let me have that cablegram."

"I'll go with you," said Copplestone. "I may be of some use—and I'm interested. But," he paused and looked questioningly at the old solicitor. "What about the other news we brought you?" he asked. "About this sale of the estate, you know? If this man is an impostor—
"

"Leave that to me," replied Petherton, with a shrewd glance at Sir Cresswell. "I know the Greyle family solicitors—highly respectable people—only a few doors away, in fact—and I'm going round to have a quiet little chat with them in a few minutes. There will be no sale! Leave me to deal with that matter—and if you young men are going to Falmouth, off you go!"

It was late that night when Copplestone and Gilling arrived at this far-off Cornish seaport, and nothing could be done until the following morning. To Copplestone it seemed as if they were in for a difficult task. Over twelve months had elapsed since the real Marston Greyle left America for England; he might not have stayed in Falmouth, might not have held any conversation with anybody there who would recollect him! how were they going to trace him? But Gilling—now free of his clerical attire and presenting himself as a smart young man of the professional classes type—was quick to explain that system, accurate and definite system, would expedite matters.

"We know the approximate date on which the Araconda would touch here," he said as they breakfasted together. "As things go, it would be from October 4th to 6th, according to the quickness of her run across the Atlantic. Very well—if Marston Greyle stayed here, he'd have to stay at some hotel. Accordingly, we visit all the Falmouth hotels and examine their registers of that date—first week of October, 1912. If we find his name—good! We can then go on to make inquiries. If we don't find any trace of him, then we know it's all up—he probably went straight away by train after landing. We'll begin with this hotel first."

There was no record of any Marston Greyle at that hotel, nor at the next half-dozen at which they called. A visit to the shipping office of the line to which the Araconda belonged revealed the fact that she reached Falmouth on October 5th at half-past ten in the evening, and that the name of Marston Greyle was on the list of first-class passengers. Gilling left the office in cheery mood.

"That simplifies matters," he said. "As the Araconda reached here late in the evening, the passengers who landed from her would be almost certain to stay the night in Falmouth. So we've only to resume our round of these hotels in order to hit something pertinent. This is plain and easy work, Copplestone—no corners in it. We'll strike oil before noon."

122

They struck oil at the very next hotel they called at—an old-fashioned house in close proximity to the harbour. There was a communicative landlord there who evidently possessed and was proud of a retentive memory, and he no sooner heard the reason of Gilling's call upon him than he bustled into activity, and produced the register of the previous year.

"But I remember the young gentleman you're asking about," he remarked, as he took the book from a safe and laid it open on the table in his private room. "Not a common name, is it? He came here about eleven o'clock of the night you've mentioned—there you are!—there's the entry. And there—higher up—is the name of the man who came to meet him. He came the day before—to be here when the Araconda got in."

The two visitors, bending over the book, mutually nudged each other as their eyes encountered the signatures on the open page. There, in the handwriting of the letters which Mr. Dennie had so fortunately preserved, was the name Marston Greyle. But it was not the sight of that which surprised them; they had expected to see it. What made them both thrill with the joy of an unexpected discovery was the sight of the signature inserted some lines above it, under date October 4th. Lest they should exhibit that joy before the landlord, they mutually stuck their elbows into each other and immediately affected the unconcern of indifference.

But there the signature was—Peter Chatfield. Peter Chatfield!—they both knew that they were entering on a new stage of their quest; that the fact that Chatfield had travelled to Falmouth to meet the new owner of Scarhaven meant much—possibly meant everything.

"Oh!" said Gilling, as steadily as possible. "That gentleman came to meet the other, did he? Just so. Now what sort of man was he?"

"Big, fleshy man—elderly—very solemn in manner and appearance," answered the landlord. "I remember him well. Came in about five o'clock in the afternoon of the 4th just after the London train arrived—and booked a room. He told me he expected to meet a gentleman from New York, and was very fidgety about fixing it up to go off in the tender to the Araconda when she came into the Bay. However, I found out for him that she wouldn't be in until next evening, so of course he settled down to wait. Very quiet, reserved old fellow—never said much."

"Did he go off on the tender next night?" asked Gilling.

"He did—and came back with this other gentleman and his baggage—this
Mr. Greyle," answered the landlord. "Mr. Chatfield had booked a room for
Mr. Greyle."
"And what sort of man was Mr. Greyle?" inquired Gilling. "That's really the important thing. You've an exceptionally good memory—I can see that. Tell us all you can recollect about him."

"I can recollect plenty," replied the landlord, shaking his head. "As for his looks—a tallish, slightly-built young fellow, between, I should say, twenty-five and twenty-eight. Stooped a good bit. Very dark hair and eyes—eyes a good deal sunken in his face. Very pale— good-looking—good features. But ill—my sakes! he was ill!"

"Ill!" exclaimed Gilling, with a glance at Copplestone. "Really ill!"

"He was that ill," said the landlord, "that me and my wife never expected to see him get up that next morning. We wanted them to have a doctor but Mr. Greyle himself said that it was nothing, but that he had some heart trouble and that the voyage had made it worse. He said that if he took some medicine which he had with him, and a drop of hot brandy-and-water, and got a good night's sleep he'd be all right. And next morning he seemed better, and he got up to breakfast—but my wife said to me that if she'd seen death on a man's face it was on his! She's a bit of a persuasive tongue, has my wife, and when she heard that these two gentlemen were thinking of going a long journey—right away to the far north, it was, I believe—she got 'em to go and see the doctor first, for she felt that Mr. Greyle wasn't fit for the exertion."

"Did they go?" asked Gilling.

"They did! I talked, myself, to the old gentleman," replied the landlord. "And I showed them the way to our own doctor—Dr. Tretheway. And as a result of what he said to them, I heard them decide to break up their journey into stages, as you might term it. They left here for Bristol that afternoon—to stay the night there."

"You're sure of that?—Bristol?" asked Gilling.

"Ought to be," replied the landlord, with laconic assurance. "I went to the station with them and saw them off. They booked to Bristol—anyway—first class."

Gilling looked at his companion.

"I think we'd better see this Dr. Tretheway," he remarked.

Dr. Tretheway, an elderly man of grave manners and benevolent aspect, remembered the visit of Mr. Marston Greyle well enough when he had turned up its date in his case book. He also remembered the visitor's companion, Mr. Chatfield, who seemed unusually anxious and concerned about Mr. Greyle's health.

"And as to that," continued Dr. Tretheway, "I learnt from Mr. Greyle that he had been seriously indisposed for some months before setting out for England. The voyage had been rather a rough one; he had suffered much from sea-sickness, and, in his state of health, that was unfortunate for him. I made a careful examination of him, and I came to the conclusion that he was suffering from a form of myocarditis which was rapidly assuming a very serious complexion. I earnestly advised him to take as much rest as possible, to avoid all unnecessary fatigue and all excitement, and I strongly deprecated his travelling in one journey to the north, whither I learnt he was bound. On my advice, he and Mr. Chatfield decided to break that journey at Bristol, at Birmingham, and at Leeds. By so doing, you see, they would only have a short journey each day, and Mr. Greyle would be

125

able to rest for a long time at a stretch. But—I formed my own conclusions."

"And they were—what?" asked Gilling.

"That he would not live long," said the doctor. "Finding that he was going to the neighbourhood of Norcaster, where there is a most excellent school of medicine, I advised him to get the best specialist he could from there, and to put himself under his treatment. But my impression was that he had already reached a very, very serious stage."

"You think he was then likely to die suddenly?" suggested Gilling.

"It was quite possible. I should not have been surprised to hear of his death," answered Dr. Tretheway. "He was, in short, very ill indeed."

"You never heard anything?" inquired Gilling.

"Nothing at all—though I often wondered. Of course," said the doctor with a smile, "they were only chance visitors—I often have trans-atlantic passengers drop in—and they forget that a physician would sometimes like to know how a case submitted to him in that way has turned out. No, I never heard any more."

"Did they give you any address, either of them?" asked Copplestone, seeing that Gilling had no more to ask.

"No," replied the doctor, "they did not. I knew of course, from what they told me that Mr. Greyle had come off the Araconda the night before, and that he was passing on. No—I only gathered that they were going to the neighbourhood of Norcaster from the fact that Mr. Greyle asked if a journey to that place would be too much for him— he said with a laugh, that over there in the United States a journey of five hundred miles would be considered a mere jaunt! He was very plucky, poor fellow, but—"

Dr. Tretheway ended with a significant shake of the head, and his two visitors left him and went out into the autumn sunlight.

"Copplestone!" said Gilling as they walked away. "That chap—the real Marston Greyle—is dead! That's as certain as that we're alive! And now the next thing is to find out where he died and when. And by George, that's going to be a big job!"

"How are you going to set about it?" asked Copplestone. "It seems as if we were up against a blank wall, now."

"Not at all, my son!" retorted Gilling, cheerfully. "One step at a time—that's the sure thing to go on, in my calling. We've found out a lot here, and quickly, too. And—we know where our next step lies. Bristol! Like looking for needles in a bundle of hay? Not a bit of it. If those two broke their journey at Bristol, they'd have to stop at an hotel. Well, now we'll adjourn to Bristol—bearing in mind that we're on the track of Peter Chatfield!"

CHAPTER XVII
THE OLD PLAYBILL

Gilling's cheerful optimism was the sort of desirable quality that is a good thing to have, but all the optimism in the world is valueless in face of impregnable difficulty. And the difficulty of tracing Chatfield and his sick companion in a city the size of Bristol did indeed seem impregnable when Gilling and Copplestone had been attacking it for twenty-four hours. They had spent a whole day in endeavouring to get news; they had gone in and out of hotels until they were sick of the sight of one; they had made exhaustive inquiries at the railway station and of the cabmen who congregated there; nobody remembered anything at all about a big, heavy-faced man and a man in his company who seemed to be very ill. And on the second night Copplestone intimated plainly that in his opinion they were wasting their time.

"How do we even know that they ever came to Bristol?" he asked, as he and Gilling refreshed themselves with a much needed dinner. "The Falmouth landlord saw Chatfield take tickets for Bristol! That's nothing to go on! Put it to yourself in this way. Greyle may have found even that journey too much for him. They may, in that case, have left the train at Plymouth—or at Exeter—or at Taunton: it would stop at each place. Seems to me we're wasting time here—far better get nearer more tangible things. Chatfield, for instance. Or, go back to town and find out what your friend Swallow has done."

"Swallow," replied Gilling, "has done nothing so far, or I should have heard. Swallow knows exactly where I am, and where I shall be until I give him further notice. Don't be discouraged, my friend—one is often on the very edge of a discovery when one seems to be miles away from it. Give me another day—and if we haven't found out something by tomorrow evening I'll consult with you as to our next step. But I've a plan for tomorrow morning which ought to yield some result."

"What?" demanded Copplestone, doubtfully.

"This! There is in every centre of population an official who registers births, marriages, and deaths. Now we believe the real Marston Greyle to be dead. Let us suppose, for argument's sake, that he did die here, in Bristol, whither he and Chatfield certainly set off when they left Falmouth. What would happen? Notice of his death would have to be given to the Registrar—by the nearest relative or by the person in attendance on the deceased. That person would, in this case, be Chatfield. If the death occurred suddenly, and without medical attendance, an inquest would have to be held. If a doctor had been in attendance he would give a signed certificate of the cause of death, which he would hand to the relatives or friends in attendance, who, in their turn, would have to hand it to the Registrar. Do you see the value of these points? What we must do tomorrow morning is to see the Registrar—or, as there will be more than one in a place this size—each of them in turn, in the endeavour to find out if, early in October, 1912, Peter Chatfield registered the death of Marston Greyle here. But remember—he may not have registered it under that name. He may, indeed, not have used his own name—he's deep enough for anything. That however, is our next best chance—search of the registers. Let's try it, anyway, first thing in the morning. And as we've had a stiff day, I propose we dismiss all thought of this affair for the rest of the evening and betake ourselves to some place of amusement—theatre, eh?"

Copplestone made no objection to that, and when dinner was over, they walked round to the principal theatre in time for the first act of a play which having been highly successful in London had just started on a round of the leading provincial theatres. Between the second and third acts of this production there was a long interval, and the two companions repaired to the foyer to recuperate their energies with a drink and a cigarette. While thus engaged, Copplestone encountered an old school friend with whom he exchanged a few words: Gilling, meanwhile strolled about, inspecting the pictures, photographs and old playbills on the walls of the saloon and its adjacent apartments. And suddenly, he turned back, waited until Copplestone's acquaintance had gone away, and then hurried up and smacked his co-searcher on the shoulder.

"Didn't I tell you that one's often close to a thing when one seems furthest off it!" he exclaimed triumphantly. "Come here, my son, and look at what I've just found."

He drew Copplestone away to a quiet corner and pointed out an old playbill, framed and hung on the wall. Copplestone stared at it and saw nothing but the title of a well-known comedy, the names of one or two fairly celebrated actors and actresses and the usual particulars which appear on all similar announcements.

"Well?" he asked. "What of this?"

"That!" replied Gilling, flicking the tip of his finger on a line in the bill. "That my boy!"

Copplestone looked again. He started at what he read.

Margaret Sayers.......MISS ADELA CHATFIELD.

"And now look at that!" continued Gilling, with an accentuation of his triumphal note. "See! These people were here for a fortnight — from October 3rd to 17th—1912. Therefore—if Peter Chatfield brought Marston Greyle to Bristol on October 6th, Peter Chatfield's daughter would also be in the town!"

Copplestone looked over the bill again, rapidly realizing possibilities.

"Would Chatfield know that?" he asked reflectively.

"It's only likely that he would," replied Gilling. "Even if father and daughter don't quite hit things off in their tastes, it's only reasonable to suppose that Peter would usually know his daughter's whereabouts. And if he brought Greyle here, ill, and they had to stop, it's only likely that Peter would turn to his daughter for help. Anyway, Copplestone, here are two undoubted facts:—Chatfield and Greyle booked from Falmouth for Bristol on October 6th, 1912, and may therefore be supposed to have come here. That's one fact.

130

The other is—Addie Chatfield was certainly in Bristol on that date and for eleven days after it."

"Well—what next?" asked Copplestone.

"I've been thinking that over while you stared at the bill," answered Gilling. "I think the best thing will be to find out where Addie Chatfield put herself up during her stay. I daresay you know that in most of these towns there are lodgings which are almost exclusively devoted to the theatrical profession. Actors and actresses go to them year after year; their owners lay themselves out for their patrons— what's more, your theatrical landlady always remembers names and faces, and has her favourites. Now, in my stage experience, I never struck Bristol, so I don't know much about it, but I know where we can get information—the stage door-keeper. He'll tell us where the recognized lodgings are—and then we must begin a round of inquiry. When? Just now, my boy!—and a good time, too, as you'll see."

"Why?" asked Copplestone.

"Best hour of the evening," replied Gilling with glib assurance. "Landladies enjoying an hour of ease before beginning to cook supper for their lodgers, now busy on the stage. Always ready to talk, theatrical landladies, when they've nothing to do. Trust me for knowing the ropes!—come round to the stage door and let's ask the keeper a question or two."

But before they had quitted the foyer an interruption came in the shape of a shrewd-looking gentleman in evening dress, who wore his opera hat at a rakish angle and seemed to be very much at home as he strolled about, hands in pockets, looking around him at all and sundry. He suddenly caught sight of Gilling, smiled surprisedly and expansively, and came forward with outstretched hand.

"Bless our hearts, is it really yourself, dear boy!" exclaimed this apparition. "Really, now? And what brings you here—God bless my soul and eyes—why I haven't seen you this—how long is it, dear boy!"

"Three years," answered Gilling, promptly clasping the outstretched hand.
"But what are you doing here—boss, eh?"
"Lessee's manager, dear boy—nice job, too," whispered the other.
"Been here two years—good berth." He deftly steered Gilling towards the refreshment bar, and glanced out of his eye corner at Copplestone. "Friend of yours?" he suggested hospitably. "Introduce us, dear boy—my name is the same as before, you know!"

"Mr. Copplestone, Mr. Montmorency," said Gilling. "Mr. Montmorency, Mr. Copplestone."
"Servant, sir," said Mr. Montmorency. "Pleased to meet any friend of my friend! And what will you take, dear boys, and how are things with you, Gilling, old man—now who on earth would have thought of seeing you here?"

Copplestone held his peace while Gilling and Mr. Montmorency held interesting converse. He was sure that his companion would turn this unexpected meeting to account, and he therefore felt no surprise when Gilling, after giving him a private nudge, plumped the manager with a direct question.

"Did you see Addie Chatfield when she was here about a year ago?" he asked. "You remember—she was here in Mrs. Swayne's Necklace—here a fortnight."

"I remember very well, dear boy," responded Mr. Montmorency, with a judicial sip at the contents of his tumbler. "I saw the lady several times. More by token, I accidentally witnessed a curious little scene between Miss Addie and a gentleman whom Nature appeared to have specially manufactured for the part of heavy parent—you know the type. One morning when that company was here, I happened to be standing in the vestibule, talking to the box-office man, when a large, solemn-faced individual, Quakerish in attire, and evidently not accustomed to the theatre walked in and peered about him at our rich carpets and expensive fittings—pretty much as if he was appraising their value. At the same time, I observed that he was in what one calls a state—a little, perhaps a good deal, upset about something. Wherefore I addressed myself to him in my politest manner and inquired if I could serve him. Thereupon he asked if he could see Miss Adela Chatfield on very important business. Now, I wasn't going to let him see Miss Addie, for I took him to be a man who might have a writ about him, or something nasty of that sort. But at that very moment, Miss Addie, who had been rehearsing, and had come out by the house instead of going through the stage door, came tripping into the vestibule and let off a sharp note of exclamation. After which she and old wooden-face stepped into the street together, and immediately exchanged a few words. And that the old man told her something very serious was abundantly evident from the expression of their respective countenances. But, of course, I never knew what it was, nor who he was, dear boy—not my business, don't you know."

"They went away together, those two?" asked Gilling, favouring Copplestone with another nudge.
"Up the street together, certainly, talking most earnestly," replied Mr. Montmorency.
"Ever see that old chap again?" asked Gilling.

"I never did, dear boy,—once was sufficient," said Mr. Montmorency, lightly. "But," he continued, dropping his bantering tone, "are these questions pertinent?—has this to do with this new profession of yours, dear boy? If so—mum's the word, you know."

"I'll tell you what, Monty," answered Gilling. "I wish you'd find out for me where Addie Chatfield lodged when she was here that time. Can it be done? Between you and me, I do want to know about that, old chap. Never mind why, now—I will tell you later. But it's serious."

Mr. Montmorency tapped the side of his handsome nose.

"All right, my boy!" he said. "I understand—wicked, wicked world! Done? Dear boy, it shall be done! Come down to the stage door—our man knows every landlady in the town!"

By various winding ways and devious passages he led the two young men down to the stage door. Its keeper, not being particularly busy at that time, was reading the evening newspaper in his glass-walled box, and glanced inquiringly at the strangers as Mr. Montmorency pulled them up before him.

"Prickett," said Mr. Montmorency, leaning into the sanctum over its half-door and speaking confidentially. "You keep a sort of register of lodgings don't you, Prickett? Now I wonder if you could tell me where Miss Adela Chatfield, of the Mrs. Swayne's Necklace Company stopped when she was last here?—that's a year ago or about it. Prickett," he went on, turning to Gilling, "puts all this sort of thing down, methodically, so that he can send callers on, or send up urgent letters or parcels during the day—isn't that it, Prickett?"

"That's about it, sir," answered the door-keeper. He had taken down a sort of ledger as the manager spoke, and was now turning over its leaves. He suddenly ran his finger down a page and stopped its course at a particular line.

"Mrs. Salmon, 5, Montargis Crescent—second to the right outside," he announced briefly. "Very good lodgings, too, are those."

Gilling promised Mr. Montmorency that he would look him up later on, and went away with Copplestone to Montargis Crescent. Within five minutes they were standing in a comfortably furnished, old-fashioned sitting-room, liberally ornamented with the photographs of actors and actresses and confronting a stout, sharp-eyed little woman who listened intently to all that Gilling said and sniffed loudly when he had finished.

"Remember Miss Chatfield being here!" she exclaimed. "I should think I do remember! I ought to! Bringing mortal sickness into my house—and then death—and then a funeral—and her and her father going away never giving me an extra penny for the trouble!"

CHAPTER XVIII
THE LIE ON THE TOMBSTONE

Gilling's glance at his companion was quiet enough, but it spoke volumes.

Here, by sheer chance, was such a revelation as they had never dreamed of

hearing!—here was the probable explanation of at least half the mystery.

He turned composedly to the landlady.

"I've already told you who and what I am," he said, pointing to the card which he had handed to her. "There are certain mysterious circumstances about this affair which I want to get at. What you've said just now is abundant evidence that you can help. If you do and will help, you'll be well paid for your trouble. Now, you speak of sickness—death—a funeral. Will you tell us all about it?"

"I never knew there was any mystery about it," answered the landlady, as she motioned her visitors to seat themselves. "It was all above-board as far as I knew. Of course, I've always been sore about it—I'd a great deal of trouble, and as I say, I never got anything for it—that is, anything extra. And me doing it really to oblige her and her father!"

"They brought a sick man here?" suggested Gilling.

"I'll tell you how it was," said Mrs. Salmon, seating herself and showing signs of a disposition to confidence. "Miss Chatfield, she'd been here, I think, three days that time—I'd had her once before a year or two previous. One morning—I'm sure it was about the third day that the Swayne Necklace Company was here—she came in from rehearsal in a regular take-on. She said that her father had just called on her at the theatre. She said he'd been to Falmouth to meet a relation of theirs who'd come from America and had found him to be very ill on landing—so ill that a Falmouth doctor had given strict orders that he mustn't travel any further than Bristol, on his way wherever he wanted to go. They'd got to Bristol and the young man was so done up that Mr. Chatfield had had to drive him to another doctor—one close by here—Dr. Valdey—as soon as they arrived. Dr. Valdey said he must go to bed at once and have at least two days' complete rest in bed, and he advised Mr. Chatfield to get quiet rooms instead of going to a hotel. So Mr. Chatfield, knowing that his daughter was here, do you see, sought her out and told her all about it. She came to me and asked me if I knew where they could get rooms. Well now, I had my drawing-room floor empty that week, and as it was only for two or three days that they wanted rooms I offered to take Mr. Chatfield and the young man in. Of course, if I'd known how ill he was, I shouldn't. What I understood—and mind you, I don't say they wilfully deceived me, for I don't think they did—what I understood was that the young man simply wanted a real good rest. But he was evidently a deal worse than what even Dr. Valdey thought. He'd stopped at Dr. Valdey's surgery while Mr. Chatfield went to see about rooms, and they moved him from there straight in here. And as I say, he was a deal worse than they thought, much worse, and the doctor had to be fetched to him more than once during the afternoon. Still Dr. Valdey himself never said to me that there was any immediate danger. But that's neither here nor there— the young fellow died that night."

"That night!" exclaimed Gilling, "the night he came here?"

"Very same night," assented Mrs. Salmon. "Brought in here about two in the afternoon and died just before midnight—soon after Miss Chatfield came in from the theatre. Went very suddenly at the end."

"Were you present?" asked Copplestone.

"I wasn't. Nobody was with him but Mr. Chatfield—Miss Chatfield was getting her supper down here," replied Mrs. Salmon. "And I was busy elsewhere."

"Was there an inquest then," inquired Gilling?"

"Oh, no!" said Mrs. Salmon, shaking her head. "Oh, no!—there was no need for that—the doctor, ye see, had been seeing him all day.

Oh, no—the cause of death was evident enough, in a way of speaking. Heart."

"Did they bury him here, then?" asked Gilling.

"Two days after," replied Mrs. Salmon. "Kept everything very quiet, they did. I don't believe Miss Chatfield told any of the theatre people—she went to her work just the same, of course. The old gentleman saw to everything—funeral and all. I'll say this for them— they gave me no unnecessary trouble, but still, there's trouble that is necessary when you've death in a house and a funeral at the door, and they ought to have given me something for what I did. But they didn't, so I considered it very mean. Mr. Chatfield, he stayed two days after the funeral, and when he left he just said that his daughter would settle up with me. But when she came to pay she added nothing to my bill, and she walked out remarking that if her father hadn't given me anything extra she was sure she shouldn't. Shabby!"

"Very shabby!" agreed Gilling. "Well, you won't find my clients quite so mean, ma'am. But just a word—don't mention this matter to anybody until you hear from me. And as I like to give some earnest of payment here's a bank-note which you can slip into your purse— on account, you understand. Now, just a question or two:—Did you hear the young man's name?"

The landlady, whose spirits rose visibly on receipt of the bank-note, appeared to reflect on hearing this question, and she shook her head as if surprised at her own inability to answer it satisfactorily.

"Well, now," she said, "it may seem a queer thing to say, but I don't recollect that I ever did! You see, I didn't see much of him after he once got here. I was never in his room with them, and they didn't mention his name—that I can remember—when they spoke about him before me. I understood he was a relative—cousin or something of that sort."

"Didn't you see any name on the coffin?" asked Gilling.

"I didn't," replied Mrs. Salmon. "You see, the undertaker fetched him away when him and his men brought the coffin—the next day. He took charge of the coffin for the second night, and the funeral took place from there. But I'll tell you what—the undertaker'll know the name, and of course the doctor does. They're both close by."

Gilling took names and addresses and once more pledging the landlady to secrecy, led Copplestone away.

"That's the end of another chapter," he said when they were clear of that place. "We know now that Marston Greyle died there—in that very house, Copplestone!—and that Peter Chatfield was with him. That's fact!"

"And it's fact, too, that the daughter knows," observed Copplestone in a low voice.

"Fact, too, that Addie Chatfield was in it," agreed Gilling. "Well—but what happened next? However, before we go on to that, there are three things to do in the morning. We must see this Dr. Valdey, and the undertaker—and Marston Greyle's grave."

"And then?" asked Copplestone.

"Stiff, big question," sighed Gilling. "Go back to town and report, I think—and find out if Swallow has discovered anything. And egad! there's a lot to discover! For you see we're already certain that at the stage at which we've arrived a conspiracy began—conspiracy between Chatfield, his daughter, and the man who's been passing himself off as Marston Greyle. Now, who is the man? Where did they get hold of him? Is he some relation of theirs? All that's got to be found out. Of course, their object is very clear, Marston Greyle, the real Simon Pure, was dead on their hands. His legal successor was his cousin, Miss Audrey. Chatfield knew that when Miss Audrey came into power his own reign as steward of Scarhaven would be brief. And so—but the thing is so plain that one needn't waste breath on it. And I tell you what's plain too, Copplestone—Miss Audrey

Greyle is the lady of Scarhaven! Good luck to her! You'll no doubt be glad to communicate the glad tidings!"

Copplestone made no answer. He was utterly confounded by the recent revelations and was wondering what the mother and daughter in the little cottage so far away in the grey north would say when all these things were told them.

"Let's make dead certain of everything," he said after a long pause. "Don't let's leave any loophole."
"Oh, we'll leave nothing—here at any rate," replied Gilling, confidently. "But you'll find in the morning that we already know almost everything."

In this he was right. The doctor's story was a plain one. The young man was very ill indeed when brought to him, and though he did not anticipate so early or sudden an end, he was not surprised when death came, and had of course, no difficulty about giving the necessary certificate. Just as plain was the undertaker's account of his connection with the affair—a very ordinary transaction in his eyes. And having heard both stories, there was nothing to do but to visit one of the adjacent cemeteries and find a certain grave the number of which they had ascertained from the undertaker's books. It was easily found—and Copplestone and Gilling found themselves standing at a new tombstone, whereon the monumental mason had carved four lines:—

MARK GREY
BORN APRIL 12TH, 1884
DIED OCTOBER 6TH, 1912
AGED 28 YEARS.

"Short, simple, eminently suited to the purpose," murmured Gilling as the two turned away. "Somebody thought things out quickly and well, Copplestone, when this poor fellow died. Do you know I've been thinking as we walked up here that if Bassett Oliver had never taken it into his head to visit Scarhaven that Sunday this fraud would never have been found out! The chances were all against its ever being found out. Consider them! A young man who is an absolute stranger in England comes to take up an inheritance, having on him no doubt, the necessary proofs of identification. He's met by one person only—his agent. He dies next day. The agent buries him, under a false name, takes his effects and papers, gets some accomplice to personate him, introduces that accomplice to everybody as the real man—and there you are! Oh, Chatfield knew what he was doing! Who on earth, wandering in this cemetery, would ever connect Mark Grey with Marston Greyle?"

"Just so—but there was one danger-spot which must have given Chatfield and his accomplices a good many uneasy hours," answered Copplestone. "You know that Marston Greyle actually registered in his own name at Falmouth and was known to the land lord and the doctor there."

"Yes—and Falmouth is three hundred miles from London and five hundred from Scarhaven," replied Gilling dryly. "And do you suppose that whoever saw Marston Greyle at Falmouth cared two pins—comparatively—what became of him after he left there? No— Chatfield was almost safe from detection as soon as he'd got that unfortunate young fellow laid away in that grave. However we know now—what we do know. And the next thing, now that we know Marston Greyle lies behind us there, is to get back to town and catch the chap who took his place. We'll wire to Swallow and to Petherton and get the next express."

Sir Cresswell Oliver and Petherton were in conference with Swallow at the solicitor's office when Gilling and Copplestone arrived there in the early afternoon. Gilling interrupted their conversation to tell the result of his investigations. Copplestone, watching the effect, saw that neither Sir Cresswell nor Petherton showed surprise. Petherton indeed, smiled as if he had anticipated all that Gilling had to say.

"I told you that I knew the Greyle family solicitors," he observed. "I find that they have only once seen the man whom we will call the Squire. Chatfield brought him there. He produced proofs of identification—papers which Chatfield no doubt took from the dead man. Of course, the solicitors never doubted for a moment that he was the real Marston Greyle! —never dreamed of fraud: Well—the next step. We must concentrate on finding this man. And Swallow has nothing to tell—yet. He has never seen anything more of him. You'd better turn all your attention to that, Gilling—you and Swallow. As for Chatfield and his daughter, I suppose we shall have to approach the police."

Copplestone presently went home to his rooms in Jermyn Street, puzzled and wondering; And there, lying on top of a pile of letters, he found a telegram—from Audrey Greyle. It had been dispatched from Scarhaven at an early hour of the previous day, and it contained but three words—Can you come?

CHAPTER XIX
THE STEAM YACHT

Copplestone had seen and learned enough of Audrey Greyle during his brief stay at Scarhaven to make him assured that she would not have sent for him save for very good and grave reasons. It had been with manifest reluctance that she had given him her promise to do so: her entire behaviour during the conference with Mr. Dennie and Gilling had convinced him that she had an inherent distaste for publicity and an instinctive repugnance to calling in the aid of strangers. He had never expected that she would send for him—he himself knew that he should go back to her, but the return would be on his own initiative. There, however, was her summons, definite as it was brief. He was wanted—and by her. And without opening one of his letters, he snatched up the whole pile, thrust it into his pocket, hurriedly made some preparation for his journey and raced off to King's Cross.

He fumed and fretted with impatience during the six hours' journey down to Norcaster. It was ten o'clock when he arrived there, and as he knew that the last train to Scarhaven left at half-past-nine he hurried to get a fast motor-car that would take him over the last twenty miles of his journey. He had wired to Audrey from Peterborough, telling her that he was on his way and should motor out from Norcaster, and when he had found a car to his liking he ordered its driver to go straight to Mrs. Greyle's cottage, close by Scarhaven church. And just then he heard a voice calling his name, and turning saw, running out of the station, a young, athletic-looking man, much wrapped and cloaked, who waved a hand at him and whose face he had some dim notion of having seen before.

"Mr. Copplestone?" panted the new arrival, coming up hurriedly. "I almost missed you—I got on the wrong platform to meet your train. You don't know me, though you may have seen me at the inquest on Mr. Bassett Oliver the other day—my name's Vickers—Guy Vickers."

"Yes?" said Copplestone. "And—"

"I'm a solicitor, here in Norcaster," answered Vickers. "I—at least, my firm, you know—we sometimes act for Mrs. Greyle at Scarhaven. I got a wire from Miss Greyle late this evening, asking me to meet you here when the London train got in and to go on to Scarhaven with you at once. She added the words urgent business so—"

"Then in heaven's name, let's be off!" exclaimed Copplestone. "It'll take us a good hour and a quarter as it is. Of course," he went on, as they moved away through the Norcaster streets, "of course, you haven't any notion of what this urgent business is?"

"None whatever!" replied Vickers. "But I'm quite sure that it is urgent, or Miss Greyle wouldn't have said so. No—I don't know what her exact meaning was, but of course, I know there's something wrong about the whole thing at Scarhaven—seriously wrong!"

"You do, eh?" exclaimed Copplestone. "What now?"

"Ah, that I don't know!" replied Vickers, with a dry laugh. "I wish I did. But—you know how people talk in these provincial places— ever since that inquest there have been all sorts of rumours. Every club and public place in Norcaster has been full of talk—gossip, surmise, speculation. Naturally!"

"But—about what?" asked Copplestone.

"Squire Greyle, of course," said the young solicitor; "that inquest was enough to set the whole country talking. Everybody thinks—they couldn't think otherwise—that something is being hushed up. Everybody's agog to know if Sir Cresswell Oliver and Mr. Petherton are applying for a re-opening of the inquest. You've just come from town, I believe! Did you hear anything?"

Copplestone was wondering whether he ought to tell his companion of his own recent discoveries. Like all laymen, he had an idea that you can tell anything to a lawyer, and he was half-minded to pour out the whole story to Vickers, especially as he was Mrs. Greyle's solicitor. But on second thoughts he decided to wait until he had ascertained the state of affairs at Scarhaven.

"I didn't hear anything about that," he replied. "Of course, that inquest was a mere travesty of what such an inquiry should have been."

"Oh, an utter farce!" agreed Vickers. "However, it produced just the opposite effect to that which the wire-pullers wanted. Of course, Chatfield had squared that jury! But he forgot the press—and the local reporters were so glad to get hold of what was really spicy news that all the Norcaster and Northborough papers have been full of it. Everybody's talking of it, as I said—people are asking what this evidence from America is; why was there such mystery about the whole thing, and so on. And, since then, everybody knows that Squire Greyle has left Scarhaven."

"Have you seen Mrs. or Miss Greyle since the inquest?" asked Copplestone, who was anxious to keep off subjects on which he might be supposed to possess information. "Have you been over there?"

"No—not since that day," replied Vickers. "And I don't care how soon we do see them, for I'm a bit anxious about this telegram. Something must have happened."

Copplestone looked out of the window on his side of the car. Already they were clear of the Norcaster streets and on the road which led to Scarhaven. That road ran all along the coast, often at the very edge of the high, precipitous cliffs, with no more between it and the rocks far beneath than a low wall. It was a road of dangerous curves and corners which needed careful negotiation even in broad daylight, and this was a black, moonless and starless night. But Copplestone had impressed upon his driver that he must get to Scarhaven as quickly as possible, and he and his companion were both so full of their purpose that they paid no heed to the perpetual danger which they ran as the car tore round propections and down deep cuts at a speed which at other times they would have considered suicidal. And at just under the hour they ran on the level stretch by the "Admiral's Arms" and looking down at the harbour saw the lighted port-holes of some ship which lay against the south quay, and on the quay itself men moving about in the glare of lamps.

"What's going on there?" said Vickers. "Late for a vessel to be loading at a place like this where time's of no great importance."

Copplestone offered no suggestion. He was hotly impatient to reach the cottage, and as soon as the car drew up at its gate he burst out, bade the driver wait, and ran eagerly up to the path to Audrey, who opened the door as he advanced. In another second he had both her hands in his own—and kept them there.

"You're all right?" he demanded in tones which made clear to the girl how anxious he had been. "There's nothing wrong—with you or your mother—personally, I mean? You see, I didn't get your wire until this afternoon, and then I raced off as quick—"

"I know," she said, responding a little to the pressure of his hands. "I understand. You may be sure I shouldn't have wired if I hadn't felt it absolutely necessary. Somebody was wanted—and you'd made me promise, and so—Yes," she continued, drawing back as Vickers came up, "we are all right, personally, but—there's something very wrong indeed somewhere. Will you both come in and see mother?"

Mrs. Greyle, looking worn and ill, appeared just then in the hall, and called to them to come in. She preceded them into the parlour and turned to the young men as soon as Audrey closed the door.

"I'm more thankful to see you gentlemen than I've ever been in my life—for anything!" she said. "Something is happening here which needs the attention of men—we women can't do anything. Let me tell you what it is. Yesterday morning, very early the Squire's steam-yacht, the Pike, was brought into the inner harbour and moored against the quay just opposite the park gates. We, of course, could see it, and as we knew he had gone away we wondered why it was brought in there. After it had been moored, we saw that preparations of some sort were being made. Then men—estate labourers—began coming down from the house, carrying packing-cases, which were taken on board. And while this was going on, Mrs. Peller, the housekeeper, came hurrying here, in a state of great consternation. She said that a number of men, sailors and estate men, were packing up and removing all the most valuable things in the house—the finest pictures, the old silver, the famous collection of china which Stephen John Greyle made—and spent thousands upon thousands of pounds in making!—the rarest and most valuable books out of the library—all sorts of things of real and great value. Everything was being taken down to the Pike—and the estate carpenter, who was in charge of all this, said it was by the Squire's orders, and produced to Mrs. Peller his written authority. Of course, Mrs. Peller could do nothing against that, but she came hurrying to tell us, because she, like everybody else, is much exercised by these recent events. And so Audrey and I pocketed our pride, and went to see Peter Chatfield. But Peter Chatfield, like his master, had gone! He had left home the previous evening, and his house was locked up."

Copplestone and Vickers exchanged glances, and the young solicitor signed
Mrs. Greyle to proceed.
"Then," she added, "to add to that, as we came away from Chatfield's house, we met Mr. Elkin, the bank-manager from Norcaster. He had come over in a motor-car, to see me—privately. He wanted to tell me—in relation to all these things—that within the last few days, the Squire and Peter Chatfield had withdrawn from the bank the very large balances of two separate accounts. One was the Squire's own account, in his name—the other was an estate account, on which Chatfield could draw. In both cases the balances withdrawn were of very large amount. Of course, as Mr. Elkin pointed out, it was all in order, and no objection could be raised. But it was unusual, for a large balance had always existed on both these accounts. And, Mr. Elkin added, so many strange rumours are going about Norcaster and the district, that he felt seriously uneasy, and thought it his duty to see me at once. And now—what is to be done? The house is being stripped of the best part of its valuables, and in my opinion when that yacht sails it will be for some foreign port. What other object can

there be in taking these things away? Of course, as nothing is entailed, and there are no heirlooms, everything is absolutely the Squire's property, so—"

Copplestone, who had been realizing the serious significance of these statements, saw that it was time to speak, if energetic methods were to be taken at once.

"I'd better tell you the truth," he said interrupting Mrs. Greyle. "I might have told you, Vickers, as we came along, but I decided to wait, until we got here and found out how things were. Mrs. Greyle, the man you speak of as the Squire, is no more the owner of Scarhaven than I am! He is not Marston Greyle at all. The real Marston Greyle who came over from America, died the day after he landed, in lodgings at Bristol to which Peter Chatfield and his daughter had taken him, and he is buried in a Bristol cemetery under the name of Mark Grey; Gilling and I found that out during these last few days. It's an absolute fact. So the man who has been posing here as the rightful owner is—an impostor!"

A dead silence followed this declaration. The mother and daughter after one long look at Copplestone turned and looked at each other. But Vickers, quick to realize the situation, started from his seat, with evident intention of doing something.

"That's—the truth?" he exclaimed, turning to Copplestone. "No possible flaw in it?"

"None," replied Copplestone. "It's sheer fact."

"Then in that case," said Vickers, "Miss Greyle is the owner of Scarhaven, of everything in the house, of every stick, stone and pebble, about the place! And we must act at once. Miss Greyle, you will have to assert yourself. You must do what I tell you to do. You must get ready at once—this minute!—and come down with me and Mrs. Greyle to that yacht and stop all these proceedings. In our presence you must lay claim to everything that's been taken from the house—yes, and to the yacht itself. Come, let's hurry!"

Audrey hesitated and looked at Mrs. Greyle.

"Very well," she said quietly. "But—not my mother."

"No need!" said Vickers. "You will have us with you."

Audrey hurried from the room, and Mrs. Greyle turned anxiously to Vickers.
"What shall you do?" she asked.

"Warn all concerned," answered Vickers, with a snap of the jaw which showed Copplestone that he was a man of determination. "Warn them, if necessary, that the man they have known as Marston Greyle is an impostor, and that everything they are handling belongs to Miss Greyle. The Scarhaven people know me, of course—there ought not to be any great difficulty with them—and as regards the yacht people—"

"You know," interrupted Mrs. Greyle, "that this man—the impostor—has made himself very popular with the people here? You saw how they cheered him after the inquest? You don't think there is danger in Audrey going down there?"

"Wouldn't it be enough if you and I went?" suggested Copplestone. "It's very late to drag Miss Greyle out."

"I'm sorry, but it's absolutely necessary," said Vickers. "If your story is true—I mean, of course, since it is true—Miss Greyle is owner and mistress, and she must be on the spot. It's all we can do, anyway," he continued, as Audrey, wrapped in a big ulster, came back to the parlour. "Even now we may be too late. And if that yacht once sails away from here—"

There were signs that the yacht's departure was imminent when they went down to the south quay and came abreast of her. The lights on the shore were being extinguished; the estate labourers were gone; only two or three sailors were busy with ropes and gear. And

149

Vickers hurried his little party up a gangway and on to the deck. A hard-faced, keen-eyed, man, evidently in authority, came forward.

"Are you the captain of this vessel?" demanded Vickers in tones of authority. "You are? I am Mr. Vickers, solicitor, of Norcaster. I give you formal warning that the man you have known as Marston Greyle is not Marston Greyle at all, but an impostor. All the property which you have removed from the house, and now have on this vessel, belongs to this lady, Miss Audrey Greyle, Lady of the Manor of Scarhaven. It is at your peril that you move it, or that you cause this vessel to leave this harbour. I claim the vessel and all that is on it on behalf of Miss Greyle."

The man addressed listened in silent attention, and showed no sign of any surprise. As soon as Vickers had finished he turned, hurried down a stairway, remained below for a few minutes, and came up again.

"Will you kindly step this way, Miss Greyle and gentlemen?" he said politely. "You must remember that I am only a servant. If you will come down—"

He led them down the stairs, along a thickly-carpeted passage, and opened the door of a lighted saloon. All unthinking, the three stepped in—to hear the door closed and locked behind them.

CHAPTER XX
THE COURTEOUS CAPTAIN

Vickers sprang back at that door as the sharp click of the turning key caught his ear, and Copplestone, preceding him and following Audrey, who had advanced fearlessly into the cabin, pulled himself up with a sudden, sickening sense of treachery. The two young men looked at each other, and a dead silence fell on them and the girl. Then Vickers laid his hand on the door and shook it.

"Locked in!" he muttered with a queer glance at his companions. "What does that mean?"

"Nothing good!" growled Copplestone who was secretly cursing his own folly in allowing Audrey to leave the quay. "We're trapped!—that's what it means. Why we're trapped isn't a question that matters very much under the circumstances—the serious thing is that we certainly are trapped."

Vickers turned to Audrey.

"My fault!" he said contritely. "All my fault! But I meant it for the best—it was the thing to do—and who on earth could have foreseen this. Look here!—we've got to think pretty quick, Copplestone, that captain, now? Has he done this on his own hook, or—is there somebody on board who's at the top of things?"

"I don't see any good in thinking quick, or asking one's self questions," replied Copplestone. "We're locked in here. We've got Miss Greyle into this mess—and her mother will be anxious and alarmed. I wish we'd let this confounded yacht go where it liked before ever we'd—"

"Don't!" broke in Audrey. "That's no good. Mr. Vickers certainly did what he felt to be best—and who could foresee this? And I'm not afraid—and as for my mother, if we don't return very soon, why, she knows where we are and there are police in Scarhaven, and—"

"How long are we going to be where we are?" asked Copplestone, grimly.

"The thing's moving!"

There was no doubt of that very pertinent fact. Somewhere beneath them, machinery began to work; above them there was hurry and scurry as ropes and stays were thrown off. But so beautifully built was that yacht, and so almost sound-proof the luxurious cabin in which they were prisoners, that little of the noise of departure came to them. However, there was no mistaking the increasing throb of the engines nor the fact that the vessel was moving, and Vickers suddenly sprang on a lounge seat and moved away a silken screen which curtained a port-hole window.

"There's no doubt of that!" he exclaimed.

"We're going through the outer harbour—we've passed the light at the end of the quay. What do these people mean by carrying us out to sea? Copplestone!—with all submission to you—whether it's relevant or not, I wish we knew more of that captain chap!"

"I know him," remarked Audrey. "I have been on this yacht before. His name is Andrius. He's an American—or American-Norwegian, or something like that."

"And the crew?" asked Vickers. "Are they Scarhaven men?"

"No," replied Audrey. "There isn't a Scarhaven man amongst them. My cousin—I mean—you know whom I mean—bought this yacht just as it stood, from an American millionaire early this spring, and he took over the captain, crew, and everything."

"So—we're in the hands of strangers!" exclaimed Vickers, while Copplestone dug his hands into his pockets and began to stamp about. "I wish I'd known all that before we came on board."

"But what harm can they do us?" said Audrey, incredulous of danger. "You don't suppose they'll want to murder us, surely! My own belief is that we never should have been locked up here if you hadn't let them know how much we know, Mr. Vickers."

"Let them—I don't understand," said Vickers, turning a puzzled glance on her.

"Why," replied Audrey with a laugh which convinced both men of her fearlessness, "you let the captain see that we know a great deal and he thereupon ran downstairs—presumably to tell somebody of what you said. And—here's the result!"

"You think, then—" suggested Vickers. "You think that—"

"I think the somebody—whoever he is—wants to know exactly how much we do know," answered Audrey with another laugh. "And so we're being carried off to be cross-examined—at somebody's leisure. Let's hope they won't use thumb-screws and that sort of thing. And anyway," she continued, looking from one to the other, "hadn't we better make the best of it? We're going out to sea, that's certain— here's the bar!"

A sudden lifting of the thickly-carpeted floor, a dip to the left, another to the right, a plunge forward, a drop back, then a settling down to a steady persistent roll, showed her companions that Audrey was right—the yacht was crossing the bar which lay at the mouth of Scarhaven Bay. Outside that lay the North Sea, and Copplestone suddenly wondered which course the vessel was going to take, north, east, or south. But before he could put his thoughts into words, the door was suddenly unlocked, and Captain Andrius, suave, polite, deprecating, walked into the cabin.

"A thousands pardons—and two words of explanation!" he exclaimed, as he executed a deep bow to his lady prisoner. "First— Miss Greyle, I have sent a message to your mother that you are quite safe and will join her in due course. Second—this is merely a temporary detention—you shall all be landed—all in good time."

Vickers as a legal man, assumed his most professional air.

"Do you know what you are rendering yourself liable to, sir, by detaining us at all?" he demanded. "An action—"

Captain Andrius bowed again; again assumed his deprecating smile. He waved the two men to seats and himself took a chair with his back to the door by which he entered.

"My dear sir!" he said courteously. "You forget that I am but a servant. I am under orders. However, I give my word that no harm shall come to you, that you shall be treated with every polite attention, and that you shall be landed."

"When—and where?" asked Vickers.

"Tomorrow, certainly," replied Andrius. "As to where, I cannot exactly say. But—where you will be in touch with—shall we say civilization?"

He showed a set of fine white teeth in such a curious fashion as he spoke the last word that Copplestone and Vickers instinctively glanced at each other, with a mutual instinct of distrust.

"Won't do!" said Vickers. "I insist that you put about and go into Scarhaven again."
Andrius spread out his open palms and shook his head "Impossible!" he answered. "We are already en voyage. Time presses. Be placable—tomorrow you shall be released."

Vickers was about to answer this appeal with an angry refusal to be either placable or tractable, but he suddenly stopped the words which rose to his tongue. There was something in all this—some mystery, some queer game, and it might be worth while to find it out.

"Where are you taking this yacht?" he demanded brusquely. "Come, now!"

"I am under—orders," said Andrius, with another smile.

"Whose orders?" persisted Vickers. "Look here—it's no use trying to burke facts. Who's on board this vessel? You know what I mean. Is the man who calls himself Squire of Scarhaven here?"

Andrius shook his head quietly and gave his questioner a shrewd glance.

"Mr. Vickers," he said meaningly, "I know you! You are a lawyer—though a young one. Lawyers are guarded in their speech. Now—we are alone—we four. No one can hear anything we say. Tell me—is that right what you said to me on deck, that the man who has called himself Marston Greyle is not so at all?"

"Absolutely right," replied Vickers.

"An impostor?" demanded Andrius.

"He is!"

"And never had any right to—anything?"

"No right whatever!"

"Then," said Andrius, with a polite inclination of his head and shoulders to Audrey, "the truth is that everything of the Scarhaven property belongs to this lady?"

"Everything!" exclaimed Vickers. "Land, houses, furniture, valuables—everything. All the property which you have on this yacht—pictures, china, silver, books, objects of art, as I am instructed, removed from the house—are Miss Greyle's sole property. Once more I warn you of what you are doing, and I demand that you immediately return to Scarhaven. This very yacht belongs to Miss Greyle!"

Andrius nodded, looked fixedly at the young solicitor for a moment, and then rose.

"I am obliged to you," he said. "That, of course, is your claim. But—the other one, eh? It seems to me there might be something to be said for that, you know? So, all I can do is to renew my assurance of polite attention, offer you our best accommodation—which is luxurious—and promise to land you—somewhere—tomorrow. Miss Greyle, we have two women servants on board—I shall send them to you at once and they will attend to you—please consider them your own. You, gentlemen, will perhaps join me in my quarters?—I have two spare cabins close to my own which are at your service."

Copplestone and Vickers looked at each other and at Audrey—undecided and vaguely suspicious. But Audrey was evidently neither alarmed nor uneasy—she nodded a ready assent to the Captain's proposal.

"Thank you, Captain Andrius," she said coolly. "I know the two women. You may send one of them. Do what he suggests," she murmured, turning to Copplestone, who had moved close to her, "I'm not one scrap afraid of anything—and it's only until tomorrow. He'll land us—I'm sure of it."

There was nothing for it, then, but to follow Andrius to his own comfortable quarters. There, utterly ignoring the strange circumstances under which they met, he played the part of host with genuine desire to make his guests feel at ease, and when he showed them to their berths, a little later, he emphasized his assurance of their absolute safety and liberty.

"You see, gentlemen, your movements are untrammelled," he said. "You can go in and out of your quarters as you like. You can go where you like on the yacht tomorrow morning. There is no restriction on you. Sleep well—and tomorrow you are all free again, eh?"

Copplestone got a word or two with Vickers—alone.

"What do you think?" he muttered. "Shall you sleep?"

"My impression—for I know what you're thinking about," said Vickers, "is that Miss Greyle's as safe as if she were in her mother's house! She's no fear, herself, anyway. There's some mystery, somewhere, and I can't make this Andrius man out at all, but I believe all's right as regards personal safety. There's Miss Greyle's cabin, anyhow, right opposite ours—and I can keep an eye and an ear open even when I'm asleep!"

But in spite of these assurances, Copplestone slept little. He was up, dressed, and on deck by sunrise, staring around him in a fresh autumn morning to get some notion of the yacht's whereabouts, and he had just managed to make out a mere filmy line of land far to the westward when Audrey appeared at his elbow. There was no one of any importance near them and Copplestone impulsively seized her hands.

"I've scarcely slept!" he blurted out, gazing intently at her. "Couldn't! Blaming myself for letting you get into this confounded mess!
You're all right?"
Audrey responded a little to the pressure of his hands before she disengaged her own.

"It wasn't your fault," she said. "It's nobody's fault. Don't blame Mr. Vickers—he couldn't foresee this. Yes, I'm all right—and I slept like a top. What's the use of worrying? Do you know," she went on, lowering her voice and drawing nearer to him, "I believe something's going to come of all this—something that'll clear matters up once and for all."

"Why?" asked Copplestone, wonderingly. "What makes you think that?"

"Don't know—instinct, intuitiveness, perhaps," she answered. "Besides—I'm dead certain we're not the only people—I don't mean crew and Captain—aboard the Pike. I believe there's somebody else. There's some mystery, anyway. Keep that to yourself," she said as Andrius and Vickers appeared from below. "Don't show any sign— wait to see how things turn out."

She turned away from him to greet the other two as unconcernedly as if there were nothing unusual in the situation, and Copplestone marvelled at her coolness. He himself, not so well equipped with patience, was feverishly anxious to know how things would turn out, and when. But the day went by and nothing happened, except that Captain Andrius was very polite to his guests and that the yacht, a particularly fast sailer, continued to make headway through the grey seas, sometimes in bare sight of land and sometimes out of it. To one or two inquiries as to the fulfilment of his promise Andrius made no more answer than a reassuring nod; once when Vickers pressed him, he replied curtly that the day was not yet over. Vickers drew Copplestone aside on hearing that.

"Look here!" he said. "I've been reckoning things up as near as I can. I make out that we've been running due north, or north-east ever since we left Scarhaven last night. I reckon, too, that this vessel makes quite twenty-two or three, knots an hour. We must be off the extreme north-east coast of Scotland. And night's coming on!"

"There are ports there that he can put into," said Copplestone. "The thing is—will he keep his promise? Remember!—he must know very well that if we once land anywhere within reach of a telegraph office, we can wire particulars about him to every port in the world if we like—and he's got to go somewhere, eventually, you know."

Vickers shook his head as if this were a problem he would give up. It was beyond him, he said, to even guess at what Andrius was after, or what was going to happen. And nothing did happen until, as the three prisoners sat at dinner with their polite gaoler, the Pike came to a sudden stop and hung gently on a quiet sea. Andrius looked up and smiled.

"A pleasant night for your landing," he remarked. "Don't hurry — but there will be a boat ready for you as soon as dinner is over."

"And where are we?" asked Vickers.

"That, my dear sir, you will see when you land." replied Andrius. "You will, at any rate, be quite comfortable for the night, and in the morning, I think, you will be able to journey — wherever you wish to go to."

There was something in the smile which accompanied the last words which made Copplestone uneasy. But the prospect of regaining their liberty was too good — he kept his own counsel. And half-an-hour later, he, Audrey and Vickers, stood on deck, looking down on a boat alongside, in which were two or three of the crew and a man holding a lanthorn. In front was the dark sea, and ahead a darker mass which they took to be land.

"You won't tell us what this place is?" said Vickers as he was about to follow the others into the boat. "It's on the mainland, of course?"

"The morning light, my good sir, will show you everything," replied Andrius. "Be content that I have kept my promise — you have come off luckily," he added with a significant look.

Vickers felt a strange sense of alarm as the boat left the yacht. He noticed two or three suspicious circumstances. As soon as they got away, he saw that all the yacht's lights had been or were being darkened or entirely obscured; at a dozen boat lengths they could see her no more. Then a boat, swiftly pulled, passed them in the darkness, evidently coming from the shore to which they were being taken: it, too, carried no light. Nor were there any lights on the shore itself; all there was in utter blackness. They were on the shingle within a quarter of an hour; within a minute or two the yachtsmen had helped all three on to the beach, had carried up certain boxes and packages which had been placed in the boat, had set down the lighted lanthorn, jumped into the boat again and vanished in the darkness. And in the silence, broken only by the drip of water from the retreating oars, and by the scarcely-noticed ripple of the waves, Audrey voiced exactly what her two companions felt.

"Andrius has kept his word—and cheated us! We're stranded!"

From somewhere out of the darkness came a groan—deep and heartfelt, as if in entire agreement with Audrey's declaration. That it proceeded from a human being was evident enough, and Vickers hastily snatched up the lanthorn and strode in the direction from which it came. And there, seated on the shingle, his whole attitude one of utter dejection and misery, the three castaways found a sharer of their sorrows—Peter Chatfield!

CHAPTER XXI
MAROONED

To each of these three young people this was the most surprising moment which life had yet afforded. It was an astonishing thing to find a fellow mortal there at all, but to find that mortal was the Scarhaven estate agent was literally short of marvellous. What was also astounding was to see Chatfield's only too evident distress. Swathed in a heavy, old-fashioned ulster, with a plaid shawl round his shoulders and a deerstalker hat tied over head and ears with a bandanna handkerchief he sat on the beach nursing his knees, slightly rocking his fleshy figure to and fro and moaning softly with the regularity of a minute bell. His eyes were fixed on the dark expanse of waters at his feet; his lips, when he was not moaning, worked incessantly; as he rocked his body he beat his toes on the shingle. Clearly, Chatfield was in a bad way, mentally. That he was not so badly off materially was made evident by the presence of a half-open kit bag which obviously contained food and a bottle of spirits.

For any notice that he took of them, Audrey, Vickers, and Copplestone might have been no more than the pebbles on which they stood. In spite of the fact that Vickers shone the light on his fat face, and that three inquisitive pairs of eyes were trained on it, Chatfield continued to stare moodily and disgustedly out to sea and to take no notice of his gratuitous company. And so utterly extraordinary was his behaviour and attitude that Audrey suddenly and almost involuntarily stepped forward and laid a hand on his shoulder.

"Mr. Chatfield!" she exclaimed. "What 's the matter? Are you ill?"

The emphasis which she gave to the last word roused some quality of Chatfield's subtle intellect. He flashed a swift look at his questioner—a look of mingled contempt and derision, spiced with a dash of sneering humour. And he found his tongue.

"Ill!" he snorted. "Ill! She asks if I'm ill—me, a respectable man what's maltreated and robbed before his own eyes by them as ought to fall in humble gratitude at his feet! Ill!—aye, ill with something that's worse nor any bodily aches and pains—let me tell you that! But not done for, neither!"

"He's all right," said Copplestone. "That's a flash of his old spirit. You're all right, Chatfield, aren't you? And who's robbed and maltreated you—and how and when—especially when—did you come here?"

Chatfield looked up at his old assailant with a glare of dislike.

"You keep your tongue to yourself, young feller!" he growled. "I shouldn't never ha' been here at all if it hadn't been for the likes of you—a pokin' your nose where it isn't wanted. It's 'cause o' you three comin' aboard o' that there yacht last night as I am here—a castaway!"

"Well, we're castaways, too, Mr. Chatfield," said Audrey. "And we can't help believing that it's all your naughty conduct that's made us so. Why don't you tell the truth?"

Chatfield uttered a few grumpy and inarticulate sounds.

"It'll be a bad day for more than one when I do that—as I will," he muttered presently. "Oh aye, I'll tell the truth—when it suits me! But I'll be out o' this first."

"You'll never get out of this first or last, until you tell us how you got in," said Vickers, assuming a threatening tone. "You'd better tell us all about it, you know. Come now!—you know me and my firm."

Chatfield laughed grimly and shook his much-swathed head.

"I ought to," he said. "I've given 'em more than one nice job and said naught about their bills o' costs, neither, my lad. You keep a civil tongue in your mouth—I ain't done for yet, noways! You let me get off this here place, wherever it is, and within touch of a telegraph office, and I'll make somebody suffer!"

"Andrius, of course," said Copplestone. "Come now, he put you ashore before he sent us off, didn't he? Why don't you own up?"

"Never you mind, young feller," retorted Chatfield. "I was feeling very cast down, but I'm better. I've something that'll keep me going—revenge! I'll show 'em, once I'm off this place—I will so!"

"Look here, Chatfield," said Vickers. "Do you know where this place is?
What is it? Is it on the mainland, or is it an island, or where are we? It's all very well talking about getting off, but when and how are we to
get off? Why don't you be sensible and tell us what you know?"
The estate agent arose slowly and ponderously, drawing his shawl about him. He looked out seawards. In that black waste the steady beat of the yacht's propellers could be clearly heard, but not a gleam of light came from her, and it was impossible to decide in which direction she was going. And Chatfield suddenly shook his fist at the throbbing sound which came in regular pulsations through the night.

"Never mind!" he said sneeringly. "We aren't at the North Pole neither—I ain't a seafaring man, but I've a good idea of where we are! And perhaps there won't be naught to take me off when it's daylight, and perhaps there won't be no telegraphs near at hand, nor within a hundred miles, and perhaps there ain't such a blessed person as that there Marconi and his wireless in the world—oh, no! Just you wait, my fine fellers—that's all!"

"He's not addressing us, Vickers," said Copplestone. "You're decidedly better, Chatfield—you're quite better. The notion of revenge and of circumvention has come to you like balm. But you'd a lot better tell us who you're referring to, and why you were put ashore. Listen, Chatfield!—there's property of your own on that yacht, eh? That it? Come, now?"

163

Chatfield gave his questioner a look of indignant scorn. He stooped for the kit-bag, picked it up, and turned away.

"I don't want to have naught to do with you," he remarked over his shoulder. "You keep yourselves to yourselves, and I'll keep myself to myself. If it hadn't been for what you blabbed out last night, them ungrateful devils 'ud never have had such ideas put into their heads!"

As if he knew his way, Chatfield plodded heavily up the beach and was lost in the darkness, and the three left behind stood helplessly staring at each other. For a long time there was silence, broken only by the agent's heavy tread on the shingle—at last Vickers spoke.

"I think I can see through all this," he said. "Chatfield's cryptic utterances were somewhat suggestive. 'Robbed'—'maltreated'— 'them as ought to have fallen in humble gratitude at his feet'— 'vengeance'— 'revenge'—'Marconi telegrams'—'ungrateful devils'— ah, I see it! Chatfield had associates on the Pike—probably the impostor himself and Andrius—probably, too, he had property of his own, as you suggested to him, Copplestone. The whole gang was doubtless off with their loot to far quarters of the globe. Very good— the other members have shelved Chatfield. They've done with him. But—not if he knows it! That man will hunt the Pike and her people—whoever they are—relentlessly when he gets off this."

"I wish we knew what it is that we're on!" said Copplestone.

"Impossible till daybreak," replied Vickers. "But I've an idea—this is probably one of the seventy-odd islands of the Orkneys: I've sailed round here before. If I'm right, it's most likely one of the outlying and uninhabited ones. Andrius—or his controlling power—has dropped us—and Chatfield—here, knowing that we may have to spend a few days on this island before we succeed in getting off. Those few days will mean a great deal to the Pike. She can be run into some safe harbourage on this coast, given a new coat of paint and a new name, and be off before we can do anything to stop her. I

164

allow Chatfield to be right in this—that my perhaps too hasty declaration to Andrius revealed to that gentleman how he could make off with other people's property."

"Nothing will make me believe that Andrius is the solely responsible person for this last development," said Copplestone, moodily. "There were other people on board—cleverly concealed. And what are we going to do?"

Audrey had stepped away from the circle of light made by the lanthorn and was gazing steadily in the direction which Chatfield had taken.

"Those are cliffs, surely," she said presently. "Hadn't we better go up the beach and see if we can't find some shelter until morning? Fortunately we're all warmly clad, and Andrius was considerate enough to throw rugs and things into the boat, as well as provisions. Come along!—after all, we're not so badly off. And we have the satisfaction of knowing that we can keep Chatfield under observation. Remember that!"

But in the morning, when the first gleam of light came across the sea, and Vickers, leaving his companions to prepare some breakfast from the store of provisions which had been sent ashore with them, set out to make a first examination of their surroundings, the agent was not to be seen. What was to be seen was a breach of rock, sand, shingle, not a mile in length, lying at the foot of high cliffs, and on the grey sea in front not a sign of a sail, nor a wisp of smoke from a passing steamer. The apparent solitude and isolation of the place was as profound as the silence which overhung everything.

Vickers made his way up the cliffs to their highest point and from its summit took a leisurely view of his surroundings. He saw at once that they were on an island, and that it was but one of many which lay spread out over the sea towards the north and the west. It was a wedge-shaped island this, and the cliffs on which he stood and the beach beneath formed the widest side of it; from thence its lines drew away to a point in the distance which he judged to be two miles off. Between him and that point lay a sloping expanse of rough land, never cultivated since creation, whereon there were vast masses of rock and boulder but no sign of human life. No curling column of smoke went up from hut or cottage; his ears caught neither the bleating of sheep nor the cry of shepherd—all was still as only such places can be still. Nor could he perceive any signs of life on the adjacent islands—which, to be sure, were not very near. From the sea mists which wrapped one of them he saw projecting the cap of a mountainous hill—that hill he recognized as being on one of the principal islands of the group, and he then knew that he and his companions had been set down on one of the outlying islands which, from its position, was not in the immediate way of passing vessels nor likely to be visited by fishermen.

He was turning away from the top of the cliff after a long and careful inspection, when he caught sight of a man's figure crossing the rocky slope between him and this far-off point. That, he said to himself, was Chatfield. Did Chatfield know of any place at that point visited by fishing craft from the other islands? Had Chatfield ever been in the Orkneys before? Was there any method in his wanderings? Or was he, too, merely examining his surroundings—considering which was the likeliest part of the island from which to attract attention? In the midst of these speculation a sudden resolution came to him—one or other of the three must keep an eye on Chatfield. Night or day, Chatfield must be watched. And having already seen that Copplestone and Audrey had an unmistakable liking for each other's society and would certainly not object to being left together, he determined to watch Chatfield himself. Hurrying down the cliffs, he hastily explained the situation to his companions, took some food in his hands, and set out to follow the agent wherever he went.

CHAPTER XXII
THE OLD HAND

Half-an-hour later, when Vickers regained the top of the cliff and once more looked across the island towards the far-off point, the figure which he had previously seen making for it had turned back, and was plodding steadily across the coarse grass and rock-strewn moorland in his own direction. Chatfield had evidently taken a bird's eye view of the situation from the vantage point of the slope and had come to the conclusion that the higher part of the island was the most likely point from which to attract attention. He came steadily forward, a big, lumbering figure in the light mist, and Vickers as he went on to meet him eyed him with a lively curiosity, wondering what secrets lay carefully locked up in the man's heart and what happened on the Pike that made its captain or its owner bundle Chatfield out of it like a box of bad goods for which there was no more use. And as he speculated, they met, and Vickers saw at once that the old fellow's mood had changed during the night. An atmosphere of smug oiliness sat upon Chatfield in the freshness of the morning, and he greeted the young solicitor in tones which were suggestive of a chastened spirit.

"Morning, Mr. Vickers," he said. "A sweetly pretty spot it is that we find ourselves in, sir—nevertheless, one's affairs sometimes makes us long to quit the side of beauty, however much we would tarry by it! In plain words, Mr. Vickers, I want to get out o' this. And I've been looking round, and my opinion is that the best thing we can do is to start as big a fire as we can find stuff for on yon bluff and keep a-feeding on it. In the meantime, while you're considering of that, I'll burn something of my own—I'm weary."

He dropped down on a convenient boulder of limestone, settled his big frame comfortably, and producing a pipe and a tobacco pouch, proceeded to smoke. Vickers himself took another boulder and looked inquisitively at his strange companion. He felt sure that Chatfield was up to something.

"You say 'we' now," he remarked suddenly. "Last night you said you didn't want to have anything to do with us. We were to keep to ourselves, and—"

"Well, well, Mr. Vickers," broke in Chatfield. "One says things at one time that one wouldn't say at another, you know. Facts is facts, sir, and Providence has made us companions in distress. I've naught against you—nor against the girl—as for t'other young man, he's of a interfering nature—but I forgive him—he's young. I don't bear no ill will—things being as they are. I've had time to reflect since last night—and I don't see no reason why Miss Greyle and me shouldn't come to terms—through you."

Vickers lighted his own pipe, and took some time over it.

"What are you after, Chatfield?" he asked at length. "Something, of course. You say you want to come to terms with Miss Greyle. That, of course, is because you know very well that Miss Greyle is the legal owner of Scarhaven, and that—"

Chatfield waved his pipe.

"I don't!" he answered, with what seemed genuine eagerness. "I don't know naught of the sort. I tell you, Mr. Vickers, I do not know that the man what we've known as the Squire of Scarhaven for a year gone by is not the rightful Squire—I do not! Fact, sir! But"—he lowered his voice, and his sly eyes became slyer and craftier—"but I won't deny that during this last week or two I may have had my suspicions aroused, that there was something wrong—I don't deny that, Mr. Vickers."

Vickers heard this with amazement. Young as he was, he had had various dealings with Peter Chatfield, and he had an idea that he knew something of him, subtle old fellow though he was, and he believed that Chatfield was now speaking the truth. But, in that case, what of Copplestone's revelation about the Falmouth and Bristol affair and the dead man? He thought rapidly, and then determined to take a strong line.

168

"Chatfield!" he said. "You're trying to bluff me. It won't do. Things are known. I know 'em! I'll be candid with you—the time's come for that. I'll tell you what I know—it'll all have to come out. You know very well that the real Marston Greyle's dead. You were with him when he died. What's more, you buried him at Bristol under the name of Mark Grey. Hang it all, man, what's the use of lying about it?—you know that's all true!"

He was watching Chatfield's big face keenly, and he was astonished to see that his dramatic impeachment produced no more effect than a slightly superior smile. Instead of being floored, Chatfield was distinctly unimpressed.

"Aye!" he said, reflectively. "Aye, I expected to hear that. That's Copplestone's work, of course—I knew he was some sort of detective as soon as I got speech with him. His work and that there Sir Cresswell Oliver's as is making a mountain out of a molehill about his brother, who, of course, broke his neck quite accidental, poor man, and of that London lawyer—Petherton. Aye—aye—but all the same, Mr. Vickers, it don't alter matters—no-how!"

"Good heavens, man, what do you mean?" exclaimed Vickers, who was becoming more and more mystified. "Do you mean to tell me— come, come, Chatfield, I'm not a fool! Why—Copplestone has found it all out—there's no need to keep it secret, now. You were with Marston Greyle when he died—you registered his death as Marston Greyle—and—"

Chatfield laughed softly and gave his companion a swift glance out of one corner of his right eye.

"And put another name on a bit of a tombstone—six months afterwards, what?" he said quietly. "Mr. Vickers, when you're as old as I am, you'll know that this here world is as full o' puzzles as yon sea's full o'fish!"

Vickers could only stare at his companion in speechless silence after that. He felt that there was some mystery about which Chatfield evidently knew a great deal while he knew nothing. The old fellow's coolness, his ready acceptance of the Bristol facts, his almost contemptuous brushing aside of them, reduced Vickers to a feeling of helplessness. And Chatfield saw it, and laughed, and drawing a pocket-flask out of his garments, helped himself to a tot of spirits — after which he good-naturedly offered like refreshment to Vickers. But Vickers shook his head.

"No, thanks," he said. He continued to stare at Chatfield much as he might have, stared at the Sphinx if she had been present — and in the end he could only think of one word. "Well?" he asked lamely. "Well?"

"As to what, now?" inquired Chatfield with a sly smile.

"About what you said," replied Vickers. "Miss Greyle, you know. I'm about thoroughly tied up with all this. You evidently know a lot. Of course you won't tell! You're devilish deep, Chatfield. But, between you and me — what do you mean when you say that you don't see why you and Miss Greyle shouldn't come to terms?"

"Didn't I say that during this last week or two I'd had my suspicions about the Squire?" answered Chatfield. "I did. I have had them suspicions — got 'em stronger than ever since last night. So — what I say is this. If things should turn out that Miss Greyle's the rightful owner of Scarhaven, and if I help her to establish her claim, and if I help, too, to recover them valuables that are on the Pike — there's a good sixty to eighty thousand pounds worth of stuff, silver, china, paintings, books, tapestry, on that there craft, Mr. Vickers! — if, I say, I do all that, what will Miss Greyle give me? That's it — in a plain way of speaking."

"I thought it was," said Vickers dryly. "Of course! Very well — you'd better come and talk to Miss Greyle. Come on — now!"

Copplestone and Audrey, having made a breakfast from the box of provisions which Andrius had been good enough to send ashore with them, had climbed to the head of the cliff after Vickers, and they were presently astonished beyond measure to see him returning with Chatfield under outward signs which suggested amity if not friendship. They paused by a convenient nook in the rocks and silently awaited the approach of these two strangely assorted companions. Vickers, coming near, gave them a queer and a knowing look.

"Mr. Chatfield," he said gravely, "has had the night in which to reflect. Mr. Chatfield desires peaceable relations. Mr. Chatfield doesn't see—now, having reflected—why he and Miss Greyle shouldn't be on good terms. Mr. Chatfield desires to discuss these terms. Is that right, Chatfield?"

"Quite right, sir," assented the agent. He had been regarding the couple who faced him benevolently and indulgently, and he now raised his hat to them. "Servant, ma'am," he said with a bow to Audrey. "Servant, sir," he continued, with another bow to Copplestone. "Ah—it's far better to be at peace one with another than to let misunderstandings exist for ever. Mr. Copplestone, sir, you and me's had words in times past—I brush 'em away, sir, like that there—the memory's departed! I desire naught but better feelings. Happen Mr. Vickers'll repeat what's passed between him and me."

Copplestone stood rooted to the spot with amazement while Vickers hastily epitomized the recent conversation; his mouth opened and his speech failed him. But Audrey laughed and looked at Vickers as if Chatfield were a new sort of entertainment.

"What do you say to this, Mr. Vickers?" she asked.

"Well, if you want to know," replied Vickers, "I believe Chatfield when he says that he does not know that the Squire is not the Squire. May seem strange, but I do! As a solicitor, I do."

171

"Great Scott!" exclaimed Copplestone, finding his tongue.
"You—believe that!"
"I've said so," retorted Vickers.

"Thank you, sir," said Chatfield. "I'm obliged to you. Mr.
Copplestone, sir, doesn't yet understand that there's a deal of
conundrum in life. He'll know better—some day. He'll know, too,
that the poet spoke truthful when he said that things isn't what they
seem."

Copplestone turned angrily on Vickers.

"Is this a farce?" he demanded. "Good heavens, man! you know what
I told you!"

"Mr. Chatfield has a version," answered Vickers. "Why not hear it?"

"On terms, Mr. Vickers," remarked Chatfield. "On terms, sir."

"What terms?" asked Audrey. "To Mr. Chatfield's personal
advantage, of course."

Chatfield, who was still the most unconcerned of the group, seated
himself on the rocks and looked at his audience.

"I've said to Mr. Vickers here that if I help Miss Greyle to the estate, I
ought to be rewarded—handsome," he said. "Mind you, I don't know
that I can, for as I say, I do not know, as a matter of strict fact, that
this man as we've called the Squire, isn't the Squire. But recent
events—very recent events!—has made me suspicious that he isn't,
and happen I can do a good bit—a very good bit—to turning him
out. Now, if I help in that there work, will Miss Greyle continue me
in my post of estate agent at Scarhaven?"

"Not for any longer than it will take to turn you out of it, Mr.
Chatfield," replied Audrey with an energy and promptitude which
surprised her companions. "So we need not discuss that. You will
never be my agent!"

"Very good, ma'am—that's quite according to my expectations," said Chatfield, meekly. "I was always a misunderstood man. However, this here proposition will perhaps be more welcome. It's always been understood that I was to have a retiring pension of five hundred pounds per annum. The family has always promised it—I've letters to prove it. Will Miss Greyle stand to that if she comes in? I've been a faithful servant for nigh on to fifty years, Mr. Vickers, as all the neighbourhood is aware."

"If I come in, as you call it, you shall have your pension," said Audrey. Chatfield slowly felt in a capacious inner pocket and produced a large notebook and a fountain pen. He passed them to Vickers.

"We'll have that there in writing, signed and witnessed," he said. "Put, if you please, Mr. Vickers, 'I agree that if I come into the Scarhaven estate, Peter Chatfield shall at once be pensioned off with five hundred pounds a year, to be paid quarterly. Same to be properly assured to him for his life.' And then if Miss Greyle'll sign that document, and you gentlemen'll witness it, I shall consider that henceforth I'm in Miss Greyle's service. And," he added, with a significant glance all round, "I shall be a deal more use as a friend nor what I should be as what you might term an enemy—Mr. Vickers knows that."

Vickers held a short consultation with Audrey, the result of which was that the paper was duly signed, witnessed, and deposited in Chatfield's pocket. And Chatfield nodded his satisfaction.

"All right," he said. "Now then, ma'am, and gentlemen, the next thing is to get away out o' this, and get on the track of them as put us here. We'd better start a big fire out o' this dry stuff—"

"But what about these revelations you were going to make?" said Vickers.
"I understood you were to tell us—"

"Sir," replied Chatfield, "I'll tell and I'll reveal in due course, and in good order. Events, sir, is the thing! Let me get to the nearest telegraph office, and we'll have some events, right smart. Let me attract attention. I've sailed in these seas before. There's steamers goes out of Kirkwall yonder frequent—we must get hold of one. A telegraph office!—that's what I want. I'm a-going to set up a blaze— and I'll set up a blaze elsewhere as soon as I can lay hands on a bundle o' telegraph forms!"

He leisurely took off his shawl and overcoat, laid them on a shelf of rock, and moved away to collect the dry stuff which lay to hand. The three young people exchanged glances.

"What's this new mystery?" asked Audrey.

"All bluff!—some deep game of his own," growled Copplestone. "He's the most consummate old liar I ever—"

"You're wrong this time, old chap!" interrupted Vickers. "He's a bad 'un—but he's on our side now—I'm convinced. It is a game he's playing, and a deep one, and I don't know what it is, but it's for our benefit—Chatfield's simply transferred his interest and influence to us—that's all. For his own purposes, of course. And"—he suddenly paused, gazed seaward, and then jumped to his feet. "Chatfield!" he called quietly. "You needn't light any fire. Here's a steamer!"

CHAPTER XXIII
THE YACHT COMES BACK

Chatfield, his arms filled with masses of dried bracken and coarse grass, turned sharply on hearing Vickers's call and stared hard and long in the direction which the young solicitor pointed out. His small, crafty eyes became dilated to their full extent—suddenly they contracted again with a look of cunning satisfaction, and throwing away his burdens he drew out a big many-coloured handkerchief and mopped his high forehead as if the perspiration which burst out were the result of intense mental relief.

"Didn't I know we should be rescued from this here imprisonment!" he cried with unctuous joy. "Thought they'd pinned me here for best part of a week, no doubt, while they could get theirselves quietly away—far away! But it's my experience 'ut them as has served the Lord's never deserted, Mr. Vickers, and if you live as long as—"

"Don't be blasphemous, Chatfield!" said Vickers, curtly. "None of that!
What we'd better think about is the chance of that steamer sighting us.
We'll light that fire, anyway!"
"She's coming straight on for the island," remarked Copplestone, who had been narrowly watching the approaching vessel. "So straight that you'd think she was actually making for it."

"She'll be some craft bound for Kirkwall," said Vickers, pointing northward to the main group of islands. "And in that case she'll probably take this channel on our west; that fire, now! Come on all of you, and let's make as big a smoke as we can get out of this stuff."

The weather being calm and the grass and bracken which they heaped together as dry as tinder, there was little difficulty about raising a thick column of smoke which presently rose high in the sky. But Audrey, turning away from the successful result of their labours, suddenly glanced at Copplestone with a look that challenged an answer to her own thoughts. They were standing a little apart from the others and she lowered her voice.

"I say!" she murmured. "I don't think we need have bothered ourselves to light that fire. That vessel, whatever it is, is making for us. Look!"

Copplestone shaded his eyes and stared out across the sea. The steamer was by that time no more than two or three miles away. But she was coming towards them in a dead straight line, and as she was accordingly bow on, and as her top deck and lamps were obscured by clouds of black smoke, pouring furiously from her funnels, they could make little out of her appearance. Copplestone's first notion was that she was a naval patrol boat, or a torpedo destroyer. Whatever she was it seemed certain that she was heading direct for the island, at that very point on which the fugitives had been landed the previous night. And it was very evident that she was in a great hurry to make her objective.

"I think you're right," he said, turning to Audrey. "But it's strange that any vessel should be making for an uninhabited island like this. What—but you've got some notion in your mind?" he broke off suddenly, seeing her glance at him again. "What is it?"

Audrey shook her head, with a cautious look at Chatfield.

"I was wondering if that's the Pike?—come back!" she whispered. "And if it is—why?"

Copplestone started, and took a longer and keener look at the vessel. Before he could speak again, Vickers called out cheerily across the rocks.

"Come on, you two!" he cried. "She's seen us—she's coming in. They'll have to send off a boat. Let's get down to the beach, so that they'll know where there's a safe landing."

He sprang over the edge of the cliff and hurried down the rough path; Chatfield, picking up his coat and shawl, prepared to follow him; Audrey and Copplestone lingered until he, too, had begun to lumber downward.

"If that is the Pike," said Audrey, "there is something—wrong. Whoever it is that is on the Pike wouldn't come back to take us!"

"You think there is somebody on the Pike—somebody other than Andrius?" suggested Copplestone.

"I believe the man who calls himself Marston Greyle was on the Pike," announced Audrey. "I've always thought so. Whether Chatfield knew that or not, I don't know. My own belief is that Chatfield did know. I believe Chatfield was in with them, as the saying is. I think they were all running away with as much of the Scarhaven property as they could lay hands on and that having got it, they bundled Chatfield out and dumped him down here, having no further use for him. And, if that's the Pike, and they're returning here, it's because they want Chatfield!"

Copplestone suddenly recognized that feminine instinct had solved a problem which masculine reason had so far left unsolved.

"By gad!" he exclaimed softly. "Then, if that is so, this is merely another of Chatfield's games. You don't believe him?"

"I would think myself within approachable distance of lunacy if I believed a word that Peter Chatfield said," she answered calmly. "Of course, he is playing a game of his own all through. He shall have his pension—if I have the power to give it—but believe him—oh, no!"

"Let's follow them," said Copplestone. "Something's going to happen—if that is the Pike."

"Look there, then," exclaimed Audrey as they began to descend the cliff.
"Chatfield's already uneasy."

She pointed to the beach below, where Chatfield, now fully overcoated and shawled again, had mounted a ridge of rock, and while gazing intently at the vessel, was exchanging remarks with Vickers, who had evidently said something which had alarmed him. They caught Chatfield's excited ejaculations as they hurried over the sand.

"Don't say that, Mr. Vickers!" he was saying imploringly. "For God's sake, Mr. Vickers, don't suggest them there sort of thoughts. You make me feel right down poorly, Mr. Vickers, to say such! It's worse than a bad dream, Mr. Vickers—no, sir, no, surely you're mistaken!"

"Bet you a fiver to a halfpenny it's the Pike," retorted Vickers. "I know her lines. Besides she's heading straight here. Copplestone!" he cried, turning to the advancing couple. "Do you know, I believe that's the Pike!"

Copplestone gave Audrey's elbow a gentle squeeze.

"Look at old Chatfield!" he whispered. "By gad!—look at him. Yes," he called out loudly, "We know it's the Pike—we saw that from the top of the cliffs. She's coming straight in."

"Oh, yes, it's the Pike," exclaimed Audrey. "Aren't you delighted, Mr. Chatfield."
The agent suddenly turned his big fat face towards the three young people, with such an expression of craven fear on it that the sardonic jest which Copplestone was about to voice died away on his lips. Chatfield's creased cheeks and heavy jowl had become white as chalk; great beads of sweat rolled down them; his mouth opened and shut silently, and suddenly, as he raised his hands and wrung them, his knees began to quiver. It was evident that the man was badly, terribly afraid—and as they watched him in amazed wonder his eyes began to search the shore and the cliffs as if he were some hunted animal seeking any hole or cranny in which to hide. A sudden swelling of the light wind brought the steady throb of the oncoming engines to his ears and he turned on Vickers with a look that made the onlookers start.

"For goodness sake, Mr. Vickers!" he said in a queer, strained voice. "For heaven's sake, let's get ourselves away! Mr. Vickers—it ain't safe for none of us. We'd best to run, sir—let's get to the other side of the island. There's caves there—places—let's hide till something comes from the other islands, or till these folks goes away—I tell you it's dangerous for us to stop here!"

"We're not afraid, Chatfield," replied Vickers. "What ails you! Why man, you couldn't be more afraid if you'd murdered somebody! What do you suppose these people want? You, of course. And you can't escape—if they want you, they'll search the island till they get you. You've been deceiving us, Chatfield—there's something you've kept back. Now, what is it? What have they come back for?"

"Yes, Mr. Chatfield, what has the Pike come back for?" repeated Audrey, coming nearer. "Come now—hadn't you better tell?"

"It is the Pike," remarked Copplestone. "Look there! And they're going to send in a boat. Better be quick, Chatfield."

The agent turned an ashen face towards the yacht. She had swung round and come to a halt, and the rattle of a boat being let down came menacingly to the frightened man's ears. He tittered a deep groan and his eyes again sought the cliffs.

"It's not a bit of good, Chatfield," said Vickers. "You can't get away. Good heavens, man!—what are you so frightened for!" Chatfield moaned and drew haltingly nearer to the other three, as if he found some comfort in their mere presence.

"It's the money!" he whispered. "The money as was in the Norcaster Bank—two lots of it. He—the Squire—gave me authority to get out his lot what was standing in his name, you know—and the other— the estate lot—that was standing in mine—some fifty thousand pounds in all, Mr. Vickers. I had it all in gold, packed in sealed chests—and they—those on board there—thought I took them chests aboard the Pike with me. I did take chests, d'ye see—but they'd lead in 'em. The real stuff is hidden—buried—never mind where. And I know what they've come back for!—they've opened the chests I took on board, and they've found there's naught but lead. And they want me—me!—me! They'll torture me to make me tell where the real chests, the money is—torture me! Oh, for God's sake, keep 'em away from me—help me to hide—help me to get away—and I'll tell Miss Greyle then where the money's hid, and—oh, Lord, they're coming! Mr. Vickers—Mr. Vickers—"

He cast himself bodily at Vickers, as if to clutch him, but Vickers stepped agilely aside, and Chatfield fell on the sand, where he lay groaning while the others looked from him to each other.

"Ah!" said Vickers at last. "So that's it, is it, Chatfield? Trying to cheat everybody all round, eh? I suppose you'd have told Miss Greyle later that these people had collared all that gold—and then you'd have helped yourself to it? And now I know what you were doing on that yacht when we boarded it—you were one of the gang, and you meant to hook it with them—"

"I didn't—I didn't!" screamed Chatfield, beating the sand with his hands and feet. "I meant to slip away from 'em at a Scotch port we was to call at, and then—"

"Then you'd have gone back to the hidden chests and helped yourself," sneered Vickers. "Chatfield, you're a wicked old scoundrel, and an unmitigated liar! Give me that paper that Miss Greyle signed, this instant!"

"No!" interjected Audrey. "Let him keep it. He'll have trouble enough presently. It's very evident they mean to have him."

Chatfield heard the last few words and looked round at the edge of the surf. The boat had grounded on the shingle, and half a dozen men had leapt from it and were coming rapidly up the beach.

"Armed, by George!" exclaimed Copplestone. "No chance for you, Chatfield!"

The agent suddenly sprang to his feet with a howl of terror. He gave one more glance at the men and then he ran, clumsily, but with a speed made desperate by terror. He made straight for the rocks — and at that, two of the men, at a word from their leader, raised their rifles and fired. And with a shriek that set all the echoes ringing, the sea-birds screaming, and made Audrey clap her hands to her ears, Chatfield threw up his arms and dropped heavily on the sands.

"That's sheer murder!" exclaimed Vickers, as the yachtsmen came running up. "You'll answer for that, you know. Unless you mean to murder all of us."

The leader, a smiling-faced fellow, touched his cap respectfully, and grinned from ear to ear.

"Lor' bless you, sir, we shot twenty feet over his head!" he said. "He's too precious to shoot: they want him badly on board there. Now then, men, pick him up and get him into the boat—he'll come round quick enough when he finds he hasn't even a pellet in him. Handy, now! Captain's compliments, sir," he went on, turning again to Vickers, and pointing to certain things which were being unloaded from the boat, "and as he understands that no vessel will pass here for two more days, sir, he's sent you further provisions, some more wraps, and some books and papers."

CHAPTER XXIV
THE TORPEDO-BOAT DESTROYER

Before Vickers and his companions had recovered from the surprise
which this extraordinary cool message had given them, the men had
bundled Chatfield across the beach and into the boat and were
pulling quickly back to the Pike.

Audrey broke the silence with a ringing laugh.

"Captain Andrius is certainly the perfection of polite pirates," she
exclaimed. "More food—more wraps—and books and papers! Was
any marooned mariner ever one-half so well treated?"

"What's the fellow mean about no vessel passing here for two more
days?" growled Copplestone, who was glaring angrily at the yacht.
"What's he so meticulously correct for?"

"I should say that he's referring to some weekly or bi-weekly steamer
which runs between Kirkwall and the mainland," replied Vickers.
"Well—it's good to know that, anyhow. But wait until the Pike's
vamoosed again, and we'll make up such a column of smoke that it'll
be seen for many a mile. In fact, I'll go and gather a lot of dried stuff
now—you two can drag those boxes and things up the beach and see
what our gaolers have been good enough to send us."

He went away up the cliffs, and Audrey and Copplestone, once
more left alone, looked at each other and laughed.

"That's right," said Copplestone. "What I like about you is that you
take things that way."

"Is it any use taking them any other way?" she asked. "Besides I've
never been at all frightened nor particularly concerned. I've always
felt that we were only put here so that we should be out of the way
while our captors got safely away with their booty, and as regards
my mother, I know her well enough to feel sure that she quickly
sized things up, and that she'll have taken measures of her own.

Don't be surprised if we're rescued through her means or if she has set somebody to work to catch the predatory Pike."

"Good!" said Copplestone. "But as regards the Pike, I wonder if you observed something during the few minutes she was here. I'm sure Vickers didn't—he was too busy, watching Chatfield."

"So was I," replied Audrey. "What was it?"

"I believe I'm unusually observant," answered Copplestone. "I seem to see things—all at once, don't you know. I saw that since we made her acquaintance—and were unceremoniously bundled off her—the Pike has got a new and quite different coat of paint. And I daresay she's changed her name, too. From all of which I argue that when they got rid of us here, the people who are working all this slipped quietly back to some cove or creek on the Scotch coast, did a stiff turn at repainting, and meant to be off to the other side of the world under new colours. And while this was going on, Andrius, or his co-villain, found time to examine those chests that Chatfield told us of, and when they found that Chatfield had done them, they came back here quick. Now they're off to make him reveal the whereabouts of the real chests."

"Won't they be rather running their necks into a noose?" suggested Audrey. "I'm dead certain that my mother will have raised a hue and cry after them."

"They're cute enough," said Copplestone. "Anyway, they'll run a good many risks for the sake of fifty thousand pounds. What they may do is to run into some very quiet inlet—there are hundreds on these northern coasts—and take Chatfield to his hiding-place. Chatfield's like all scoundrels of his type—a horrible coward if a pistol's held to his head. Now they've got him, they'll force him to disgorge. Hang this compulsory inactivity!—my nerves are all a-tingle to get going at things!"

"Let's occupy ourselves with the things our generous gaolers have been kind enough to send us, then," suggested Audrey. "We'd better carry them up to our shelter."

Copplestone went down to the things which the boat's crew had deposited on the beach—a couple of small packing-cases, a bundle of wraps and cushions, and some books, magazines and newspapers. He picked up a paper with a cry which suggested a discovery of importance.

"Look at that!" he exclaimed. "Do you see? A Scotsman! Today's date! And here—Aberdeen Free Press—same date!"
"Well?" asked Audrey. "And what then?"

"What then?" demanded Copplestone. "Where are your powers of deduction? Why, that shows that the Pike was somewhere this morning where she could get the morning papers from Aberdeen and Edinburgh—therefore, she's been, as I suggested, somewhere on the Scotch coast all night. It's now noon—she's a fast sailer—I guess she's been within sixty miles of us ever since she left us."

"Isn't it more pertinent to speculate on where she'll be when we want to find her?" asked Audrey.

"More pertinent still to wonder when somebody will come to find us," answered Copplestone as he shouldered one of the cases. "However, there's a certain joy in uncertainty, so they say—we're tasting it."

The joys of uncertainty, however, were not to endure. They had scarcely completed the task of carrying up the newly-arrived stores to the shelter which they had made in an angle of the rocks when Vickers hailed them from a spur of the cliffs and waved his arms excitedly.

"I say, you two!" he shouted. "There's a craft coming—from the south-west. Come up! There!" he added, a few minutes later, when they arrived, breathless, at his side. "Out yonder—a mere black blot—but unmistakable! Do you know what that is, either of you? You don't? All right, I do—ought to, because I'm a R.N.V.R. man myself. That's a T.B.D., my friends!—torpedo-boat destroyer. What's more, far off as she is, my experienced eye and sure knowledge tell me exactly what she is. She's a class H. boat built last year—oil fuel—turbines—runs up to thirty knots—and she's doing 'em, too, just now! Come on, Copplestone—more stuff on this fire!"

"I don't think we need be uneasy," said Copplestone. "Miss Greyle thinks that her mother will have raised a hue and cry after the Pike. This torpedo thing is probably looking round for us. She—what's that?"

The sudden sharp crack of a gun came across the calm surface of the sea, and the watchers turning from their fire towards the black object in the distance saw a cloud of white smoke drifting away from it.

"Hooray!" shouted Vickers. "She's seen our smoke-pillar! Shove more on, just to let her know we understand. Saved!—this time, anyway."

Half-an-hour later, a spick and span and eminently youthful-looking naval lieutenant raised his cap to the three folk who stood eagerly awaiting his approach at the edge of the surf.

"Miss Greyle? Mr. Vickers? Mr. Copplestone?" he asked as he sprang from his boat and came up. "Right!—we're searching for you—had wireless messages this morning. Where's the pirate, or whatever he is?"

"Somewhere away to the southward," answered Vickers, pointing into the haze. "He was here two hours ago—but he's about as fast as they make 'em, and he's good reason to show a clean pair of heels. However, we've ample grounds for believing him to have gone due south again. Where are you from?"

"Got the message off Dunnett Head, and we'll run you to Thurso," replied the rescuer, motioning them to enter the boat. "Come on—our commander's got some word or other for you. What's all this been?" he went on, gazing at Audrey with youthful assurance as they moved away from the shore. "You don't mean to say you've actually been kidnapped?"

"Kidnapped and marooned," replied Vickers. "And I hope you'll catch our kidnapper—he's got a tremendous amount of property on him which belongs to this lady, and he'll make tracks for the other side of the Atlantic as soon as he gets hold of some more which he's gone to collect."

The lieutenant regarded Audrey with still more interest. "Oh, all right," he said confidently. "He'll not get away. I guess they've wirelessed all over the place—our message was from the Admiralty!"

"That's Sir Cresswell's doing," said Copplestone, turning to Audrey. "Your mother must have wired to him. I wonder what the message is?" he asked, facing the lieutenant. "Do you know?"

"Something about if you're found to tell you to get south as fast as possible," he answered. "And we've worked that out for you. You can get on by train from Thurso to Inverness, and from Inverness, of course, you'll get the southern express. Well put you off at Thurso by two o'clock—just time to give you such lunch as our table affords—bit rough, you know. So you've really been all night on that island?" he went on with unaffected curiosity. "What a lark!"

"You'd have had an opportunity of studying character if you'd been with us," replied Vickers. "We lost a fine specimen of humanity two hours ago."

"Tell about it aboard," said the lieutenant. "We'll be thankful—we've been round this end-of-everywhere coast for a month and we're tired. It's quite a Godsend to have a little adventure."

Copplestone had been right in surmising that Sir Cresswell Oliver had bestirred himself to find him and his companions. They were presently shown his message. They were to get to Norcaster as quickly as possible, and to wire their whereabouts as soon as they were found. If, as seemed likely, they were picked up on the north coast of Scotland, they were to ask at Inverness railway station for telegrams. And to Inverness after being landed at Thurso they betook themselves, while the torpedo-boat destroyer set off to nose round for the Pike, in case she came that way back from wherever she had gone to.

Copplestone came out of the station-master's office at Inverness with a couple of telegrams and read their contents over to his companions in the dining-room to which they adjourned.

"This is from Mrs. Greyle," he said. "'All right and much relieved by wire from Thurso. Bring Audrey home as quick as possible.' That's good! And this—Great Scott! This is from Gilling! Listen!—'Just heard from Petherton of your rescue. Come straight and sharp Norcaster. Meet me at the "Angel." Big things afoot. Spurge most anxious see you. Important news. Gilling.' So things have been going on," he concluded, turning the second telegram over to Vickers. "I suppose we'll have to travel all night?"

"Night express in an hour," replied Vickers. "We shall make Norcaster about five-thirty tomorrow morning."

"Then let us wire the time of our arrival to Gilling. I'm anxious to know what has brought him up there," said Copplestone. "And we'll wire to Mrs. Greyle, too," he added, turning to Audrey. "She'll know then that you're absolutely on the way."

"I wonder what we're on the way to?" remarked Vickers with a grim smile. "It strikes me that our recent alarms and excursions will have been as nothing to what awaits us at Norcaster."

What did await them on a cold, dismal morning at Norcaster was Gilling, stamping up and down a windswept platform. And Gilling seized on Copplestone almost before he could alight from the train.

"Come to the 'Angel' straight off!" he said. "Mrs. Greyle's there awaiting her daughter. I've work for you and Vickers at once—that chap Spurge is somewhere about the 'Angel,' too—been hanging round there since yesterday, heavy with news that he'll give to nobody but you."

CHAPTER XXV
THE SQUIRE

Such of the folk of the "Angel" hotel—a night porter, a waiter, a chamber-maid—as were up and about that grey morning, wondered why the two old gentlemen who had arrived from London the day before should rise from their beds to hold a secret and mysterious conference with the three young ones who, with a charming if tired-looking young lady, drove up before the city clocks had struck six. But Sir Cresswell Oliver and Mr. Petherton knew that there was no time to be lost, and as soon as Audrey had been restored to and carried off by her mother to Mrs. Greyle's room, they summoned Vickers and Copplestone to a private parlour and demanded their latest news. Sir Cresswell listened eagerly, and in silence, until Copplestone described the return of the Pike; at that he broke his silence.

"That's precisely what I feared!" he exclaimed. "Of course, if she's been hurriedly repainted and renamed, she stands a fair chance of getting away. Our instructions to the patrol boats up there are to look for a certain vessel, the Pike—naturally they won't look for anything else. We must get the wireless to work at once."

"But there's this," said Copplestone. "They certainly fetched old Chatfield to make him hand over the gold! They won't go away without
that! And he said that he'd hidden the gold somewhere near Scarhaven.
Therefore, they'll have to come down this coast to get it."
"Not necessarily," replied Sir Cresswell, with a knowing shake of the head. "You may be sure they're alive to all the exigencies of the situation. They could do several things once they'd got Chatfield on board again. Some of them could land with him at some convenient port and make him take them to where he's hidden the money; they could recapture that and go off to some other port, to which the yacht had meanwhile been brought round. If we only knew where Chatfield had planted that money—"

189

"He said near Scarhaven, unmistakably," remarked Vickers.

"Near Scarhaven!" repeated Sir Cresswell, laughing dismally. "That's a wide term—a very wide one. Behind Scarhaven, as you all know, are hills and moors and valleys and ravines in which one could hide a Dreadnought! Well, that's all I can think of—getting into communication with patrol boats and coastguard stations all along the coast between here and Wick. And that mayn't be the least good. Somebody may have escorted Chatfield ashore after they left you yesterday, brought him hereabouts by rail or motor-car, and the yacht may have made a wide detour round the Shetlands and be now well on her way to the North Atlantic."

"But in that case—the money?" asked Copplestone.

"They would get hold of the money, take it clean away, and ship it from Liverpool, or Glasgow, or—anywhere," replied Sir Cresswell. "You may be sure they've plenty of resources at command, and that they'll work secretly. Of course, we must keep a look out round about here for any sign or reappearance of Chatfield, but, as I say, this country is so wild that he and his companions can easily elude observation, especially as they're sure to come by night. Still, we must do what we can, and at once. But first, there are one or two things I want to ask you young men—you said, Mr. Vickers, that Chatfield solemnly insisted to you that he did not know that the man who had posed as Marston Greyle was not Marston Greyle?"

"He did," replied Vickers, "and though Chatfield is an unmitigated old scoundrel, I believe him."

"You do!" exclaimed Gilling, who was listening eagerly. "Oh, come!"

"I do—as a professional man," answered Vickers, stoutly, and with an appealing glance at his brother solicitor. "Mr. Petherton will tell you that we lawyers have a curious gift of intuition. With all Chatfield's badness, I do really believe that the old fellow does not know whether the man we'll call the Squire is Marston Greyle or not! He's doubtful—he's puzzled—but he doesn't know."

190

"Odd!" murmured Sir Cresswell, after a minute's silence. "Odd! Very, very odd! That shows that there's still some extraordinary mystery about this which we haven't even guessed at. Well, now, another question—you got the idea that some one else was aboard the yacht?"

"Some one other than Andrius—in authority—yes!" answered Vickers. "We certainly thought that."

"Did you think it was the man we know as the Squire?" asked Sir Cresswell.
"We had a notion that he might be there," replied Vickers, with a glance at Copplestone. "Especially after what happened to Chatfield. Of course, we never saw him, or heard his voice, or saw a sign of him. Still, we fancied—"

Sir Cresswell rose from his chair and motioned to Petherton.

"Well," he said, "I think you and I, Petherton, had better complete our toilets, and then give a look in at the authorities here and find out if anything has been received by wireless or from the coastguard stations about the yacht. In the meantime," he added, turning to Vickers and Copplestone, "Gilling can tell you what's been going on in your absence—you'll learn from it that our impression is that the Squire, as we call him, was on the Pike with you."

The two elder men went away, and Copplestone turned to Gilling.

"What have you got?" he asked eagerly. "Live news!"

"Might have been livelier and more satisfactory," answered Gilling, "if it hadn't been for the factor which none of us can help—luck! We tracked the Squire."

"You did?" exclaimed Copplestone. "Where?"

"When I said we I should have said Swallow," continued Gilling. "You remember that afternoon of our return from Bristol, Copplestone? It seems ages away now, though as a matter of time it's only four days ago! — Well, that afternoon Swallow, who had had two or three more keeping a sharp look out for the Squire, got a telephone message from one of 'em saying that he'd tracked his man to the Fragonard Club. I'd gone home to my chambers, to rest a bit after our adventures at Bristol and Falmouth, so Swallow had to act on his own initiative. He set off for the Fragonard Club, and outside it met his man. This particular man had been keeping a watch for days on that tobacconist's shop in Wardour Street. That afternoon he suddenly saw the Squire leave it, by a side door. He followed him to the Fragonard Club, watched him enter; then he himself turned into a neighbouring bar and telephoned to Swallow. The Squire was still in the Fragonard when Swallow got there: from that time he kept a watch. The Squire remained in the Club for an hour—"

"Which proves," interrupted Copplestone, "that he's a member, and that I ought to have followed up my attempt to get in there."

"Well, anyway," continued Gilling, "there he was, and thence he eventually emerged, with a kit-bag. He got into a taxi, and Swallow heard him order its driver to go to King's Cross. Now Swallow was there alone—and he had just before that met his man scooting round to see if there was a rear exit from the Fragonard, and he hadn't returned. Swallow, of course, couldn't wait—every minute was precious. He followed the Squire to King's Cross, and heard him book for Northborough."

"Northborough!" exclaimed Copplestone, in surprise. "Not Norcaster? Ah, well, Northborough's a port, too, isn't it?"

"Northborough is as near to Scarhaven as Norcaster is, you know," said
Gilling. "To Northborough he booked, anyhow. So did Swallow, who, now
that he'd got him, was going to follow him to the North Pole, if need be.

The train was just starting—Swallow had no time to communicate with me.

Also, the train didn't stop until it reached Grantham. There he sent me a

wire, saying he was on the track of his man. Well, they went on to Northborough, where they arrived late in the evening. There—what is it,

Copplestone," he broke off, seeing signs of a desire to speak on Copplestone's part.

"You're talking of the very same afternoon and evening that I came down—four evenings ago," said Copplestone. "My train was the four o'clock—I got to Norcaster at ten—surely they didn't come on the same train!"

"I feel sure they did, but anyhow, these trains to the North are usually very long ones, and you were probably in a different part," replied Gilling. "Anyway, they got to Northborough soon after nine. Swallow followed his man on to the platform, out to some taxi-cabs, and heard him commission one of the chauffeurs to take him to Scarhaven. When they'd gone Swallow got hold of another taxi, and told its driver to take him to Scarhaven, too. Off they went—in a pitch-black night, I'm told—"

"We know that!" said Vickers with a glance at Copplestone. "We motored from Norcaster—just about the same time."

"Well," continued Gilling, "it was at any rate so dark that Swallow's driver, who appears to have been a very nervous chap, made very poor progress. Also he took one or two wrong turnings. Finally he ran his car into a guide post which stood where two roads forked—and there Swallow was landed, scarcely halfway to Scarhaven. They couldn't get the car to move, and it was some time before Swallow could persuade the landlord at the nearest inn to hire out a horse and trap to him. Altogether, it was near or just past midnight when he reached Scarhaven, and when he did get there, it was to see the lights of a steamer going out of the bay."

"The Pike, of course," muttered Copplestone.

"Of course—and some men on the quay told him," continued Gilling. "Well, that put Swallow in a fix. He was dead certain, of course, that his man was on that yacht. However, he didn't want to rouse suspicion, so he didn't ask any of those quayside men if they'd seen the Squire. Instead, remembering what I'd told him about Mrs. Greyle he asked for her house and was directed to it. He found Mrs. Greyle in a state of great anxiety. Her daughter had gone with you two to the yacht and had never returned; Mrs. Greyle, watching from her windows, had seen the yacht go out to sea. Swallow found her, of course, seriously alarmed as to what had happened. Of course, he told her what he had come down for and they consulted. Next morning—"

"Stop a bit," interrupted Vickers. "Didn't Mrs. Greyle get any message from the yacht about her daughter—Andrius said he'd sent one, anyway."

"A lie!" replied Gilling. "She got no message. The only consolation she had was that you and Copplestone were with Miss Greyle. Well; first thing next morning Swallow and Mrs. Greyle set every possible means to work. They went to the police—they wired to places up the coast and down the coast to keep a look out—and Swallow also wired full particulars to Sir Cresswell Oliver, with the result that Sir Cresswell went to the naval authorities and got them to set their craft up north to work. Having done all this, and finding that he could be of no more service at Scarhaven, Swallow returned to town to see me and to consult. Now, of course, we were in a position by then to approach that Fragonard Club—"

"Ah!" exclaimed Copplestone. "Just so!"

"The man, whoever he is, had been there an hour on the day Swallow and his man tracked him," continued Gilling. "Therefore, something must be known of him. Swallow and I, armed with certain credentials, went there. And—we could find out next to nothing. The hall porter there said he dimly remembered such a gentleman coming in and going upstairs, but he himself was new to

his job, didn't know all the members—there are hundreds of 'em—
and he took this man for a regular habitue. A waiter also had some
sort of recollection of the man, and seeing him in conversation with
another man whom he, the waiter, knew better, though he didn't
know his name. Swallow is now moving everything to find that
man—to find anybody who knows our man—and something will
come of it, in the end—must do. In the meantime I came down here
with Sir Cresswell and Mr. Petherton, to be on the spot. And, from
your information, things will happen here! That hidden gold is the
thing—they'll not leave that without an effort to get it. If we could
only find out where that is and watch it—then our present object
would be achieved."

"What is the present object?" asked Copplestone.

"Why," replied Gilling, "we've got warrants out against both
Chatfield and the Squire for the murder of Bassett Oliver!—the
police here have them in hand. Petherton's seen to that. And if they
can only be laid hands on—What is it?" he asked turning to a sleepy-
eyed waiter who, after a gentle tap at the door, put a shock head into
the room. "Somebody want me?"

"That there man, sir—you know," said the waiter. "Here again, sir—
stable-yard, sir."

Gilling jumped up and gave Copplestone a look.

"That's Spurge!" he muttered. "He said he'd be back at day-break.
Wait here—I'll fetch him."

CHAPTER XXVI
THE REAVER'S GLEN

Zachary Spurge, presently ushered in by Gilling, who carefully closed the door behind himself and his companion, looked as if his recent lodging had been of an even rougher nature than that in which Copplestone had found him at their first meeting. The rough horseman's cloak in which he was buttoned to the edge of a red neckerchief and a stubbly chin was liberally ornamented with bits of straw, scraps of furze and other odds and ends picked up in woods and hedge-rows. Spurge, indeed, bore unmistakable evidence of having slept out in wild places for some nights and his general atmosphere was little more respectable than that of a scarecrow. But he grinned cheerfully at Copplestone—and then frowned at Vickers.

"I didn't count for to meet no lawyers, gentlemen," he said, pausing on the outer boundaries of the parlour, "I ain't a-goin' to talk before 'em, neither!"

"He's a grudge against me—I've had to appear against him once or twice," whispered Vickers to Copplestone. "You'd better soothe him down—I want to know what he's got to tell."

"It's all right, Spurge," said Copplestone. "Come—Mr. Vickers is on our side this time; he's one of us. You can say anything you like before him—or Mr. Gilling either. We're all in it. Pull your chair up—here, alongside of me, and tell us what you've been doing."

"Well, of course, if you puts it that way, Mr. Copplestone," replied Spurge, coming to the table a little doubtfully. "Though I hadn't meant to tell nobody but you what I've got to tell. However, I can see that things is in such a pretty pass that this here ain't no one-man job—it's a job as'll want a lot o' men! And I daresay lawyers and such-like is as useful men in that way as you can lay hands on—no offence to you, Mr. Vickers, only you see I've had experience o' your sort before. But if you are taking a hand in this here—well, all right. But now, gentlemen," he continued dropping into a chair at the table and laying his fur cap on its polished surface, "afore ever I says a word, d'ye think that I could be provided with a cup o' hot coffee, or tea, with a stiff dose o' rum in it? I'm that cold and starved—ah, if you'd been where I been this last twelve hours or so, you'd be perished."

The sleepy waiter was summoned to attend to Spurge's wants—until they were satisfied the poacher sat staring fixedly at his cap and occasionally shaking his head. But after a first hearty gulp of strongly fortified coffee the colour came back into his face, he sighed with relief, and signalled to the three watchful young men to draw their chairs close to his.

"Ah!" he said, setting down his cup. "And nobody never wanted aught more badly than I wanted that! And now then—the door being shut on us quite safe, ain't it, gentlemen?—no eavesdroppers?—well, this here it is. I don't know what you've been a-doing of these last few days, nor what may have happened to each and all—but I've news. Serious news—as I reckons it to be. Of— Chatfield!"

Copplestone kicked Vickers under the table and gave him a look.

"Chatfield again!" he murmured. "Well, go on, Spurge."

"There's a lot to go on with, too, guv'nor," said Spurge, after taking another evidently welcome drink. "And I'll try to put it all in order, as it were—same as if I was in a witness-box," he added, with a sly glance at Vickers. "You remember that day of the inquest on the actor gentleman, guv'nor? Well, of course, when I went to give evidence at Scarhaven, at that there inquest, I never expected but what the police 'ud collar me at the end of it. However, I didn't mean that they should, if I could help it, so I watched things pretty close, intending to slip off when I saw a chance. Well, now, you'll bear in mind that there was a bit of a dust-up when the thing was over— some on 'em cheering the Squire and some on 'em grousing about the verdict, and between one and t'other I popped out and off, and you yourself saw me making for the moors. Of course, me, knowing them moors back o' Scarhaven as I do, it was easy work to make

myself scarce on 'em in ten minutes—not all the police north o' the
Tees could ha' found me a quarter of an hour after I'd hooked it out
o' that schoolroom! Well, but the thing then was—where to go next?
'Twasn't no good going to Hobkin's Hole again—now that them
chaps knew I was in the neighbourhood they'd soon ha' smoked me
out o' there. Once I thought of making for Norcaster here, and going
into hiding down by the docks—I've one or two harbours o' refuge
there. But I had reasons for wishing to stop in my own country—for
a bit at any rate. And so, after reckoning things up, I made for a spot
as Mr. Vickers there'll know by name of the Reaver's Glen."

"Good place, too, for hiding," remarked Vickers with a nod.

"Best place on this coast—seashore and inland," said Spurge. "And as
you two London gentlemen doesn't know it, I'll tell you about it. If
you was to go out o' Scarhaven harbour and turn north, you'd sail
along our coast line up here to the mouth of Norcaster Bay and you'd
think there was never an inlet between 'em. But there is. About halfway between Scarhaven and Norcaster there's a very narrow
opening in the cliffs that you'd never notice unless you were close in
shore, and inside that opening there's a cove that's big enough to
take a thousand-ton vessel—aye, and half-a-dozen of 'em! It was a
favourite place for smugglers in the old days, and they call it
Darkman's Dene to this day in memory of a famous old smuggler
that used it a good deal. Well, now, at the land end of that cove
there's a narrow valley that runs up to the moorland and the hills,
full o' rocks and crags and precipices and such like—something o'
the same sort as Hobkin's Hole but a deal wilder, and that's known
as the Reaver's Glen, because in other days the cattle-lifters used to
bring their stolen goods, cattle and sheep, down there where they
could pen 'em in, as it were. There's piles o' places in that glen where
a man can hide—I picked out one right at the top, at the edge of the
moors, where there's the ruins of an old peel tower. I could get
shelter in that old tower, and at the same time slip out of it if need be
into one of fifty likely hiding places amongst the rocks. I got into
touch with my cousin Jim Spurge—the one-eyed chap at the
'Admiral's Arms,' Mr. Copplestone, that night—and I got in a supply

of meat and drink, and there I was. And—as things turned out, Chatfield had got his eye on the very same spot!"

Spurge paused for a minute, and picking out a match from a stand which stood on the table, began to trace imaginary lines on the mahogany.

"This is how things is there," he said, inviting his companions' attention. "Here, like, is where this peel tower stands—that's a thick wood as comes close up to its walls—that there is a road as crosses the moors and the wood about, maybe, a hundred yards or so behind the tower on the land side. Now, there, one afternoon as I was in that there tower, a-reading of a newspaper that Jim had brought me the night before, I hears wheels on that moorland road, and I looked out through a convenient loophole, and who should I see but Peter Chatfield in that old pony trap of his. He was coming along from the direction of Scarhaven, and when he got abreast of the tower he pulled up, got out, left his pony to crop the grass and came strolling over in my direction. Of course, I wasn't afraid of him—there's so many ways in and out of that old peel as there is out of a rabbit-warren—besides, I felt certain he was there on some job of his own. Well, he comes up to the edge of the glen, and he looks into it and round it, and up and down at the tower, and he wanders about the heaps of fallen masonry that there is there, and finally he puts thumbs in his armhole and went slowly back to his trap. 'But you'll be coming back, my old swindler!' says I to myself. 'You'll be back again I doubt not at all!' And back he did come—that very night. Oh, yes!"

"Alone?" asked Copplestone.

"A-lone!" replied Spurge. "It had got to be dark, and I was thinking of going to sleep, having nought else to do and not expecting cousin Jim that night, when I heard the sound of horses' feet and of wheels. So I cleared out of my hole to where I could see better. Of course, it was Chatfield—same old trap and pony—but this time he came from Norcaster way. Well, he gets out, just where he'd got out before, and he leads the pony and trap across the moor to close by the tower. I could tell by the way that trap went over the grass that there was some sort of a load in it and it wouldn't have surprised me, gentlemen, if the old reptile had brought a dead body out of it. After a bit, I hear him taking something out, something which he bumped down on the ground with a thump—I counted nine o' them thumps. And then after a bit I heard him begin a moving of some of the loose masonry what lies in such heaps at the foot o' the peel tower—dark though it was there was light enough in the sky for him to see to do that. But after he'd been at it some time, puffing and groaning and grunting, he evidently wanted to see better, and he suddenly flashed a light on things from one o' them electric torches. And then I see— me being not so many yards away from him—nine small white wood boxes, all clamped with metal bands, lying in a row on the grass, and I see, too, that Chatfield had been making a place for 'em amongst the stones. Yes—that was it—nine small white wood boxes—so small, considering, that I wondered what made 'em so heavy."

Copplestone favoured Vickers with another quiet kick. They were, without doubt, hearing the story of the hidden gold, and it was becoming exciting.

"Well," continued Spurge. "Into the place he'd cleared out them boxes went, and once they were all in he heaped the stones over 'em as natural as they were before, and he kicked a lot o' small loose stones round about and over the place where he'd been standing. And then the old sinner let out a great groan as if something troubled him, and he fetched a bottle out of his pocket and took a good pull at whatever was in it, after which, gentlemen, he wiped his forehead with his handkerchief and groaned again. He'd had his bit of light on all that time, but he doused it then, and after that he led the old pony away across the bit of moor to the road, and presently in he gets and drives slowly away towards Scarhaven. And so there was I, d'ye see, Mr. Copplestone, left, as it were, sold guardian of—what?"

The three young men exchanged glances with each other while Spurge refreshed himself with his fortified coffee, and their eyes asked similar questions.

"Ah!" observed Copplestone at last. "You don't know what, Spurge? You haven't examined one of those boxes?"

Spurge set his cup down and gave his questioner a knowing look.

"I'll tell you my line o' conduct, guv'nor," he said. "So certain sure have I been that something 'ud come o' this business of hiding them boxes and that something valuable is in 'em that I've taken partiklar care ever since Chatfield planted 'em there that night never to set foot within a dozen yards of 'em. Why? 'Cause I know he'll ha' left footprints of his own there, and them footprints may be useful. No, sir!—them boxes has been guarded careful ever since Chatfield placed 'em where he did. For—Chatfield's never been back!"

"Never back, eh?" said Copplestone, winking at the other two.

"Never been back—self nor spirit, substance nor shadow!—since that night," replied Spurge. "Unless, indeed, he's been back since four o'clock this morning, when I left there. However, if he's been 'twixt then and now, my cousin Jim Spurge, he was there. Jim's been helping me to watch. When I first came in here to see if I could hear anything about you—Jim having told me that some London gentlemen was up here again—I left him in charge. And there he is now. And now you know all I can tell you, gentlemen, and as I understand there's some mystery about Chatfield and that he's disappeared, happen you'll know how to put two and two together. And if I'm of any use—"

"Spurge," said Gilling. "How far is it to this Reaver's Glen—or, rather to that peel tower?"

"Matter of eight or nine miles, guv'nor, over the moors," replied Spurge.

"How did you come in then?" asked Gilling.

"Cousin Jim Spurge's bike—down in the stable-yard, now," answered
Spurge. "Did it comfortable in under the hour."
"I think we ought to go out there—some of us," said Gilling. "We
ought—"

At that moment the door opened and Sir Cresswell Oliver came in,
holding a bit of flimsy paper in his hand. He glanced at Spurge and
then beckoned the three young men to join him.

"I've had a wireless message from the North Sea—and it puzzles
me," he said. "One of our ships up there has had news of what is
surely the Pike from a fishing vessel. She was seen late yesterday
afternoon going due east—due east, mind you! If that was she—and
I'm sure of it!—our quarry's escaping us."

CHAPTER XXVII
THE PEEL TOWER

Gilling took the message from Sir Cresswell and thoughtfully read it over. Then he handed it back and motioned the old seaman to look at Spurge.

"I think you ought to know what this man has just told us, sir," he said. "We've got a story from him that exactly fits in with what Chatfield told Mr. Vickers when the Pike returned to carry him off yesterday. Chatfield, you'll remember, said that the gold he'd withdrawn from the bank is hidden somewhere—well, there's no doubt that this man Zachary Spurge knows where it is hidden. It's there now—and the presumption is, of course, that these people on the Pike will certainly come in to this coast—somehow!—to get it. So in that case—eh?"

"Gad!—that's valuable!" said Sir Cresswell, glancing again at Spurge, and with awakened interest. "Let me hear this story."

Copplestone epitomized Spurge's account, while the poacher listened admiringly, checking off the main points and adding a word or two where he considered the epitome lacking.

"Very smart of you, my man," remarked Sir Cresswell, nodding benevolently at Spurge when the story was over. "You're in a fair way to find yourself well rewarded. Now gentlemen!" he continued, sitting down at the table, and engaging the attention of the others, "I think we had better have a council of war. Petherton has just gone to speak to the police authorities about those warrants which have been taken out against Chatfield and the impostor, but we can go on in his absence. Now there seems to be no doubt that those chests which Spurge tells us of contain the gold which Chatfield procured from the bank, and concerning which he seems to have played his associates more tricks than one. However, his associates, whoever they are—and mind you, gentlemen, I believe there are more men than Chatfield and the Squire in all this!—have now got a tight grip on Chatfield, and they'll force him to show them where that gold is—they'll certainly not give up the chances of fifty thousand pounds without a stiff try to get it. So—I'm considering all the possibilities and probabilities—we may conclude that sooner or later—sooner, most likely—somebody will visit this old peel tower that Spurge talks of. But—who? For we're faced with this wireless message. I've no doubt the vessel here referred to is the Pike—no doubt at all. Now she was seen making due east, near this side of the Dogger Bank, late last night—so that it would look as if these men were making for Denmark, or Germany, rather than for this coast. But since receiving this message, I have thought that point out. The Pike is, I believe, a very fast vessel?"

"Very," answered Vickers. "She can do twenty-seven or eight knots an hour."

"Exactly," said Sir Cresswell. "Then in that case they may have put in at some Northern port, landed Chatfield and two or three men to keep an eye on him and to accompany him to this old tower, while the Pike herself has gone off till a more fitting opportunity arises of dodging in somewhere to pick up the chests which Chatfield and his party will in the meantime have removed. From what I have seen of it this is such a wild part of the coast that Chatfield and such a small gang as I am imagining, could easily come back here, keep themselves hidden and recover the chests without observation. So our plain duty is to now devise some plan for going to the Reaver's Glen and keeping a watch there until somebody comes. Eh?"

"There's another thing that's possible, sir," said Vickers, who had listened carefully to all that Sir Cresswell had said. "The Pike is fitted for wireless telegraphy."

"Yes?" said Sir Cresswell expectantly. "And you think—?"

"You suggested that there may be more people than Chatfield and the Squire in at this business," continued Vickers. "Just so! We—Copplestone and myself—know very well that the skipper of the Pike, Andrius, is in it: that's undeniable. But there may be others—or one other, or two—on shore here. And as the Pike can communicate by wireless, those on board her may have sent a message to their shore confederates to remove those chests. So—"

"Capital suggestion!" said Sir Cresswell, who saw this point at once. "So we'd better lose no time in arranging our expedition out there. Spurge—you're the man who knows the spot best—what ought we to do about getting there—in force?"

Spurge, obviously flattered at being called upon to advise a great man, entered into the discussion with enthusiasm.

"Your honour mustn't go in force at all!" he said. "What's wanted, gentlemen, is—strategy! Now if you'll let me put it to you, me knowing the lie of the land, this is what had ought to be done. A small party ought to go—with me to lead. We'll follow the road that cuts across the moorland to a certain point; then we'll take a by-track that gets you to High Nick; there we'll take to a thick bit o' wood and coppice that runs right up to the peel tower. Nobody'll track us, nor see us from any point, going that way. Three or four of us—these here young gentlemen, now, and me—'ll be enough for the job—if armed. A revolver apiece your honour—that'll be plenty. And as for the rest—what you might call a reserve force—your honour said something just now about some warrants. Is the police to be in at it, then?"

"The police hold warrants for the two men we've been chiefly talking about," replied Sir Cresswell.

"Well let your honour come on a bit later with not more than three police plain-clothes fellows—as far as High Nick," said Spurge. "The police'll know where that is. Let 'em wait there—don't let 'em come further until I send back a message by my cousin Jim, You see, guv'nor," he added, turning to Copplestone, whom he seemed to regard as his own special associate, "we don't know how things may be. We might have to wait hours. As I view it, me having listened careful to what his honour the Admiral there says—best respects to your honour—them chaps'll never come a-nigh that place till it's night again, or at any rate, dusk, which'll be about seven o'clock this evening. But they may watch, during the day, and it 'ud be a foolish thing to have a lot of men about. A small force such as I can hide in that wood, and another in reserve at High Nick, which, guv'nor, is a deep hole in the hill-top—that's the ticket!"

"Spurge is right," said Sir Cresswell. "You youngsters go with him—get a motor-car—and I'll see about following you over to High Nick with the detectives. Now, what about being armed?"

"I've a supply of service revolvers at my office, down this very street," replied Vickers. "I'll go and get them. Here! Let's apportion our duties. I'll see to that. Gilling, you see about the car. Copplestone, you order some breakfast for us—sharp."

"And I'll go round to the police," said Sir Cresswell. "Now, be careful to take care of yourselves—you don't know what you've got to deal with, remember."

The group separated, and Copplestone went off to find the hotel people and order an immediate breakfast. And passing along a corridor on his way downstairs he encountered Mrs. Greyle, who came out of a room near by and started at sight of him.

"Audrey is asleep," she whispered, pointing to the door she had just left. "Thank you for taking care of her. Of course I was afraid—but that's all over now. And now the thing is—how are things?"

"Coming to a head, in my opinion," answered Copplestone. "But how or in what way, I don't know. Anyway, we know where that gold is—and they'll make an attempt on it—that's sure! So—we shall be there."

"But what fools Peter Chatfield and his associates must be—from their own villainous standpoint—to have encumbered themselves with all that weight of gold!" exclaimed Mrs. Greyle. "The folly of it seems incredible when they could have taken it in some more easily portable form!"

"Ah!" laughed Copplestone. "But that just shows Chatfield's extraordinary deepness and craft! He no doubt persuaded his associates that it was better to have actual bullion where they were going, and tricked them into believing that he'd actually put it aboard the Pike! If it hadn't been that they examined the boxes which he put on the Pike and found they contained lead or bricks, the old scoundrel would have collared the real stuff for himself."

"Take care that he doesn't collar it yet," said Mrs. Greyle with a laugh as she went into her own room. "Chatfield is resourceful enough for—anything. And—take care of yourselves!"

That was the second admonition to be careful, and Copplestone thought of both, as, an hour later, he, Gilling, Vickers and Spurge sped along the desolate, wind-swept moorland on their way to the Reaver's Glen. It was a typically North Country autumnal morning, cold, raw, rainy; the tops of the neighbouring hills were capped with dark clouds; sea-birds called dismally across the heather; the sea, seen in glimpses through vistas of fir and pine, looked angry and threatening.

"A fit morning for a do of this sort!" exclaimed Gilling suddenly. "Is it pretty bare and bleak at this tower of yours, Spurge?"

"You'll be warm enough, guv'nor, where I shall put you," answered Spurge. "One as has knocked about these woods and moors as much as I've had to knows as many places to hide his nose in as a fox does! I'll put you by that tower where you'll be snug enough, and warm enough, too—and where nobody'll see you neither. And here's High Nick and out we get."

Leaving the car in a deep cutting of the hills and instructing the driver to await the return of one or other of them at a wayside farmstead a mile back, the three adventurers followed Spurge into the wood which led to the top of the Beaver's Glen. The poacher guided them onward by narrow and winding tracks through the undergrowth for a good half-mile; then he led them through thickets in which there was no paths at all; finally, after a gradual and cautious advance behind a high hedge of dense evergreen, he halted them at a corner of the wood and motioned them to look out through a loosely-laced network of branches.

"Here we are!" he whispered. "Tower—Reaver's Glen—sea in the distance.
Lone spot, ain't it, gentlemen?"
Copplestone and Gilling, who had never seen this part of the coast before, looked out on the scene with lively interest. It was certainly a prospect of romance and of wild, almost savage beauty on which they gazed. Immediately in front of them, at a distance of twenty to thirty yards, stood the old peel tower, a solid square mass of grey stone, intact as to its base and its middle stories, ruinous and crumbling from thence to what was left of its battlements and the turret tower at one angle. The fallen stone lay in irregular heaps on the ground at its foot; all around it were clumps of furze and bramble. From the level plateau on which it stood the Glen fell away in horseshoe formation gradually narrowing and descending until it terminated in a thick covert of fir and pine that ran down to the land end of the cove of which Spurge had told them. And beyond that stretched the wide expanse of sea, with here and there a red-sailed fishing boat tossing restlessly on the white-capped waves, and over that and the land was a chill silence, broken only by the occasional cry of the sea-birds and the bleating of the mountain sheep.

"A lone spot indeed!" said Gilling in a whisper. "Spurge, where is that stuff hidden?"

"Other side of the tower—in an angle of the old courtyard," replied Spurge, "Can't see the spot from here."
"And where's that road you told us about?" asked Copplestone. "The moor road?"

"Top o' the bank yonder—beyond the tower," said Spurge. "Runs round yonder corner o' this wood and goes right round it to High Nick, where we've cut across from. Hush now, all of you, gentlemen—I'm going to signal Jim."

Screwing up his mobile face into a strange contortion, Spurge emitted from his puckered lips a queer cry—a cry as of some trapped animal—so shrill and realistic that his hearers started.

"What on earth's that represent?" asked Gilling. "It's blood-curdling?"

"Hare, with a stoat's teeth in its neck," answered Spurge. "H'sh—I'll call him again."

No answer came to the first nor to the second summons—after a third, equally unproductive, Spurge looked at his companions with a scared face.

"That's a queer thing, guv'nors!" he muttered. "Can't believe as how our Jim 'ud ever desert a post. He promised me faithfully as how he'd stick here like grim death until I came back. I hope he ain't had a fit, nor aught o' that sort—he ain't a strong chap at the best o' times, and—"

"You'd better take a careful look round, Spurge," said Vickers. "Here—shall I come with you?"
But Spurge waved a hand to them to stay where they were. He himself crept along the back of the hedge until he came to a point opposite the nearest angle of the tower. And suddenly he gave a great cry—human enough this time!—and the three young men rushing forward found him standing by the body of a roughly-clad man in whom Copplestone recognized the one-eyed odd-job man of the "Admiral's Arms."

CHAPTER XXVIII
THE FOOTPRINTS

The man was lying face downwards in the grass and weeds which clustered thickly at the foot of the hedgerow, and on the line of rough, weatherbeaten neck which showed between his fur cap and his turned-up collar there was a patch of dried blood. Very still and apparently lifeless he looked, but Vickers suddenly bent down, laid strong hands on him and turned him over.

"He's not dead!" he exclaimed. "Only unconscious from a crack on his skull. Gilling!—where's that brandy you brought?—hand me the flask."

Zachary Spurge watched in silence as Vickers and Gilling busied themselves in reviving the stricken man. Then he quickly pulled Copplestone's sleeve and motioned him away from the group.

"Guv'nor!" he muttered. "There's been foul play here—and all along of them nine boxes—that I'll warrant. Look you here, guv'nor—Jim's been dragged to where we found him—dragged through this here gap in the hedge and flung where he's lying. See—there's the plain marks, all through the grass and stuff. Come on, guv'nor—let's see where they lead."

The marks of a heavy, inanimate body having been dragged through the wet grass were evidence enough, and Copplestone and Spurge followed them to a corner of the old tower where they ceased. Spurge glanced round that corner and uttered a sharp exclamation.

"Just what I expected!" he said. "Leastways, what I expected as soon as I see Jim a-lying there. Guv'nor, the stuff's gone!"

He drew Copplestone after him and pointed to a corner of the weed-grown courtyard where a cavity had been made in the mass of fallen masonry and the stones taken from it lay about just as they had been displaced and thrown aside.

"That's where the nine boxes were," he continued. "Well, there ain't one of 'em there now! Naught but the hole where they was! Well—this must ha' been during the early morning—after I left Jim to go into Norcaster. And of course him as put the stuff there must be him as fetched it away—Chatfield. Let's see if there's footmarks about, guv'nor."

"Wait a bit," said Copplestone. "We must be careful about that. Move warily. We 'd better do it systematically. There'd have to be some sort of a trap, a vehicle, to carry away those chests. Where's the nearest point of that road you spoke of?"

"Up there," replied Spurge, pointing to a flanking bank of heather. "But they—or him—wasn't forced to come that way, guv'nor. He—or them—could come up from that cove down yonder. It wouldn't surprise me if that there yacht—the Pike, you know—had turned on her tracks and come in here during the night. It's not more than a mile from this tower down to the shore, and—"

At that moment Vickers called to them, and they went back to find Jim
Spurge slowly opening his eyes and looking round him with consciousness
of his company. His one eye lightened a little as he caught sight of Zachary, and the poacher bent down to him.
"Jim, old man!" he said soothingly. "How are yer, Jim? Yer been hit by somebody. Who was it, Jim?"

"Give him a drop more brandy and lift him up a bit," counselled Gilling.
"He's improving."
But it needed more than a mere drop of brandy, more than cousinly words of adjuration, to bring the wounded man back to a state of speech. And when at last he managed to make a feeble response, it was only to mutter some incoherent and disjointed sentences about and being struck down from behind—after which he again relapsed into semi-unconsciousness.

"That's it guv'nor," muttered Spurge, nudging Copplestone. "That's the ticket! Struck down from behind—that's what happened to him. Unawares, so to speak, I can reckon of it up—easy. They comes in the darkness—after I'd left him here. He hears of 'em, as he says, a-moving about. Then he no doubt starts moving about—watching 'em, as far as he can see. Then one of 'em gives him this crack on the skull—life-preserver if you ask me—and down he goes! And then—they drag him in here and leaves him. Don't care whether he's a goner or not—not they! Well, an' what does it prove? That there's been more than one of 'em, guv'nor. And in my opinion, where they've come from is—down there!"

He pointed down the glen in the direction of the sea, and the three young men who were considerably exercised by this sudden turn of events and the disappearance of the chests, looked after his out-stretched hand and then at each other.

"Well, we can't stand here doing nothing," said Gilling at last. "Look here, we'd better divide forces. This chap'll have to be removed and got to some hospital. Vickers!—I guess you're the quickest-footed of the lot—will you run back to High Nick and tell that chauffeur to bring his car round here? If Sir Cresswell and the police are there, tell them what's happened. Spurge—you go down the glen there, and see if you can see anything of any suspicious-looking craft in that bay you told us of. Copplestone, we can't do any more for this man just now—let's look round. This is a queer business," he went on when they had all departed, and he and Copplestone were walking towards the tower. "The gold's gone, of course?"

"No sign of it here, anyway," answered Copplestone, leading him into the ruinous courtyard and pointing to the cavity in the fallen masonry. "That's where it was placed by Chatfield, according to Zachary Spurge."

"And of course Chatfield's removed it during the night," remarked Gilling. "That message which Sir Cresswell read us must have been all wrong—the Pike's come south and she's been somewhere about—maybe been in that cove at the end of the glen—though she'll have cleared out of it hours ago!" he concluded disappointedly. "We're too late!"

"That theory's not necessarily correct," replied Copplestone. "Sir Cresswell's message may have been quite right. For all we know the folks on the Pike had confederates on shore. Go carefully, Gilling — let's see if we can make out anything in the way of footprints."

The ground in the courtyard was grassless, a flooring of grit and loose stone, on which no impression could well be made by human foot. But Copplestone, carefully prospecting around and going a little way up the bank which lay between the tower and the moorland road, suddenly saw something in the black, peat-like earth which attracted his attention and he called to his companion.

"I say!" he exclaimed. "Look at this! There! — that's unmistakable enough.
And fresh, too!"
Gilling bent down, looked, and stared at Copplestone with a question in his eyes.

"By Gad!" he said. "A woman!"

"And one who wears good and shapely footwear, too," remarked Copplestone. "That's what you'd call a slender and elegant foot. Here it is again — going up the bank. Come on!"

There were more traces of this wearer of elegant foot-gear on the soft earth of the bank which ran between the moorland and the stone-strewn courtyard — more again on the edges of the road itself. There, too, were plain signs that a motor-car of some sort had recently been pulled up opposite the tower — Gilling pointed to the indentations made by the studded wheels and to droppings of oil and petrol on the gravelly soil.

"That's evident enough," he said. "Those chests have been fetched away during the night, by motor, and a woman's been in at it!

Confederates, of course. Now then, the next thing is, which way did that motor go with its contents?"

They followed the tracks for a short distance along the road, until, coming to a place where it widened at a gateway leading into the wood, they saw that the car had there been backed and turned. Gilling carefully examined the marks.

"That car came from Norcaster and it's gone back to Norcaster," he affirmed presently. "Look here! —they came up the hill at the side of the wood—here they backed the car towards that gate, and then ran it backwards till they were abreast of the tower—then, when they'd loaded up with those chests they went straight off by the way they'd come. Look at the tracks—plain enough."

"Then we'd better get down towards Norcaster ourselves," said Copplestone. "Call Spurge back—he'll find nothing in that cove. This job has been done from land. And we ought to be on the track of these people—they've had several hours start already."

By this time Zachary Spurge had been recalled, Vickers had brought the car round from High Nick, and the injured man was carefully lifted into it and driven away. But at High Nick itself they met another car, hurrying up from Norcaster, and bringing Sir Cresswell Oliver and three other men who bore the unmistakable stamp of the police force. In one of them Copplestone recognized the inspector from Scarhaven.

The two cars met and stopped alongside each other, and Sir Cresswell, with one sharp glance at the rough bandage which Vickers had fastened round Jim Spurge's head, rapped out a question.

"Gone!" replied Gilling, with equal brusqueness. "Came in a motor, during the night, soon after Zachary Spurge left Jim. They hit him pretty hard over his head and left him unconscious. Of course they've carried off the boxes. Car appears to have gone to Norcaster. Hadn't you better turn?"

Sir Cresswell pointed to the Scarhaven police inspector.

"Here's news from Scarhaven," he said, bending forward to the other car,
"The inspector's just brought it. The Squire—whoever he was—is dead.
They found his body this morning, lying at the foot of a cliff near the Keep. Foul play?—that's what you don't know, eh, inspector?"
"Can't say at all, sir," answered the inspector. "He might have been thrown down, he might have fallen down—it's a bad place. Anyway, what the doctor said, just before I hurried in here to tell Mrs. Greyle, as the next relative that we know of, is that he'd been dead some days—the body, you see, was lying in a thicket at the foot of the cliff."

"Some days!" exclaimed Copplestone, with a look at Gilling. "Days?"

"Four or five days at least, sir," replied the inspector. "So the doctor thinks. The place is a cliff between the high road from Northborough and the house itself. There's a short cut across the park to the house from that road. It looks as if—"

"Ah!" interrupted Gilling. "It's clear how that happened, then. He took that short cut, when he came from Northborough that night! But—if he's dead, who's engineering all this? There's the fact, those chests of gold have been removed from that old tower since Zachary Spurge left his cousin in charge there early this morning. Everything looks as if they'd been carried to Norcaster. Therefore—"

"Turn this car round," commanded Sir Cresswell. "Of course, we must get back to Norcaster. But what's to be done there?"

The two cars went scurrying back to the old shipping town. When at last they had deposited the injured man at a neighbouring hospital and came to a stop near the "Angel," Zachary Spurge pulled Copplestone's sleeve, and with a look full of significance, motioned him aside to a quiet place.

CHAPTER XXIX
SCARVELL'S CUT

The quiet place was a narrow alley, which opening out of the Market Square in which the car had come to a halt, suddenly twisted away into a labyrinth of ancient buildings that lay between the centre of the town and the river. Not until Spurge had conducted Copplestone quite away from their late companions did he turn and speak; when he spoke his words were accompanied by a glance which suggested mystery as well as confidence.

"Guv'nor!" he said. "What's going to be done?"

"Have you pulled me down here to ask that?" exclaimed Copplestone, a little impatiently. "Good heavens, man, with all these complications arising—the gold gone, the Squire dead—why, there'll have to be a pretty deep consultation, of course. We'd better get back to it."

But Spurge shook his head.

"Not me, guv'nor!" he said resolutely. "I ain't no opinion o' consultations with lawyers and policemen—plain clothes or otherwise. They ain't no mortal good whatever, guv'nor, when it comes to horse sense! 'Cause why? 'Tain't their fault—it's the system. They can't do nothing, start nothing, suggest nothing! —they can only do things in the official, cut-and-dried, red-tape way, Guv'nor—you and me can do better."

"Well?" asked Copplestone.

"Listen!" continued Spurge. "There ain't no doubt that that gold was carried off early this morning—must ha' been between the time I left Jim and sun-up, 'cause they'd want to do the job in darkness. Ain't no reasonable doubt, neither, that the motor-car what they used came here into Norcaster. Now, guv'nor, I ask you—where is it possible they'd make for? Not a railway station, 'cause them boxes 'ud be conspicuous and easy traced when inquiry was made. And yet they'd want to get 'em away—as soon as possible. Very well—what's the other way o' getting any stuff out o' Norcaster? What? Why—that!"

He jerked his thumb in the direction of a patch of grey water which shone dully at the end of the alley and while his thumb jerked his eye winked.

"The river!" he went on. "The river, guv'nor! Don't this here river, running into the free and bounding ocean six miles away, offer the best chance? What we want to do is to take a look round these here docks and quays and wharves—keeping our eyes open—and our ears as well. Come on with me, guv'nor—I know places all along this riverside where you could hide the Bank of England till it was wanted—so to speak."

"But the others?" suggested Copplestone. "Hadn't we better fetch them?"

"No!" retorted Spurge, assertively. "Two on us is enough. You trust to me, guv'nor—I'll find out something. I know these docks—and all that's alongside 'em. I'd do the job myself, now—but it'll be better to have somebody along of me, in case we want a message sending for help or anything of that nature. Come on—and if I don't find out before noon if there's any queer craft gone out o' this since morning—why, then, I ain't what I believe myself to be."

Copplestone, who had considerable faith in the poacher's shrewdness, allowed himself to be led into the lowest part of the town—low in more than one sense of the word. Norcaster itself, as regards its ancient and time-hallowed portions, its church, its castle, its official buildings and highly-respectable houses, stood on the top of a low hill; its docks and wharves and the mean streets which intersected them had been made on a stretch of marshland that lay between the foot of that hill and the river. And down there was the smell of tar and of merchandise, and narrow alleys full of sea-going men and raucous-voiced women, and queer nooks and corners, and ships being laden and ships being stripped of their cargoes and such noise and confusion and inextricable mingling and elbowing that Copplestone thought it was as likely to find a needle in a haystack as to make anything out relating to the quest they were engaged in.

But Zachary Spurge, leading him in and out of the throngs on the wharves, now taking a look into a dock, now inspecting a quay, now stopping to exchange a word or two with taciturn gentlemen who sucked their pipes at the corners of narrow streets, now going into shady-looking public houses by one door and coming out at another, seemed to be remarkably well satisfied with his doings and kept remarking to his companion that they would hear something yet. Nevertheless, by noon they had heard nothing, and Copplestone, who considered casual search of this sort utterly purposeless, announced that he was going to more savoury neighborhoods.

"Give it another turn, guv'nor," urged Spurge. "Have a bit o' faith in me, now! You see, guv'nor, I've an idea, a theory, as you might term it, of my very own, only time's too short to go into details, like. Trust me a bit longer, guv'nor—there's a spot or two down here that I'm fair keen on taking a look at—come on, guv'nor, once more!—this is Scarvell's Cut."

He drew his unwilling companion round a corner of the wharf which they were just then patrolling and showed him a narrow creek which, hemmed in by ancient buildings, some of them half-ruinous, sail-lofts, and sheds full of odds and ends of merchandise, cut into the land at an irregular angle and was at that moment affording harbourage to a mass of small vessels, just then lying high and dry on the banks from which the tide had retreated. Along the side of this creek there was just as much crowding and confusion as on the wider quays; men were going in and out of the sheds and lofts; men were busy about the sides of the small craft. And again the feeling of uselessness came over Copplestone.

"What's the good of all this, Spurge!" he exclaimed testily. "You'll never—"

Spurge suddenly laid a grip on his companion's elbow and twisted him aside into a narrow entry between the sheds.

"That's the good!" he answered in an exulting voice. "Look there, guv'nor! Look at that North Sea tug—that one, lying out there! Whose face is, now a-peeping out o' that hatch? Come, now?"

Copplestone looked in the direction which Spurge indicated. There, lying moored to the wharf, at a point exactly opposite a tumble-down sail-loft, was one of those strongly-built tugs which ply between the fishing fleets and the ports. It was an eminently business-looking craft, rakish for its class, and it bore marks of much recent sea usage. But Copplestone gave no more than a passing glance at it—what attracted and fascinated his eyes was the face of a man who had come up from her depths and was looking out of a hatchway on the top deck—looking expectantly at the sail-loft. There was grime and oil on that face, and the neck which supported the unkempt head rose out of a rough jersey, but Copplestone recognized his man smartly enough. In spite of the attempt to look like a tug deck-hand there was no mistaking the skipper of the Pike.

"Good heavens!" he muttered, as he stared across the crowded quay. "Andrius!"

"Right you are, guv'nor," whispered Spurge. "It's that very same, and no mistake! And now you'll perhaps see how I put things together, like. No doubt those folk as sent Sir Cresswell that message did see the Pike going east last evening—just so, but there wasn't no reason, considering what that chap and his lot had at stake why they shouldn't put him and one or two more, very likely, on one of the many tugs that's to be met with out there off the fishing grounds. What I conclude they did, guv'nor, was to charter one o' them tugs and run her in here. And I expect they've got the stuff on board her, now, and when the tide comes up, out they'll go, and be off into the free and open again, to pick the Pike up somewhere 'twixt here and the Dogger Bank. Ah!—smart 'uns they are, no doubt. But—we've got 'em!"

"Not yet," said Copplestone. "What are we to do. Better go back and get help, eh?"

He was keenly watching Andrius, and as the skipper of the Pike suddenly moved, he drew Spurge further into the alley.

"He's coming out of that hatchway!" whispered Copplestone. "If he comes ashore he'll see us, and then—"

"No matter, guv'nor," said Spurge reassuringly. "They can't get out o' Scarvell's Cut into the river till the tide serves. Yes, that's Cap'n Andrius right enough—and he's coming ashore."
Andrius had by that time drawn himself out of the hatchway and now revealed himself in the jersey, the thick leg-wear, and short sea-boots of an oceangoing man. Copplestone's recollection of him as he showed himself on board the Pike was of a very smartly attired, rather dandified person—only some deep scheme, he knew, would have caused him to assume this disguise, and he watched him with interest as he rolled ashore and disappeared within the lower story of the sail-loft. Spurge, too, watched with all his eyes, and he turned to Copplestone with a gleam of excitement.

"Guv'nor!" he said. "We've trapped 'em beautiful! I know that place—I've worked in there in my time. I know a way into it, from the back—we'll get in that way and see what's being done. 'Tain't worked no longer, that sail-loft—it's all falling to pieces. But first—help!"

"How are we to get that?" asked Copplestone, eagerly.

"I'll go it," replied Spurge. "I know a man just aback of here that'll run up to the town with a message—chap that can be trusted, sure and faithful. 'Bide here five minutes, sir—I'll send a message to Mr. Vickers—this chap'll know him and'll find him. He can come down with the rest—and the police, too, if he likes. Keep your eyes skinned, guv'nor."

He twisted away like an eel into the crowd of workers and idlers, and left Copplestone at the entrance to the alley, watching. And he had not been so left more than a couple of minutes when a woman slipped past the mouth of the alley, swiftly, quietly, looking neither to right nor left, of whose veiled head and face he caught one glance. And in that glance he recognized her—Addie Chatfield!

But in the moment of that glance Copplestone also recognized something vastly more important. Here was the explanation of the mystery of the early-morning doings at the old tower. The footprints of a woman who wore fashionable and elegant boots? Addie Chatfield, of course! Was she not old Peter's daughter, a chip of the old block, even though a feminine chip? And did not he and Gilling know that she had been mixed up with Peter at the Bristol affair? Great Scott!—why, of course. Addie was an accomplice in all these things!

If Copplestone had the least shadow of doubt remaining in his mind as to this conclusion, it was utterly dissipated when, peering cautiously round the corner of his hiding-place, he saw Addie disappear within the old sail-loft into which Andrius had betaken himself. Of course, she had gone to join her fellow-conspirators. He began to fume and fret, cursing himself for allowing Spurge to bring him down there alone—if only they had had Gilling and Vickers with them, armed as they were—

"All right, guv'nor!" Spurge suddenly whispered at his shoulder. "They'll be here in a quarter of an hour—I telephoned to 'em."

"Do you know what?" exclaimed Copplestone, excitedly. "Old Chatfield's daughter's gone in there, where Andrius went. Just now!"

"What—the play-actress!" said Spurge. "You don't say, guv'nor? Ha!—that explains everything—that's the missing link! Ha! But we'll soon know what they're after, Mr. Copplestone. Follow me—quiet as a mouse."

Once more submitting to be led, Copplestone followed his queer guide along the alley.

CHAPTER XXX
THE GREENGROCER'S CART

Spurge led Copplestone a little way up the narrow alley from the mouth of which they had observed the recent proceedings, suddenly turned off into a still narrower passage, and emerged at the rear of an ancient building of wood and stones which looked as if a stout shove or a strong wind would bring it down in dust and ruin.

"Back o' that old sail-loft what looks out on this cut," he whispered, glancing over his shoulder at Copplestone. "Now, guv'nor, we're going in here. As I said before, I've worked in this place—did a spell here when I was once lying low for a month or two. I know every inch of it, and if that lot are under this roof I know where they'll be."

"They'll show fight, you know," remarked Copplestone.

"Well, but ain't we got something to show fight with, too?" answered Spurge, with a knowing wink. "I've got my revolver handy, what Mr. Vickers give me, and I reckon you can handle yours. However, it ain't come to no revolver yet. What I want is to see and hear, guv'nor—follow me."

He had opened a ramshackle door in the rear of the premises as he spoke and he now beckoned his companion to follow him down a passage which evidently led to the front. There was no more than a dim light within, but Copplestone could see that the whole place was falling to pieces. And it was all wrapped in a dead silence. Away out on the quay was the rattle of chains, the creaking of a windlass, the voices of men and shrill laughter of women, but in there no sound existed. And Spurge suddenly stopped his stealthy creeping forward and looked at Copplestone suspiciously.

"Queer, ain't it?" he whispered. "I don't hear a voice, nor yet the ghost of one! You'd think that if they was in here they'd be talking. But we'll soon see."

Clambering up a pile of fallen timber which lay in the passage and beckoning Copplestone to follow his example, Spurge looked through a broken slat in the wooden partition into an open shed which fronted the Cut. The shed was empty. Folk were passing to and fro in front of it; the North Sea tug still lay at the wharf beyond; a man who was evidently its skipper sat on a tub on its deck placidly smoking his short pipe—but of Addie Chatfield or of Andrius there was no sign. And the silence in that crumbling, rat-haunted house was deeper than ever.

"Guv'nor!" muttered Spurge, "How long is it since you see—her?"

"Almost as soon as you'd gone," answered Copplestone.

"Ten minutes ago!" sighed Spurge. "Guv'nor—they've done us! They're off! I see it—she must ha' caught sight o' me, nosing round, and she came here and gave the others the office, and they bucked out at the back. The back, Guv'nor! and Lord bless you, at the back o' this shanty there's a perfect rabbit-warren o' places—more by token, they call it the Warren. If they've got in there, why, all the police in Norcaster'll never find 'em—leastways, I mean, to speak truthful, not without a deal o' trouble."

"What about upstairs?" asked Copplestone.

"Upstairs, now?" said Spurge with a doubtful glance at the ramshackle stairway. "Lord, mister!—I don't believe nobody could get up them stairs! No—they've hooked it through the back here, into the Warren. And once in there—"

He ended with an eloquent gesture, and dismounting from his perch made his way along the passage to a door which opened into the shed. Thence he looked out on the quay, and along the crowded maze of Scarvell's Cut.

"Here's some of 'em, anyway, guv'nor," he announced. "I see Mr. Vickers and t'other London gentleman, and the old Admiral, at all events. There they are—getting out of a motor at the end. But go to

224

meet 'em, Mr. Copplestone, while I keep my eye on this here tug and its skipper."

Copplestone elbowed his way through the crowd until he met Sir Cresswell and his two companions. All three were eager and excited: Copplestone could only respond to their inquiries with a gloomy shake of the head.

"We seem to have the devil's own luck!" he growled dismally. "Spurge and I spotted Andrius by sheer accident. He was on a North Sea tug, or trawler, along the quay here. Then Spurge ran off to summon you. While he was away Miss Chatfield appeared—"

"Addie Chatfield!" exclaimed Vickers.

"Exactly. And that of course," continued Copplestone, glancing at Gilling, "that without doubt—in my opinion, anyway—explains those elegant footprints up at the tower. Addie Chatfield, I tell you! She passed me as I was hiding at the entrance to an alley down the Cut here, and she went into an old sail-loft, outside which the tug I spoke of is moored, and into which Andrius had strolled a minute or two previously. But—neither she nor Andrius are there now. They've gone! And Spurge says that at the back of this quay there's a perfect rabbit-warren of courts and alleys, and if—or, rather as they've escaped into that—eh?"

The detectives who had accompanied Sir Cresswell on the interrupted expedition to the old tower and who had now followed him and his companions in a second car and arrived in time to hear Copplestone's story, looked at each other.

"That's right enough—comparatively speaking," said one. "But if they're in the Warren we shall get 'em out. The first thing to do, gentlemen, is to take a look at that tug."

"Exactly!" exclaimed Sir Cresswell. "Just what I was thinking. Let us find out what its people have to say."

The man who smoked his pipe in placid contentment on the deck of the tug looked up in astonishment as the posse of eight crossed the plank which connected him with the quay. Nevertheless he preserved an undaunted front, kept his pipe in his tightly closed lips, and cocked a defiant eye at everybody.

"Skipper o' this craft?" asked the principal detective laconically. "Right? Where are you from, then, and when did you come in here?" The skipper removed his pipe and spat over the rail. He put the pipe back, folded his arms and glared.

"And what the dickens may that be to do with you?" he inquired. "And who may you be to walk aboard my vessel without leave?"

"None of that, now!" said the detective. "Come on—we're police officers. There's something wrong round here. We've got warrants for two men that we believe to have been on your tug—one of 'em was seen here not so many minutes ago. You'd far better tell us what you know. If you don't tell now, you'll have to tell later. And—I expect you've been paid already. Come on—out with it!"

The skipper, whose gnarled countenance had undergone several changes during this address, smote one red fist on top of the other.

"Darned if I don't know as there was something on the crook in this here affair!" he said, almost cheerily. "Well, well—but I ain't got nothing to do with it. Warrants?—you say? Ah! And what might be the partiklar' natur' o' them warrants?"

"Murder!" answered the detective. "That's one charge, anyhow—for one of 'em, at any rate. There's others."

"Murder's enough," responded the skipper. "Well, of course, nobody can tell a man to be a murderer by merely looking at his mug. Not at all!—nobody! However, this here is how it is. Last night it were—evening, to be c'rect—dark. I was on the edge o' the fleet, out there off the Dogger. A yacht comes up—smart 'un—very fast sailer—and hails me. Was I going into Norcaster or anywheres about? Being a

Northborough tug, this, I wasn't. Would I go for a consideration—
then and there? Whereupon I asked what consideration? Then we
bargains. Eventual, we struck it at thirty pounds—cash down, which
was paid, prompt. I was to take two men straight and slick into
Norcaster, to this here very slip, Scarvell's Cut, to wait while they
put a bit of a cargo on board, and then to run 'em back to the same
spot where I took 'em up. Done! they come aboard—the yacht goes
off east—I come careenin' west. That's all! That part of it anyway."

"And the men?" suggested the detective. "What sort were they, and
where are they?"

"The men, now!" said the skipper. "Ah! Two on 'em—both done up
in what you might call deep-sea-style. But hadn't never done no
deep-sea nor yet any other sort o' sea work in their mortial days—
hands as white and soft as a lady's. One, an old chap with a dial like
a full moon on him—sly old chap, him! T'other a younger man,
looked as if he'd something about him—dangerous chap to cross.
Where are they? Darned if I know. What I knows, certain, is this—
we gets in here about eight o'clock this morning, and makes fast
here, and ever since then them two's been as it were on the fret and
the fidge, allers lookin' out, so to speak, for summun as ain't come
yet. The old chap, he went across into that there sail-maker's loft an
hour ago, and t'other, he followed of him, recent. I ain't seen 'em
since. Try there. And I say?"

"Well?" asked the detective.

"Shall I be wanted?" asked the skipper. "'Cause if not, I'm off and
away as soon as the tide serves. Ain't no good me waitin' here for
them chaps if you're goin' to take and hang 'em!"

"Got to catch 'em first," said the detective, with a glance at his two
professional companions. "And while we're not doubting your word
at all, we'll just take a look round your vessel—they might have
slipped on board again, you see, while your back was turned."

But there was no sign of Peter Chatfield, nor of his daughter, nor of the captain of the Pike on that tug, nor anywhere in the sailmaker's loft and its purlieus. And presently the detectives looked at one another and their leader turned to Sir Cresswell.

"If these people—as seems certain—have escaped into this quarter of the town," he said, "there'll have to be a regular hunt for them! I've known a man who was badly wanted stow himself away here for weeks. If Chatfield has accomplices down here in the Warren, he can hide himself and whoever's with him for a long time—successfully. We'll have to get a lot of men to work."

"But I say!" exclaimed Gilling. "You don't mean to tell me that three people—one a woman—could get away through these courts and alleys, packed as they are, without being seen? Come now!"

The detectives smiled indulgently.

"You don't know these folks," said one of them, inclining his head towards a squalid street at the end of which they had all gathered. "But they know us. It's a point of honour with them never to tell the truth to a policeman or a detective. If they saw those three, they'd never admit it to us—until it's made worth their while."

"Get it made worth their while, then!" exclaimed Gilling, impatiently.

"All in due course, sir," said the official voice. "Leave it to us."

The amateur searchers after the iniquitous recognized the futility of their own endeavours in that moment, and went away to discuss matters amongst themselves, while the detectives proceeded leisurely, after their fashion, into the Warren as if they were out for a quiet constitutional in its salubrious byways. And Sir Cresswell Oliver remarked on the difficulty of knowing exactly what to do once you had red-tape on one side and unusual craftiness on the other.

"You think there's no doubt that gold was removed this morning by Chatfield's daughter?" he said to Copplestone as they went back to the centre of the town together, Gilling and Vickers having turned aside elsewhere and Spurge gone to the hospital to ask for news of his cousin. "You think she was the woman whose footprints you saw up there at the Beaver's Glen?"

"Seeing that she's here in Norcaster and in touch with those two, what else can I think?" replied Copplestone. "It seems to me that they got in touch with her by wireless and that she removed the gold in readiness for her father and Andrius coming in here by that North Sea tug. If we could only find out where she's put those boxes, or where she got the car from in which she brought it down from the tower—"

"Vickers has already started some inquiries about cars," said Sir Cresswell. "She must have hired a car somewhere in the town. Certainly, if we could hear of that gold we should be in the way of getting on their track."

But they heard nothing of gold or of fugitives or of what the police and detectives were doing until the middle of the afternoon. And then Mr. Elkin, the manager of the bank from which Chatfield had withdrawn the estate and the private balance, came hurrying to the "Angel" and to Mrs. Greyle, his usually rubicund face pale with emotion, his hand waving a scrap of crumpled paper. Mrs. Greyle and Audrey were at that moment in consultation with Sir Cresswell Oliver and Copplestone—the bank manager burst in on them without ceremony.

"I say, I say!" he exclaimed excitedly. "Will you believe it!—the gold's come back! It's all safe—every penny. Bless me!—I scarcely know whether I'm dreaming or not. But—we've got it!"

"What's all this?" demanded Sir Cresswell. "You've got—that gold?"

"Less than an hour ago," replied the bank manager, dropping into a chair and slapping his hand on his knees in his excitement, "a man

229

who turned out to be a greengrocer came with his cart to the bank and said he'd been sent with nine boxes for delivery to us. Asked who had sent him he replied that early this morning a lady whom he didn't know had asked him to put the boxes in his shed until she called for them—she brought them in a motor-car. This afternoon she called again at two o'clock, paid him for the storage and for what he was to do, and instructed him to put the boxes on his cart and bring them to us. Which," continued Mr. Elkin, gleefully rubbing his hands together, "he did! With—this! And that, my dear ladies and good gentlemen, is the most extraordinary document which, in all my forty years' experience of banking matters, I have ever seen!"

He laid a dirty, crumpled half-sheet of cheap note-paper on the table at which they were all sitting, and Copplestone, bending over it, read aloud what was there written.

"MR. ELKIN—Please place the contents of the nine cases sent herewith to the credit of the Greyle Estate.

"PETER CHATFIELD, Agent."

Amidst a chorus of exclamations Sir Cresswell asked a sharp question.

"Is that really Chatfield's signature?"

"Oh, undoubtedly!" replied Mr. Elkin. "Not a doubt of it. Of course, as soon as I saw it, I closely questioned the greengrocer. But he knew nothing. He said the lady was what he called wrapped up about her face—veiled, of course—on both her visits, and that as soon as she'd seen him set off with his load of boxes she disappeared. He lives, this greengrocer, on the edge of the town—I've got his address. But I'm sure he knows no more."

"And the cases have been examined?" asked Copplestone.

"Every one, my dear sir," answered the bank manager with a satisfied smirk. "Every penny is there! Glorious!"

"This is most extraordinary!" said Sir Cresswell. "What on earth does it all mean? If we could only trace that woman from the greengrocer's place—"

But nothing came of an attempt to carry out this proposal, and no news arrived from the police, and the evening had grown far advanced, and Mrs. Greyle and Audrey, with Sir Cresswell, Mr. Petherton and Vickers, Copplestone, and Gilling, were all in a private parlour together at a late hour, when the door suddenly opened and a woman entered, who threw back a heavy veil and revealed herself as Addie Chatfield.

CHAPTER XXXI
AMBASSADRESS EXTRAORDINARY

If Copplestone had never seen Addie Chatfield before, if he had not known that she was an actress of some acknowledged ability, her entrance into that suddenly silent room would have convinced him that here was a woman whom nature had undoubtedly gifted with the dramatic instinct. Addie's presentation of herself to the small and select audience was eminently dramatic, without being theatrical. She filled the stage. It was as if the lights had suddenly gone down in the auditorium and up in the proscenium, as if a hush fell, as if every ear opened wide to catch a first accent. And Addie's first accents were soft and liquid—and accompanied by a smile which was calculated to soften the seven hearts which had begun to beat a little quicker at her coming. With the smile and the soft accent came a highly successful attempt at a shy and modest blush which mounted to her cheek as she moved towards the centre table and bowed to the startled and inquisitive eyes.

"I have come to ask—mercy!"

There was a faint sigh of surprise from somebody. Sir Cresswell Oliver, only realizing that a pretty woman, had entered the room, made haste to place a chair for her. But before Addie could respond to his old-fashioned bow, Mr. Petherton was on his legs.

"Er!—I take it that this is the young wom—the Miss Chatfield of whom we have had occasion to speak a good deal today," he said very stiffly. "I think, Sir Cresswell—eh?"

"Yes," said Sir Cresswell, glancing from the visitor to the old lawyer. "You think, Petherton—yes?"
"The situation is decidedly unpleasant," said Mr. Petherton, more icily than ever. "Mr. Vickers will agree with me that it is most unpleasant—and very unusual. The fact is—the police are now searching for this—er, young lady."

"But I am here!" exclaimed Addie. "Doesn't that show that I'm not afraid of the police. I came of my own free will—to explain. And—to ask you all to be merciful."

"To whom?" demanded Mr. Petherton.

"Well—to my father, if you want to know," replied Addie, with another softening glance. "Come now, all of you, what's the good of being so down on an old man who, after all hasn't got so very long to live? There are two of you here who are getting on, you know—it doesn't become old men to be so hard. Good doctrine, that, anyway—isn't it, Sir Cresswell?"

Sir Cresswell turned away, obviously disconcerted; when he looked round again, he avoided the eyes of the young men and glanced a little sheepishly at Mr. Petherton.

"It seems to me, Petherton," he said, "that we ought to hear what Miss
Chatfield has to say. Evidently she comes to tell us—of her own free will—something. I should like to know what that something is. I think
Mrs. Greyle would like to know, too."
"Decidedly!" exclaimed Mrs. Greyle, who was watching the central figure with great curiosity. "I should indeed, like to know— especially if Miss Chatfield proposes to tell us something about her father."

Mr. Petherton, who frowned very much and appeared to be greatly disturbed by these irregularities, twisted sharply round on the visitor.

"Where is your father?" he demanded.

"Where you can't find him!" retorted Addie, with a flash of the eye that lit up her whole face. "So's Andrius. They're off, my good sir! — both of 'em. Neither you nor the police can lay hands on 'em now. And you'll do no good by laying hands on me. Come now," she went on, "I said I'd come to ask for mercy. But I came for more. This game's all over! It's—up. The curtain's down—at least it's going down. Why don't you let me tell you all about it and then we can be friends?"

Mr. Petherton gazed at Addie for a moment as if she were some extraordinary specimen of a new race. Then he took off his glasses, waved them at Sir Cresswell and dropped into a chair with a snort.

"I wash my hands of the whole thing!" he exclaimed. "Do what you like—all of you. Irregular—most irregular!"

Vickers gave Addie a sly look.

"Don't incriminate yourself, Miss Chatfield," he said. "There's no need for you to tell anything against yourself, you know."

"Me!" exclaimed Addie. "Why, I've been playing good angel all day long—me incriminate myself, indeed! If Miss Greyle there only knew what I'd done for her!—look here," she continued, suddenly turning to Sir Cresswell. "I've come to tell all about it. And first of all—every penny of that money that my father drew from the bank has been restored this afternoon."

"We know that," said Sir Cresswell.

"Well, that was me!—I engineered that," continued Addie. "And second—the Pike will be back at Scarhaven during the night, to unload everything that was being carried away. My doing, again! Because, I'm no fool, and I know when a game's up."

"So—there was a game?" suggested Vickers.

Addie leaned forward from the chair which Sir Cresswell had given her at the end of the table and planting her elbows on the table edge began to check off her points on the tips of her slender fingers. She was well aware that she had the stage to herself by that time and she showed her consciousness of it.

234

"You have it," she answered. "There was a game—and perhaps I know more of it than anybody. I'll tell now. It began at Bristol. I was playing there. One morning my father fetched me out from rehearsal to tell me that he'd been down to Falmouth to meet the new Squire of Scarhaven, Marston Greyle, and that he found him so ill that they'd had to go to a doctor, who forbade Greyle to travel far at a time. They'd got to Bristol—there, Greyle was so much worse that my father didn't know what to do with him. He knew that I was in the town, so he came to me. I got Greyle a quiet room at my lodgings. A doctor saw him—he said he was very bad, but he didn't say that he was in immediate danger. However, he died that very night."

Addie paused for a moment, and Copplestone and Gilling exchanged glances.
So far, this was all known to them—but what was coming?
"Now, I was alone with Greyle for awhile that evening," continued Addie. "It was while my father was getting some food downstairs. Greyle said to me that he knew he was dying, and he gave me a pocket-book in which he said all his papers were: he said I could give it to my father. I believe he became unconscious soon after that; anyway, he never mentioned that pocket-book to my father. Neither did I. But after Greyle was dead I examined its contents carefully. And when I was in London at the end of the week, I showed them to—my husband."

Addie again paused, and at least two of the men glanced at each other with a look of surmise. Her—husband! "Who the—"

"The fact is," she went on suddenly, "Captain Andrius is my husband. But nobody knew that—not even my own father. We've been married three years—I met him when I was crossing over to America once. We got married—we kept the marriage secret for reasons of our own. Well, he met me in London the Sunday after Greyle's death, and I showed him the papers which were in Greyle's pocket-book. And—now this, of course, was where it was very wicked in me—and him—though we've tried to make up for it today, anyhow—we fixed up what I suppose you two gentlemen would call a conspiracy. My husband had a brother, an actor—not up to much, nor of much experience—who had been brought up in the States and who was then in town, doing nothing. We took him into confidence, coached him up in everything, furnished him with all the papers in the pocket-book, and resolved to pass him off as the real Marston Greyle."

Mr. Petherton stirred angrily in his chair and turned a protesting face on Sir Cresswell.

"Apart from being irregular," he exclaimed, "this is altogether outrageous! This woman is openly boasting of conspiracy and—"

"You're wrong!" said Addie. "I'm not boasting—I'm explaining. You ought to be obliged to me. And—"

"If Mrs. Andrius—to give the lady her real name—cares to unburden her secrets to us, I really don't see why we shouldn't listen to them, Mr. Petherton," observed Vickers. "It simplifies matters greatly."

"That's what I say," agreed Addie. "I'm done with all this and I want to clear things up, whatever comes of it. Well—I say we fixed that up with my brother-in-law."

"His name—his real name, if you please," inquired Vickers.

"Oh—ah!—well, his real name was Martin Andrius, but he'd another name for the stage," replied Addie. "We gave him the papers and arranged for him to go down to Scarhaven to my father. Now I want to assure you all, right here, that my father never did really know that Martin was an imposter. He began to suspect something at the end, but he didn't know for a fact. Martin went down to him at Scarhaven, just a week after the real Marston Greyle had died. He claimed to be Marston Greyle, he produced his papers. My father told about the Marston Greyle he'd buried. Martin pooh-poohed that—he said that that man must be a secretary of his, Mark Grey, who, after stealing some documents had left him in New York and slipped across here, no doubt meaning to pass himself off as the real man until he could get something substantial out of the estate, when he'd have vanished. I tell you my father accepted that story — why? Because he knew that if Miss Greyle there came into the estate, she and her mother would have bundled Peter Chatfield out of his stewardship quick."

"Proceed, if you please," said Sir Cresswell. "There are other details about which I am anxious to hear."

"Meaning about your own brother," remarked Addie. "I'm coming to that. Well, on his story and on his production of those papers — birth certificates, Greyle papers of their life in America and so on — everybody accepted Martin as the real man, and things seemed to go on smoothly till that Sunday when Bassett Oliver had the bad luck to go to Scarhaven. And now, Sir Cresswell, I'll tell you the plain and absolute truth about your brother's death! It's the absolute truth, mind — nobody knows it better than I do. On that Sunday I was at Scarhaven. I wanted to speak privately to Martin. I arranged to meet him in the grounds of the Keep during the afternoon. I did meet him there. We hadn't been talking many minutes when Bassett Oliver came in through the door in the wall, which one of us had carelessly left open. He didn't see us. But we saw him. And we were afraid! Why? Because Bassett Oliver knew both of us. He'd met Martin several times, in London and in New York — and, of course, he knew that Martin was no more Marston Greyle than he himself was. Well! — we both shrank behind some shrubs that we were standing amongst, and we gave each other one look, and Martin went white as death. But Bassett Oliver went on across the lawn, never seeing us, and he entered the turret tower and went up. Martin just said to me 'If Bassett Oliver sees me, there's an end to all this — what's to be done?' But before I could speak or think, we saw Bassett at the top of the tower, making his way round the inside parapet. And suddenly — he disappeared!"

Addie's voice had become low and grave during the last few minutes and she kept her eyes on the table at the end. But she looked up readily enough when Sir Cresswell seized her arm and rapped out a question almost in her ear.

"Is that the truth—the real truth?"

"It's the absolute truth!" she answered, regarding him steadily. "I'm not altogether a good sort, nor a very bad sort, but I'm telling you the real truth in that. It was a sheer accident—he stepped off the parapet and fell. Martin went into the base of the tower and came back saying he was dead. We were both dazed—we separated. He went off to the house—I went to my father by a roundabout way. We decided to let things take their course. You all know a great deal of what happened. But—later—my husband and Martin began to take certain things into their own hands. They put me on one side. To this minute, I don't quite know how much my father got into their secrets or how little, but I do know that they determined to make what you might call a purse for themselves out of Scarhaven. Martin left certain powers in his brother's hands and went off to London. He was there, hidden, until Andrius got all ready for a flight on the Pike. Then he set off to Scarhaven, to join her. But he didn't join her, and none of us knew what had become of him until today, when we heard of what had been found at Scarhaven. That explained it—he had taken that short cut from the Northborough road through the woods behind the Keep, and fallen over the cliff at the Hermit's steps. But that very night, you, Mr. Vickers, and Mr. Copplestone and Miss Greyle, nearly stopped everything, and if Andrius and Chatfield hadn't carried you off, the scheme would have come to nothing. Well—you know what happened after that—"

"But," interjected Vickers, quickly, "not your share in the last development."

"My share's been to see that the thing was up, and that if I wanted to save them all, I'd best put a stop to it," rejoined Addie, with a grim smile. "I tell you, I didn't know what they'd been up to until today. I was in England—never mind where—wondering what was going on. Yesterday I got a code message from my husband. When he fetched my father away from you, he forced him to tell where that gold was—then he wired to me—by wireless—full instructions to recover it during last night. I did—never you mind the exact means I

238

took nor who it was that I got to help—I got it—and I took good care to put it where I knew it would be safe. Then this morning I went to meet the two of them at Scarvell's Cut. And I took the upper hand then! I got them away from that sail-loft—safely. I made my husband give me a code message for the man in charge of the Pike, telling him to return at once to Scarhaven; I made my father write a note to Elkin at the bank, telling him to place the gold which I sent with it to the credit of the Greyle Estate. And when all that was done—I got them away—they're gone!"

Vickers, who had never taken his eyes off Addie during her lengthy explanation, gave her a whimsical smile.

"Safely?" he asked.

"I'll defy the police to find 'em, anyway," replied Addie with a quick response of lip and eye. "I don't do things by halves. I say—they're gone! But—I'm here. Come, now—I've made a clean breast of it all. The thing's over and done with. There's nothing to prevent Miss Greyle there coming into her rights—I can prove 'em—my father can prove them. So—is it any use doing what that old gentleman's just worrying to do? You can all see what he wants—he's dying to hand me over to the police."

Sir Cresswell Oliver rose, glanced at Audrey and her mother, received some telepathic communication from them, and assumed his old quarter-deck manner.

"Not tonight, I think, Petherton," he said authoritatively. "No—certainly not tonight!"
* * * * *

Some months later, when Audrey Greyle had come into possession of Scarhaven, and had married Copplestone in the little church behind her mother's cottage, she and her husband, to satisfy a mutual and long-cherished desire, visited a certain romantic and retired part of the country. And in the course of their wanderings they came across a very pretty village, and in it a charmingly situated retreat, which looked so attractive from the road along which they were walking that they halted and peered at it through its trimly-kept boundary hedge. And there, seated in the easiest of chairs on the smoothest of lawns, roses about him, a cigar in his mouth, the newspaper in his hand, a glass at his elbow, they saw Peter Chatfield. They looked at him for a long moment; then they looked at each other and smiled delightedly, as children might smile at a pleasure-giving picture, and they passed on in silence. But when that village lay behind them, Copplestone gave his wife a sly glance, and permitted himself to make an epigram.

"Chatfield!" he said musingly. "Chatfield! sublimely ungrateful that he isn't in Dartmoor."

THE END

CPSIA information can be obtained
at www.ICGtesting.com
Printed in the USA
LVHW012342290321
682892LV00011B/281

9 781034 643173